Dear Haiti,
Love
Alaine

Books by Maika Moulite and Maritza Moulite

Dear Haiti, Love Alaine

MAIKA MOULITE AND MARITZA MOULITE

Dear Haiti, Love Alaine

ink
yard
press

ISBN-13: 978-1-335-77709-6

Dear Haiti, Love Alaine

Copyright © 2019 by Maika Moulite and Maritza Moulite

InkyardPress.com

Printed in U.S.A.

To TeTe, FiFie and LouLou.

And our soul mates Jessica and Lydi'Ann:

Huh huh

Aye yai yai yai yai

Blankety-blanks unite

Imagination

For Narnia!

Dementor, dementor!

~Oooh~

INTRODUCTION

~~~~~~~~~~~~~~~~

Dear Sister Wagner,

When I first started this assignment, I was prepared to write it off as one of the many weird projects that we always get assigned at this school. (This is, after all, the only educational institution in Florida that teaches electives like *The Joy of Physical Education & Classical Music* and *Feminist Theory Within the World of the Shire*.) I chose to register for this class in particular because I figured a course that takes a look at Latin American history would be an opportunity for me to draw on the stories of Haiti that I've heard my whole life. And after three years of projects at St. Catherine de' Ricci Academy, this fourth and final assignment should've been a cinch.

It wasn't. This research project asked us to explore the revolutionary history of a country of our choosing "while highlighting a prominent family's contribution to its early liberation and subsequent development." Since Henri Christophe, the first and only king of Haiti, is my great-great-great-great^{nth}-grandfather, the lovable narcissist in me thought that it would be cool to learn more about my family's history in the larger context of Haiti's turbulent past. But my work quickly took on a life of its own and, many times, I didn't know where it was headed or whether I was chasing the right leads.

And though I hadn't planned on it for this assignment, I got to visit Haiti for the first time. This trip opened my eyes in ways I couldn't have foreseen. I was able to deepen my relationship with my mother, explore my family history, and experience up close the country that I've loved from afar. I discovered that the choices of the past reverberate into the future and that achieving our wildest dreams often comes at a nightmare of a cost. While I was in Haiti, I was swept up in the rhythm of the culture and lost myself. I'm still shocked. The painless acceptance that you mention in our instructions between "the everyday with the fantastic" was not an idea I was familiar with. I was raised by a doctor who encouraged me to sift beneath what we see at face value and a journalist who told me to never stop asking questions. But I realize now that sometimes you won't get answers. And other times you won't like the answers you get.

Oh, and I learned that growing up means that we're not always in control. But it doesn't mean that we're completely powerless either. In fact, each of us must come to the realization that life actually lies somewhere in the middle. (Seriously, I've done so much adulting these past few weeks I've been looking into retirement options.)

I wasn't totally sure what I'd end up with or how much I was going to share. In the end, I've decided to trust you with my story, hairy warts and all. And now that I know where I've been, I know where I'm going. The notes, articles, emails, and diary entries you'll find in the following pages will take you on a twisty journey into both my family's and Haiti's past and bring you to present day. Get ready for a bumpy ride.

Alaine

FINAL PROJECT

Rasin Pye Bwa Kouri Byen Fon

or

The Roots of the Trees Run Deep

ALAINE BEAUPARLANT

LATIN AMERICAN HISTORY + CREATIVE WRITING WORKSHOP
SISTER PATRICIA WAGNER, PHD
ST. CATHERINE DE' RICCI ACADEMY

FINAL PROJECT INSTRUCTIONS

You will examine the journey of a Latin American country's revolution in three sections while highlighting a prominent family's contribution to its early liberation and subsequent development. Latin America is the birthplace of magical realism, the literary genre that juxtaposes the everyday with the fantastic and makes no apologies or explanations for it. If the Spirit moves you, write in the tradition of the greats and embrace the aspects of your chosen culture that leave you breathless. Remember: this class is equal parts Latin American history *and* creative writing.

PART 1: THE LIST
DUE - WEDNESDAY, JANUARY 6..... 10% OF FINAL PROJECT GRADE

Instructions: Create a list of notable individuals in your chosen country's revolution. Include the defining moments of five or more principal actors (at least one should be from your prominent family) and describe his or her claim to fame. Use the List as a framework for both the Presentation and Story sections of your project. Be sure to also include a short paragraph describing your presentation plans.

PART 2: THE PRESENTATION
DUE - TUESDAY, JANUARY 12..... 40% OF FINAL PROJECT GRADE

Instructions: Using the research you've conducted throughout the year on your chosen country, depict a culturally significant moment in time as it relates to your country's revolution. Costumes, photographs, dioramas, and other props are encouraged.

PART 3: THE STORY

DUE - FRIDAY, APRIL 1....... 50% OF FINAL PROJECT GRADE

Instructions: Present the information that you've collected on your chosen family in an engaging story. How did they impact the revolution? Does the family remain a significant power in the country's modern history? This section is where your creative writing should particularly shine.

PART I

NOU TOUT FOU LA

(WE'RE ALL MAD HERE)

Thursday, November 12

The Life and Times of Alaine Beauparlant

~~~~~~~~~~~~~~~~~~~~~~~~~~~~~~~~~~~

Curiouser and curiouser.

Quoting my favorite line in my favorite book (Hi, Alice) was my first reaction when I came home from school today and saw the new laptop that I'd been heavily hinting at wanting for the last few months, placed carefully in the center of the small desk in my bedroom.

Well. My first reaction was actually distrust.

Now, I know that a *normal* reaction to receiving a gift that you've wanted for an eternity and a quarter should involve something like clasping your hands on either side of your face, tears of happiness sliding down your cheeks, and a toothy grin followed by a loud exclamation of "Oh, you shouldn't have!"

But gifting at my house doesn't quite work out that way when you know for a fact that you're not due to receive said gift for another six to nine months. Not when the only thing your divorced parents agree on is that their sole child should never feel entitled to anything without earning it, no matter what their salaries could provide. I was almost positive that my parents were going to "surprise" me with the laptop as a graduation present after I'd done my part as the first-generation American daughter and gotten accepted to Mom's alma mater, Columbia University, to study journalism. This would of course be followed by the other items they'd have to get for my welcome-to-college-don't-mess-this-up package. See: mini-fridge, microwave, respectably sized television, twin XL bedding, freedom, etc.

The bright red bow that was unceremoniously attached to the cover of the laptop clashed horribly with the yellow-striped computer case surrounding it, but what caught my eye was the handwritten sticky note signed *Love, Mom & Dad*. It wasn't every day that "Mom & Dad" (or "Celeste & Jules") appeared side by side, even if it was only on paper. I ripped off the bow and tossed it onto my desk, opening the laptop slowly while I squealed to myself. I hovered my wiggling fingers impatiently above the black keys as I waited for the screen to light up. The wallpaper was of a beach and the home screen was empty, save for the recycle bin and one other shortcut of a notebook and quill. I clicked on it and found that it was a daily meditation journal app, waiting to be filled with the secrets of my hopes and daydreams. Not the biggest surprise when your dad's a psychiatrist, but still…something felt off.

"You needed a new computer, and I figured you'd want somewhere to write out your feelings," Dad said as he walked past my open bedroom door without coming inside. I wasn't sure if mentioning that I'd been journaling for years with good ol' pen and paper was the right move, so I didn't. I'd hate for my parents to change their minds about giving me the laptop. And besides, he was already gone, off to do whatever it was that single fathers did when they got home from work a little early. (Nap.)

I pulled my old laptop out of my book bag and ran my

hands along the grimy strips of duct tape holding it together. It did look pretty depressing, especially compared to the shiny new computer that was waiting for me to play. I wouldn't look this gift horse in the mouth until it bit me…for now. Instead, I'd graciously accept my present ahead of schedule and maintain the healthy dose of suspicion brewing in the back of my mind.

So, without further ado…

Behold, the written words of Alaine Beauparlant, future journalist and media personality. Here is where I keep my deepest thoughts and most [un]developed ideas.

After such a declaration, you might ask the obvious question: What do I, Alaine Beauparlant, a seventeen-year-old with *way* too little life experience, have to say about anything? Well, too little life experience or no, I'm super observant (future journalist here), equally assertive (misogynists might call it bossy), and a natural hair guru (if I do say so myself). These are all skills that come in handy as Queen of Keeping Boundary-Crossing Masked as Inquisitive Hands Out of My Lovely 'Fro. As my *tati* Estelle always says, "You can't let just anyone touch your hair. The wrong hands could make all those beautiful coils fall right out." Whether she meant someone styling my hair or a quick pat from a random stranger, I'm not sure. But I'm not about to risk losing these edges. Not after I've finally mastered all things natural hair. Seriously, you have no idea the things I can do with it. If you keep reading, you too will learn the secrets to a perfectly fluffed yet defined twist-out. But dessert comes after broccoli, which I happen to love, so you'll have to sit through my origin story.

I was born far away. You could say it was another planet. My parents knew of the imminent doom of our homeland and decided to whisk me from everything we knew. Like many sad stories go, they were killed on the way to our new home. I led a normal life with the kind souls who adopted me after they found me all alone on a park bench…

Wait. That's not right.

Everything changed on a class trip to the science museum. I needed more than a few dinosaur fossils to satiate my curiosity. As I was looking around on my own, I was bitten by a radioactive…

Let me back up.

I am the molded-from-clay daughter of a mystical queen on an island inhabited solely by women…

No.

I am from a little-known country named Waka—

Okay, okay. You got me. Here's the truth. Like I said, my name is Alaine Beauparlant. I'm seventeen years old, co-editor of my school's online newspaper, *The Riccian* (you're reading the words of an award-winning preeminent journalist in case you were wondering), the best bingo caller at the local assisted-living facility, and currently living in Miami, Florida. Saying I'm from Miami is a factually correct yet deceptive statement. When someone who isn't from here imagines a person living in the coolest city in the Sunshine State, they conjure up mental images of people on Jet Skis during hurricanes and clubbing shamelessly on South Beach. (If I had just said Florida, one would probably imagine me skipping school to tip cows or rob banks with my pet alligator. Let me disabuse you of that notion right now. I haven't had a pet alligator in years.)

The Life and Times of Alaine Beauparlant

It wasn't personal. I did the math and assessed immediately that, to get an A in my college prep seminar, I didn't need the extra credit points that having a parent speak at Career Day would provide. Dad was slightly miffed of course when I explained this before politely declining his offer to debate the merits of Freud and Jung in front of my class for the event—but that was to be expected.

"I dunno, I've got this hunch that my peers won't be that into you pontificating about two dead guys with mommy issues for a half hour," I said.

"If I did my presentation, you would know that your statement is a gross simplification of the fields of psychoanalysis and analytical psychology," he sniffed. "Pontificate... Nice word."

"I still can't shake those darn SAT vocabulary flash cards," I said, piling a mountain of scrambled eggs over my jellied toast. It wasn't a real complaint though. Those cards helped me beat my target score by 5 points. Call me Rumi and Sir, because the Ivys were calling my name. "And because I love and respect you, I won't even lie and say I forgot to give you the invitation."

"I suppose that means I haven't failed totally as a parent, then," he said wryly as he looked up from his *New York Times*. I bought him an online subscription for his birthday last year, but he still liked to do the crossword puzzles on a hard copy. He let slip once that sharing the newspaper used to be his and my mom's Sunday ritual. I could imagine Dad idling in the Health section for a couple of minutes before shuffling through for the wedding announcements, and Mom examining the front page with a magnifying glass to confirm her sources hadn't withheld even the tiniest of scoops.

Now she was too busy making news on the Sunday morning show she hosted to worry about which politician might or might not have been playing coy during the week. If she (or "the American people!") wanted to get to the bottom of something, she'd just ask said public servant about it on live TV.

"…a deep dive into the secretive health care bill that will leave millions of Americans uncovered and scrambling for a way to pay…"

Mom might have been a thousand miles away from Miami, but her voice was right there with us each weekend, emanating from the family room television to where we ate in the kitchen. Dad rarely watched *Sunday Politicos* with me unless Mom had a majorly super fancy interview subject (think POTUS), but after I grabbed my plate and hopped onto the couch, he usually pretended not to listen from the table. It was our own special ritual.

This morning though, he rounded up his puzzle and coffee mug and sat beside me in front of the flat screen. I glanced at him but stayed quiet. The guests included the usual roundtable setup plus a congressperson or two. No one majorly super fancy.

"Health care reform is an important topic," he grunted by way of explanation. "And me watching also serves as reinforcement of what it looks like to have a healthy relationship, even post-divorce."

"Sure it does."

I pulled the coffee table closer to the couch and made sure that my new laptop was safely positioned (I hadn't dropped it once yet!) so that I could skim the Tweets coming in about *Sunday Politicos* as I ate my breakfast. On Sundays at 11:00 a.m. Eastern Standard Time, the social media posts about religious services and dreading Mondays devolved into a cesspool of viewer comments regarding my mother's hosting [in]abilities, her occasionally controversial guests, and her appearance. On the one hand, I loved that there was a community of women of color out there who felt true pride in seeing someone who looked like them #representing. On the other, it never stopped being creepy when some rando shared a YouTube link of a compilation of my mother's legs in skirts "just because." What kind of sexist maniac edits something like that together? And why did it have over 100,000 views?

~~~~~~

THIS JUST IN:
SELECT ENTRIES COPIED FROM
#SUNDAYPOLITICOS TWEETS

United States Trends

Brian Hoffman | 1m
Not this chick again. What an idiot diversity hire **#SundayPo-liticos #MourningtheEndofPoliticalJournalism**

Celeste's #1 Fan Club | 2m
Celeste shut that Murphy guy down and is WORKING that press n curl **#YASqueen #imlovinit #SundayPoliticos**

Viola Printz | 4m
Idk. Please don't come for me Black Twitter, but is it just me or is Celeste a little off her game today? **#SundayPoliticos**

The Life and Times of Alaine Beauparlant

Say what you want about my mother (everybody else has), but you had to give her props. She was always the first to say that being on TV was just "the means to a greater end" and that journalism was about "upholding democracy" and giving "a voice to the voiceless" and blah, blah, blah—but the camera loved her. The way she held court at her roundtable was masterful. Straight-up Arthurian. She was the conductor who wasn't afraid to stop the train to put someone in their place and kick them off if need be.

"See, that's exactly why Americans today don't trust—"

"What Americans are *really* concerned about is making sure they have enough money to—"

"How would *you* know what Americans are concerned about? You're so far removed from—"

"Oh, please. Give me a break. You own two homes in New Canaan! You're not exactly the woman of the people you think you are. More like Marie Antoinette—"

"Now, hold on—"

If anyone interrupted beyond the admittedly higher-than-what-was-acceptable-in-real-life (but appropriate-for-cable-news) level, or started getting personal with their insults, Mom always called them out on it fast. She was even known for hounding her booking producer to stay away from the talking heads on other shows who went viral for losing their tempers in their on-screen tic-tac-toe boxes. She called it "choosing substance over spectacle." I expected her to tell the two opposing flacks who were getting into it to cut the crap in three…two…

What was the holdup?

"Oh no…" Dad muttered.

I looked up from my laptop in time to see the countenance of the confident no-nonsense ice queen I was used to flicker into a blank stare. I turned to my dad to confirm I wasn't seeing things, but his gaze was still transfixed on her.

"The name-calling will have to stop now…uh…" Mom said, touching her hand lightly to her forehead before dropping it quickly. I had never seen her so flustered. I gripped the arm of my seat, as if I could squeeze the words out for her.

"Delano?" Delano said.

"Of course. Forgive me. Let's take a time-out. We'll be right back with more *Sunday Politicos*."

The rest of the show went smoothly enough, but more than a few people online mentioned the odd moment. I (obviously) responded to some from the secret Twitter account I reserve for ratchetness and told them where they could ~~shove~~ keep their opinions. I regret nothing.

But off the record…what I didn't say online was how scary it was to watch her freeze like that. Mom never freezes.

Dear *Tati*,

Bonjour! Or should I say *hola*? Because I'm definitely writing this *en mi clase de español*. How are things in Haiti? Anything new and cool happening with PATRON PAL? I wanted to check in to find out whether you watched that *Sunday Politicos* link I sent you. I'm sure Mom was just having a brain fart but, even so, it kind of freaked me out. (The family curse strikes again, am I right?) Normally I would say that I was overreacting, but it really doesn't help that everyone keeps asking me if she's doing okay.

I picked up my friend Tatiana this morning on the way to school, and even her grandma told me—while I was speed-kissing the rest of Tatiana's family—to tell Mom that she was praying for her. I'd run in to use the bathroom, and when I walked past the kitchen, there sat Tatiana's parents, great-aunt, and a pair of grandparents. Do you know the most efficient way to greet a roomful of Haitians without offending anyone? Three words: pucker and pat. The first time I'd ever come over, Tatiana had warned me that her relatives were really snippy about manners and wouldn't like me if I just waved at them like *yon ti ameriken*. I followed her suggestion to kiss the air and give each of her relatives' cheeks a little bump. In Tatiana's words: you too would find a way to be as efficient as possible after years of having to greet every adult you run into after church.

It's weird. Everyone groups me and Tatiana together at school because we're the only two Haitian American girls in our grade, but our life experiences are way different. Sure, I speak Creole, but I can't mimic a Haitian accent the way she can. She's the only girl of five children. She's on a scholarship and I'm not. She goes to church like it's her job, while I can count the number of times I've been to a Haitian church on one hand that's had the pinkie cut off.

If I'm being honest, there are times when I don't feel as Haitian as Tatiana. Would my Zoe card be revoked if anyone found out that I'd been pretending to know who *Tonton* Bicha was? And that I'd never seen *I Love You Anne*? There've been so many times when I've felt left out of the Culture and I think it's because it's been me and Dad for most of my life. And whenever I go to Tatiana's house and see her with all those cousins and brothers and relatives, I can't help but wish I had that too.

Can you imagine a house filled with two to three variations of *me*, your favorite niece? Heaven, I know. But in all seriousness, it would've been great to have grown up with someone who knew all my secrets. Someone to pass the time with when Dad dozed off in front of the TV after taking another shift at work and Mom missed a third scheduled phone call in a week because of another breaking news story. That's not to say that I don't appreciate the moments we get to chat, *Tati*. It's just that you're so far away and Mom's always so busy. And sometimes I want someone besides Dad to talk to over dinner. Don't tell him I said that.

You know what's funny though? I shared all of this with Tatiana when we got in the car and she revealed how she was jealous of *me* for living in such a big house with only my "chill dad who is always working." And then after eating a mysterious fortune cookie one Friday night, we switched bodies, spent the next few days learning to love what we had, and turned back to our old selves wiser than we were before.

Oops—*Señora Ortega viene a tomar mi teléfono.*

Bye!
Alaine

P.S. ThankyouforthepeanutsDadsmakingabrittle—

Chérie,

I hope that emailing me in class does not become a habit. You should be focused on your lessons, young lady. Although you should never feel that you aren't Haitian enough. It's in your blood.

But to answer your questions, things at PATRON PAL are wonderful. Thank you for asking. We're getting our affairs in order to pitch to a few investors for a new round of funding. We just confirmed that we will have a new intern from Stanford joining our ranks for the spring semester. We're also working on an upcoming feature with a major media outlet that will highlight all the money we've been able to raise through the app to benefit the children of Haiti.

In regards to your mother, yes, we are all allowed to have "brain farts" as you say. However, it's understandable for people to be concerned. She is admired by so many; they will notice any change in her behavior. Have you spoken with Celeste about how you're feeling? Also, you might be onto something when you mention the family curse. I know your mom doesn't like discussing it, but I think she should. Bring it up to her. Sooner than later.

I'm happy you enjoyed the peanuts I sent. Tony Juste's *pistach* are the best. I've probably paid a year's tuition worth of school for each of his kids with the amount I buy.

Also, don't worry. I won't tell Jules a thing.

Bisous,
E
——
Estelle Dubois
Haitian Minister of Tourism
CEO of PATRON PAL
L'Union Fait La Force

Tuesday, November 24

The Life and Times of Alaine Beauparlant

Dad was going to kill me.

A decent number of days had gone by since I'd declared that the Beauparlant household would be absent from Career Day. At first, Dad was a little mopey, but he eventually made a full recovery.

But I was on the phone with Mom tonight enduring our third awkward silence in a twelve-minute span after she, yet again, stopped me from reading out the best (and worst) online viewer comments from Sunday's episode. I didn't know how she stayed above all that. I told her that if I were in her shoes, I'd probably spend a third of each show just responding to everyone who flattered or angered me enough. She said I "had a lot of growing up to do," which is always fun to hear.

I thought about bringing up the family curse like my aunt had suggested to give us something to talk about, but I knew there was no point. *Tati* Estelle had been blathering on about this curse for as long as I could remember. But she never got further than saying that we had one, because my mom insisted that she not fill my head with such nonsense.

Anyway, I didn't know what else to discuss, so I threw out the following just to say *something*:

"Um, did I mention there's a Career Day at school coming up?"

"Really? I didn't know they did those in high school." She jumped on my conversational life raft and didn't let go. "When is it? I'll have to check my schedule, but we can certainly make this work—"

"Oh. Don't worry about it. I know you're busy. Plus, the event is extra credit and won't affect my grade," I said as the thoughtful person that I am.

She paused.

"Do you not want me there?"

Jeez, not this again. She got offended if I didn't invite her to something and then felt guilty when she couldn't make it. I didn't hold it against her, but I would rather just avoid the whole routine.

"I told Dad he didn't need to come either. Seriously, it's fine. I'd love for you to do it, but I don't want to inconvenience you…"

"You're never an inconvenience! I will be at your Career Day bright and early to represent you well and make all your classmates jealous."

Visions of superiority danced in my head.

"All right, then. This will be fun! Maybe we can make a day of it? It's a Friday. December 11—"

"Hold on. The eleventh? Of December?"

The click-clack of her nails on her keyboard invaded my earpiece. She was undoubtedly scrolling through her calendar to discover a prior engagement more important than a school visit. I sighed.

"It's okay. I'll see you at Thanksgiving in a couple of days anyway."

"No!" she said sharply. "I can move things around… And didn't your father speak to you about Thanksgiving?"

Come *on*.

"He did not… What was he was supposed to tell me?"

"I thought that was why this call has been so uncomfortable."

"Really? I thought it was because we have nothing to say to each other."

"Alaine. I will not have you use that tone with me. I don't care how upset you are," she said with the steely voice she reserved for dictators and despots. "I have an important meeting I can't miss and Thanksgiving was the only date that would work."

"What's the point of hosting your own show if you still have to come in on holidays?" I asked. "Who is so busy that they don't take Thanksgiving off and then force other people to miss out on turkey?"

"I can't discuss that with you right now."

I snorted.

"Okay, Jane Bond—that was the last joke," I added hastily.

"It better be," she said. "All I can say is that I'm going to Germany for a few days."

"Tell the chancellor I say hey," I grumbled.

"Let's put a pin in it," she said. "Your father told me he's seen you typing away on your new computer. I'm glad."

"Hold up," I said. "*Of course* giving me this laptop was supposed to be some sort of consolation prize for you not showing up."

She stayed quiet.

"Well, if we're turning into the kind of family that just buys each other's love, can I get a new car the next time you can't make it to a family function? Should be around December 11."

"Alaine. I. Will. Be. There."

"Sure, sure, but if you aren't, please understand that Dad's old 1998 Toyota Camry has sufficiently built my character and I'm ready to move on," I said. "I'm not looking for luxury! Just working passenger-seat windows." Disappointment was an expected emotion when dealing with my mom, but it still exhausted me. I retreated into my cocoon of cleverness and let her off the hook. For now.

"I wouldn't be missing Thanksgiving unless I really had to. I promise I will be at Career Day."

"Sounds good," I said, unconvinced. The thing was, I've always gotten the sense that it didn't take much to miss a date with me. And sometimes I didn't feel like being the inconvenient daughter.

I hung up the phone. On the way to the kitchen to lick my wounds with a bowl of strawberry mint ice cream, I slowed down as I neared my dad's room. Might as well tell him that Mom was doing Career Day (so he could get his burning jealousy out of the way before waking up for work the next morning). Unlike my parents, I didn't wait an eternity before sharing information. His door was slightly ajar and I could hear him pacing on the large rug beside his bed.

"I'm sorry, but it isn't my responsibility to constantly break bad news to her on your behalf… You've had days to do this," he said, surely defending himself against whatever blame Mom was now trying to pin on him. Ugh. My ear was still warm from my phone and she had already called Dad to complain. "You shouldn't be afraid to talk to her. *Really* talk."

I kept walking, aware of how this conversation would play out. I'd heard it all before. She could tell him about Career Day herself.

The Life and Times of Alaine Beauparlant

My mother is late.

It was a nice surprise when she followed up with *me* a couple days after I invited her to Career Day to get more details and figure out what was actually required of her. I said she could just show up and ~~show out~~ be herself. I would work on the rest. She wouldn't take that as an answer.

"What is 'the rest'?"

"It's nothing. They just wanted the speakers to write a biography of themselves and a list of tips for us—what do you old folks call us—spring chickens."

"I have so much to say! Consider it done."

That's where we'd left things. Based on our track record, I could see it going one of two ways: either she'd write a five-hundred-page tome of all of her journalistic accomplishments, real and imagined, and film a ten-minute news package of the pieces of wisdom she'd acquired from that week she spent shadowing Sheryl Sandberg at Facebook…or she would completely forget.

To be fair, in this particular instance, she remembered...
but hadn't gotten to it yet.

Is the end of the week okay? she texted me last night.

Is it cool that the reason she didn't have time to write up
her career tip sheet was that she'd scored an exclusive interview with some whistle-blower who'd leaked sensitive government secrets to the public? Uh, duh. Is it *uncool* that days
ago I had offered to slap something together for her so she
wouldn't have to worry about it, but she insisted she wanted
to do it herself? Kinda!

I know I'm coming off a little dramatic (*quelle surprise*),
but that's how I felt. Don't get me wrong, I'm super proud
of my mom! How many people can say that they have one
of the most well-known journalists in the world as a parent?
Not many, I can tell you. And I'm definitely not saying that
I didn't want my mom to reach her ultimate career potential.

I really want her to!

Seriously!

Look at these exclamation points!

I look up to everything that she's done so far as a journalist, and I'd be lying if I said that I wanted to become a journalist myself because of anyone but her.

One of the main things that bugs me about getting so
upset whenever I think about my mom is that I always feel
strangely anti-feminist. Who am I to stop her from Leaning
In? She should go and conquer the world! Break that glass
ceiling! But is it too much to ask that she try a little harder to
fit me into her calendar somewhere between Monday's hair
appointment and Friday's quest for world domination? Especially for Thanksgiving. It's one of my favorite holidays ever,
maybe even more than my birthday. A socially acceptable

time to gorge yourself on as much delicious food as possible all in the name of gratitude? Count me in.

Every Thanksgiving before my parents divorced and a couple after they already had, the smell of turkey and perfectly marinated *pikliz* would waft around the house, driving me to madness as I waited for dinner to be ready. My mom would cook the tastiest food that I had ever had in my life. (Dad would make the biscuits and dinner rolls.) It was one of the few memories that I had of us as a cohesive, happy family. Now I can't even imagine my mom cooking anybody's meals.

This Thanksgiving, we celebrated with a few of my dad's employees from his clinic, some neighbors, my school's head nurse, Kelley Dawson, and her daughter Abigail (fellow classmate but more commonly known as the bane of my existence). Nurse Kelley was absolutely in *love* with my dad and everyone in the world knew it—except for him.

For the sake of journalistic credibility, I should make a correction—Nurse Kelley invited *herself* to Thanksgiving dinner a few weeks ago. One second Dad was making his monthly delivery of freshly baked croissants to the front office at school (yup, he's that parent), and the next Nurse Kelley was grilling him on Thanksgiving plans and insisting that he just had to taste her pumpkin pie. I tried not to gag. ~~It did not work.~~

I'm not against my dad dating; in fact, it would actually be good for him. But I'd be damned if the first person he truly considers is Nurse Kelley. There's no way on this planet ~~or any other planet in this solar system~~ that Abigail's arms would remain in their sockets if we lived in the same house. Not when I already walked through school having to dodge her as she insisted that she couldn't help but want to pat my "fluffy 'fro, girl."

But Nurse Kelley wasn't going to miss her shot at landing on my dad's radar and she did her best to pull out all the stops for dinner. She not only brought her pumpkin pie (which wasn't half-bad), but macaroni and cheese (not good—full stop), cranberry sauce (why do people eat this?), corn bread (decent), and smoked ham (honestly, she could've just brought this and we would've been fine). She definitely was a believer of the "way to a man's heart is through his stomach" doctrine. And she batted her eyelashes and stared more and more longingly at my dad with each bite of pie.

My mom checked in with me later that evening to see how dinner had gone. The conversation was more strained than it normally was, but I could tell that there was more to the tension than the fact that my dad had "casually" let slip that we had extra guests over for Thanksgiving. I couldn't even bring myself to make a joke to conceal my growing discomfort with how quiet Mom was on the other line. And she never explained why she *had* to go to Germany during Thanksgiving in the first place. I mean, come on, we all know that the only reason a renowned reporter would be traveling there during an important, albeit problematic, national holiday instead of spending quality time with her family is for a major scoop. Would it have killed her to just tell me that she was going to interview the chancellor and be done with it?

"Don't think I've forgotten that I owe you a biography," she said finally.

"Of course not. You don't forget anything," I said. "But I went ahead and ignored your wishes and made it myself. It was just easier that way."

She sighed. "I'm sorry, Alaine."

"Mom. Please. It's fine. I'm just ridiculously excited that you're even coming."

I'm proactive. I had a feeling I would need to slap something together when she missed the first fake deadline I gave her in hopes of getting her to meet the real due date for submitting this, which was this morning. What can I say? I know my mom.

Someone else who knows her is my dad, and he copied and pasted her bio from the GNN website and typed up some tips for me as well. I'd say he was pretty low sodium on the salty scale about it too. Some things don't change, I guess.

Celeste Beauparlant's Career Biography & Tip Sheet
(My Version)

Celeste Beauparlant is not a woman of the people. She probably doesn't want to stop and have a chat if you see her on the street. No, she is not "just like you and me!" That's okay. What she lacks in human warmth, she makes up for with stony resolve and an impressive résumé.

That résumé includes stints at GNN's Washington, DC, bureau as a production assistant before leaving for WLQR, a local affiliate television station in Panama City, Florida. She worked her way up to the Miami market in two short years and spent the next six at WPLJ, covering hurricanes, car chases, corrupt city council members refusing to pay parking tickets, and—on three separate occasions—a cat stuck in the grille of a sheriff's car. It was the same cat.

Her tenacity paid off. After a decade of toiling in the wilderness of local news, she returned to GNN as a political reporter. She'd vexed enough people that she started out as a Capitol Hill reporter and, shortly after, a White House correspondent. That wasn't enough for her though, so she got her own *Meet the Press* situation with *Sunday Politicos*, where she's been Queen Bey ever since. Thus, anything you can do, she can do better.

Celeste's Tips for Career Domination:

- Remember that journalism is a calling and will require long nights and missed birthdays and holidays, even Thanksgiving, which is ridiculous. Before committing yourself, make sure journalism is what you really want to do with your life, because your family will resent you for the time you must be away. Even if they say they're fine most of the time, they're totally lying. You might even get a divorce!

- Work hard and make sure the important people in charge of your career know how you've improved the company's ratings so that all the days away will be worth it—and you won't be stuck reporting on the same three stories over and over again.

- Get an assistant who is young and flexible enough that they can entertain your kid when she comes to visit and you don't have time to take her to the National Zoo or the Lincoln Memorial. Make sure said assistant is hip enough to totally get why said kid is now morally opposed to the existence of zoos and is debating whether to become a pescatarian.

- Ask open-ended questions that can't be answered with just a yes or no. On a related note: during White House

briefings, don't ask six-part questions that will prompt
the press secretary to make the same dumb joke about
long questions and then go on to choose just one part
to answer. The easy part.

Celeste Beauparlant's Career Biography & Tip Sheet
(Dad's Version)

Celeste Beauparlant joined GNN over a decade ago and currently serves as the host of the network's flagship program,
Sunday Politicos. Prior to that, Beauparlant was a regular fill-
in anchor for GNN shows such as *The Sit-Down with Mark
Scholtz* and the now-defunct *Quick Read*.

Sunday Politicos is GNN's most watched show to date. Beauparlant has interviewed notable individuals such as President
Barack Obama, Xi Jinping, and Ellen Johnson Sirleaf. She
also traveled to her birth country of Haiti to cover the mag-
nitude 7.0 Mw earthquake that devastated the island nation's
capital, Port-au-Prince. Her poignant coverage earned her
multiple accolades and cemented her role as host of *Sunday
Politicos*. No stranger to confronting the difficult, Beauparlant has spent her career bringing issues that disproportion-
ately impact marginalized communities to the mainstream.
Her ability to delve into any topic with tenacity and objec-
tivity has resulted in a devoted fan base and a combined total
of eight Emmy and Peabody Awards.

A vocal activist for minority and women's rights, Beauparlant
sits on several boards, including the International Women's
Media Foundation and the National Association of Black Journalists, and counts herself as a member of Columbia Journal-

ism School's Board of Visitors. She is a graduate of Columbia University and has one child, a daughter.

Tips:

- Never forget where you come from

- Don't be afraid to ask the hard questions—even of yourself

- Work hard, but also be sure to live

- Always keep things in perspective

- Take care of yourself

- Remember: the people who look up to you see the best version of themselves in you

Wednesday, December 2
From: Sister Samantha Bridgewater
To: College Prep Seminar List-Serv
Subject: Special Announcement from Celeste Beauparlant

Greetings students,

As you all know, Career Day is quickly approaching. In preparation for this momentous occasion, Celeste Beauparlant has sent our class a message. You can find her note below.

Many blessings,
Sister Samantha Bridgewater

———

Hello Sister Bridgewater,

Please have your students watch *Sunday Politicos* this Sunday, December 6. There will be questions and a discussion as part of my presentation based on the interview that I will be conducting with Senator Andres Venegas.

I'm looking forward to Career Day,
C

Did. You. See. That? What *was* that? Did I just imagine what went down on my television screen???

IN SHOCK,
ALAINE

BREAKING:

Video Footage and Transcript of Explosive and Baffling Moment Between Journalist Celeste Beauparlant and Florida Senator Andres Venegas on 'Sunday Politicos'

By Colt Rivers, *The Capitol Post*

CP reporters are working actively to determine what sparked the violent clash between GNN Sunday talk show host Celeste Beauparlant and Florida senator Andres Venegas this morning. If pictures are worth a thousand words, this video is worth a million. Here is the rushed transcript of the conversation excerpt leading up to what many are already calling "Slap-Gate":

CELESTE BEAUPARLANT: You're facing serious accusations, Senator.

SEN. ANDRES VENEGAS: Celeste. This is me we're talking about. I'm as honest as they come. You know, growing up, I'd get in trouble for being *too* truthful. So, when I tell you that I did not do anything improper, I mean it.

BEAUPARLANT: [*leans forward with hand under chin*] Those party-issued credit cards. You can say unequivocally that following the money will lead us to nothing…untoward?

VENEGAS: Not a thing.

BEAUPARLANT: Then why the delay in releasing the records? We have our FOIAs out all over the place, waiting.

VENEGAS: Celeste. *Celeste.* I assure you, I'm just following protocol. My constituents know of the liberal media bias that has been against me since I set foot in DC—

[*cross talk*]

BEAUPARLANT: …sir, it was your constituents that raised the issue. We report what we find and what concerns the public.

VENEGAS: Nothing personal, right?

[*pause*]

BEAUPARLANT: Exactly. So, when the public hears rumors of expensive dinners at Zuma and court-

side Miami Heat seats on their dime, let alone
claims of foreign vacations to Singapore…
it leads me to wonder what you'll do to re-
gain their trust. Your profile only continues to
rise, and the scrutiny of a potential pres—

[*cross talk*]

VENEGAS: I've been blessed with a vision since I
was a kid, Celeste. I was the youngest elected
member to my state's House of Representatives
and served there diligently before I felt my
work would be best continued in Washington. My
time in Congress only cemented my dream of representing *all* of Florida in the Senate—

[*cross talk*]

BEAUPARLANT: Your accomplishments are very impressive, Senator, and we mentioned them in our
segment intro, but with the growing calls for
your receipts or resignation, where do you re-
alistically go from *here*?

VENEGAS: [*reaches toward Beauparlant, places
hand on her forearm*] Well, Celeste, here's what
I can promise you and the American people—I'm
not going anywhere.

BEAUPARLANT: LET ME GO RIGHT NOW!

VENEGAS: What? What'd I do?

BEAUPARLANT: [*shrugs off Venegas, leaps from seat*] STOP IT! [*smacks Venegas across the face and pushes him off chair*]

VENEGAS: WHAT THE F— [*feedback from microphone*]

[*unintelligible cross talk*]

[*show cuts to commercial*]

~~~~~~~~~~~~~~~~~~~~~~~~~~~~~~~~

THIS JUST IN:
SELECT TOPICS TRENDING ON TWITTER THE DAY OF SLAP-GATE

United States Trends

#SlapGate

@nytimes, @ABCNews, and 10,000 more are Tweeting about this

#CelesteBeauparlant

35.2K Tweets

Andres Venegas

12.5K Tweets

#DamnGina

Just started trending

~~~~~~~~~~~~~~~~~~~~~~~~~~~~~~~~

Monday, December 7

The Life and Times of Alaine Beauparlant

The concluding years of adolescence mark the heightening of your maturity. As time progresses, you'll learn more and more about yourself along the way. High school in particular is a time of exploration, self-growth, and—

What a load of crap.

I folded the pamphlet that my dad had snuck into my lunch bag in half as Tatiana settled into the seat beside me in the cafeteria. He was notorious for giving me developmental handouts whenever he needed more time to get his thoughts together around a certain topic before discussing it with me. My dad thought he did a good job of masking it, but he cared about my mother. A lot more than he would ever admit to me (or her, for that matter). And with Mom now hiding in Haiti to wait out the media sharks, he was focusing all of his attention on me. I knew there was a larger conversation just looming around the corner. I could already hear him clearing his throat before looking deeply into my eyes and asking about my feelings on Slap-Gate.

It was now over twenty-four hours since Mom's on-air outburst and all Dad had done was ask me 856 times if I was doing okay and wanted to talk. Clips from what some were calling the "anchor altercation of the century" were inescapable. The evening news. The morning news. Late night shows. My classmates' cell phones. With each news alert, my dad would send another "just checking in" text, and it was driving me as Mad as the Hatter.

But I will say, the good side of Dad's incessant need to deliver a dose of optimistic self-help in the form of paper booklets commonly reserved for grief counseling and Jehovah's Witness evangelizing was that they always came with a side of freshly baked goods. Whenever feelings of worry threatened to overwhelm my father, he kneaded them into dough, where they could rise safely away from him. And while this was a delicious way for him to cope, I automatically associated those yummy carbs with heavy conversations about emotions and feeling shrinked by my own parent.

Middle school had been the worst. Dad clearly couldn't deal with being a single father to someone developing boobs, and he'd spent *a lot* of his free time in the kitchen. Once, Peter Logan grabbed my bag of raisin bread in that playful way immature boys who like someone do (at least that's what I told myself)...and out tumbled a bright red fact sheet: *Puberty is a monumental time period of physical development and discovery and it doesn't end with just periods!* He avoided eye contact for the rest of sixth grade.

As soon as a custodian wheeled by where Tatiana and I sat in the cafeteria, I tossed the pamphlet into the trash can. I debated getting rid of the bread maker when I got home. Maybe that would put a stop to Dad's well-intentioned but slightly irritating ways. It would mean no more tasty peanut butter banana kaiser rolls made from the roasted peanuts *Tati* Estelle regularly sent us from Haiti, but sometimes you have to make a sacrifice. Dad could have the bread maker back when I graduated.

Besides, I didn't need flaky, buttery pastries or a psych booklet to tell me what I already knew. With or without Mom slapping Senator Venegas, high school would always be a time of major angst and uncertainty. Some of my peers just happened to be able to navigate this dreadfully uncomfortable time better than others. In fact, quite a few of them had the I'm-going-to-act-like-I'm-much-cooler-than-I-really-am thing down to a science. But *I* was particularly terrible at this, because I couldn't help but fill awkward silences with any thought that sprouted in my mind. And now that my mom had *lost* it on air, the tiny amount of "think before you speak" that I possessed was officially depleted. Seriously, anything that anyone said only served to remind me of her outburst.

~~~~~~

DIRECT QUOTE #1
ALAINE BEAUPARLANT WITH FELLOW CLASSMATE AT
ST. CATHERINE DE' RICCI ACADEMY

Kid #1 at Locker:
Ugh, I hate this jacket.

Me:
You know what I hate? When my mom assaults a
government official on live TV.

~~~~~~

DIRECT QUOTE #2

ALAINE BEAUPARLANT WITH FELLOW CLASSMATE AT
ST. CATHERINE DE' RICCI ACADEMY

Kid #2 in AP English:
This class is the worst.

Me:
You know what's worse? When your mom asks your
class to tune in to her going bat-shit wild on
live TV.

~~~~~~

DIRECT QUOTE #3

ALAINE BEAUPARLANT WITH A VALUED STAFF MEMBER
OF ST. CATHERINE DE' RICCI ACADEMY

Lunch Lady at Lunchtime:
Rice and chicken or spaghetti?

Me:
Just juice, please. I brought my lunch. Just
like my mom brought those hands. On live TV!

~~~~~~

The Life and Times of Alaine Beauparlant

If St. Catherine de' Ricci was the setting of a cult hit teen movie, I would be the cub reporter always snooping around for a scoop. I'd take myself way too seriously and wear tortoiseshell glasses and compete with a young Jeff Goldblum for the editor-in-chief position until we would ultimately decide to share the responsibilities. (Which is actually what happened with me and my coeditor, George Finchley, who unfortunately doesn't have *any* of Jeff's droll magnetism. SAT vocab prep strikes again.)

Tatiana—whom I love and admire very deeply—would be the girl on lockdown who is always making excuses to her parents for why she has to stay late at the library. Each morning she'd walk out the door and drop the Deferential Daughter schtick as soon as she kissed her parents (and aunts and uncles and grandparents) goodbye. Just in time for homeroom.

She'd have impressive grades but also a massive yearning to be a part of the Popular Group, or the It Crowd, or, as I liked to call them, the Peaked in High School Posse. Meanwhile, I couldn't even will myself to be interested in who Nina Voltaire was no longer friends with or what college guy Kaylee Johnson was currently seeing. Not because I'm so above it all like everyone seems to think... I just have my priorities in order. How else am I supposed to follow in my mom's footsteps? She didn't get to where she was by sitting around talking about high school nonsense, so neither will I. That's part of the reason that I want to go to Columbia in the first place—to find my tribe. It's a fancy-pants school for sure, but how great would it be to make a name for myself at the great Celeste Beauparlant's alma mater? And the fact that it's in New York is amazing all on its own. I try to keep the fantasizing to a minimum, but there's no denying the allure of the Big Apple—four actual seasons, nonstop electrifying atmosphere, some of the most driven individuals in the world who are hungry and want to show everyone what they're made of. I know, I know. How woefully banal of me.

But alas, I am *not* in New York. I am at lunch in Miami and groaning inwardly as I watch Nina and Kaylee, respectively the undisputed queen and lady-in-waiting of the royal social court, make a beeline to our table because St. Catherine is the type of school that gives its students rotating assigned lunch seats "in order to foster a sense of Christlike community and camaraderie."

Tatiana lived for these days. I…did not. She took full advantage of the screen time and had her aforementioned I'm-going-to-act-like-I'm-much-cooler-than-I-really-am skills on full display. Nina and Kaylee had barely sat down before they were sucked into listening skeptically as Tatiana explained why her nonexistent relationship with some jock would never work out.

"He's on his way to being a *double* senior," Tatiana said as she took a delicate sip of her coconut water. "That's just way more baggage than I want to take on right now. Flings are supposed to be light and carefree, you know? I can't spend all my time thinking about how I'm going to move on to college and he's still going to be here."

"Yeah," I said. "That and the fact that he doesn't know who you are."

Tatiana gave me a death glare and went back to her story.

Honestly, what kind of friend would I be if I didn't tease her just a little? She made it so easy whenever ~~Tweedledumb and Tweedledumber~~ Nina and Kaylee were around. Besides,

it was part of the trade-off for being her alibi whenever her
parents demanded to know where she was or where she was
going. That's kind of the reason that Tatiana and I became
friends in the first place. It was a few days after the release
of first quarter report cards during freshman year. Tatiana's
mom (*Madam* Hippolyte, as I call her) had barged into AP
World History, the last class of the day, to demand in *very*
broken English why Tatiana had been marked tardy for nine
classes. The look on *Madam* Hippolyte's face after Mr. Berger
explained that Tatiana had been marked tardy because she
was indeed late for each of those classes was enough to make
me want to run out of the class screaming. Without a doubt,
Tatiana was about to be in a ~~world~~ galaxy of trouble. Tatiana's mom continued on, asking if this would cause Tatiana
to be held back, and I could hear the kids in class snickering
at *Madam* Hippolyte's pronunciation of *flunk*—or "floonk,"
as it sounded. Maybe it was because I couldn't bear to watch
Madam Hippolyte struggle to find her next words, or because
Tatiana looked so utterly embarrassed, but I walked right up
to the front of the class and explained in Creole to *Madam*
Hippolyte that Tatiana had been late because she was helping
me study during our lunch period. I promised not to make
Tatiana miss the start of class again and reassured *Madam* Hippolyte that Tatiana wouldn't be held back for cutting class. It
was a lie of course, but it worked. Tatiana's mom nodded her
thanks and turned to Tatiana.

"*Papa ou ap tande tout sa.*" I didn't want to know what Tatiana's dad would do to her, but Tatiana nodded and quickly
ran to her desk to gather up her belongings. On the way out,
Tatiana gave me a small smile and I knew in that moment
that we would be besties. That and the fact that she'd feel in-
debted to me for the rest of eternity. I smiled back.

Tatiana coughed exaggeratedly and elbowed me lightly in the ribs, pulling me out of my thoughts. Peter Logan had joined our table and was looking at me expectantly.

"Uh…yes?" I said sheepishly.

"I said thanks for helping me study for that calculus exam. I got a B… I couldn't have done it without your help."

"Oh," I answered, feeling my face grow hot. "You're welcome."

Peter looked at me for a bit longer than he should and smiled. Even I couldn't figure out what to do to talk my way out of this. Unrequited crushing makes me nervous and everyone knows that nerves are the kryptonite of wit. Nina, Kaylee, and Tatiana looked back and forth between the both of us like they were watching a tennis match, which didn't help either. If only I had Serena Williams's skills.

"So…uh…high five," I said and immediately regretted it. Kaylee snorted. Issa Rae in all her awkward black girl glory would be proud (or mortified). To my surprise, he held my gaze and slapped my hand. Then he frowned.

"What were you guys eating over here?" he asked, sniffing the air.

"Me?" I said quickly. "A peanut butter kaiser roll. Homemade. It was really—"

"Oh no. I have to wash my hands," Peter interrupted. "I'm super allergic to peanuts. I'll talk to you later, Alaine. Ladies."

Peter backed off from our table, but as soon as he was a few feet away, he made a beeline for his book bag. He quickly gobbled up what looked like his allergy pill and raced to the bathroom. I turned back to the girls, trying unsuccessfully to conceal my mortification.

"I hope he's okay," I said as I turned to stare after him again.

"He'll be all right," Tatiana reassured me. "I bet he just breaks out in hives or something."

"But hives are painful!" I replied, my horror growing. "And some people stop breathing!"

"He's allergic to everything. It's not his first rodeo. He'll be fine," Nina cut in. "So on to more important things. There's nothing going on between you and Penicillin Pete?"

"I couldn't have done it without your help," Kaylee said, imitating Peter's earlier statement in a low voice.

"Yeah, girl. You're the Netflix to my chill," Nina quipped.

Tatiana looked between the two of them and tried not to smile.

"What? Me and Peter? No way! Besides, peanut butter is legit a staple at my house. If he's allergic, there's no way we would ever work out. And I'm pretty sure you take an antihistamine or epinephrine for an allergy and not penicillin."

"Could you imagine their kids?" Nina went on, ignoring me. "They'd either be allergic to everything *or* think they know it all."

"Ugh. What if they're both?" Kaylee said with an eye roll. "Tragic!"

Tatiana looked like a fish out of water as she listened to Nina and Kaylee go back and forth. I could tell that she was torn between keeping up her cool factor and standing up for me as her friend. Lucky for her, I didn't particularly care about what those girls thought. And I didn't want to watch my best friend short-circuit as she struggled through what I'm sure she thought was a major crisis of conscience.

"Number one, we're, like, seventeen and this conversation is irrelevant. None of what we're doing now matters," I said as I stood up and quickly gathered my belongings. "And number two, would it really be the end of the world if our

imaginary kid *was* a highly allergic know-it-all? Much better than being a dumb—"

"Alaine!" Tatiana interjected, saving me from what some
would consider social suicide.

"I'll see you later, Tatiana."

"Don't leave now!" Kaylee shouted as I walked away. "We
wanted to see how long it would take before you snapped like
your mother!"

I didn't even bother to turn around as I gave her the finger. I may not know how to act cooler than I really am, but I
have get-out-of-my-way-you're-getting-on-my-nerves down
to a science.

Friday, December 11

ST. CATHERINE DE' RICCI ACADEMY: UPDATED SENIOR CAREER DAY AGENDA

Welcome, parents and guardians, to one of our most cherished annual traditions: Career Day! This is an opportunity for you to shine and share your passions and career wisdom with our beloved students before they head off to winter break and, soon, college. Career Day wouldn't be possible without you and we are particularly appreciative of your flexibility in light of recent updates to the schedule. Please find the complete agenda for today's activities below. We are eternally grateful for your participation.

8:30 A.M.–9:30 A.M.

Breakfast

Continental breakfast provided for all attendees

9:30 A.M.–9:45 A.M.

Welcome

Sister Gayle Pollack, Principal

9:45 A.M.–10:00 A.M.

Mindfulness Moment: What is Success?

A special virtual message of contemplation for our students from the Bishop of Rome

10:00 A.M.–10:30 A.M.

Presentation by the Honorable Constantine Logan, Chief Judge of the Eleventh Judicial Circuit of Florida

The role of law and order and unbiased sentencing in the Florida judicial system

10:30 A.M.–11:00 A.M.

Presentation by Luciana Martinez, Latin Grammy Award-Winning International Pop Star

So you want to be famous? Do you even lift? Because dancing on stage is a workout

11:00 A.M.–11:30 A.M.

Presentation by Brenda Johnson, Head Coach and Lead Recruiter of the Miami Dolphins Cheerleaders

How to ask for what you deserve in salary negotiations and look good doing it

11:30 A.M.–12:00 P.M.

Mindfulness Moment: A Conversation with Class President Nina Voltaire and Prescott Voltaire, Executive Producer of *Will You Be Mine?*

What did you just say to me? A lesson in conflict negotiation and anger management on the set of America's biggest reality show

12:00 P.M.–1:00 P.M.

Keynote Luncheon: Josephine Kobayashi

*What happens when your baby is no longer yours? The tech maven
and St. Catherine alum on her company's IPO*

1:00 P.M.–3:00 P.M.

Networking and Summer Internship Career Fair
*Parents, guardians, and students come together for an opportunity
to mix and mingle*

The Life and Times of Alaine Beauparlant

I knew I was going to have a crappy day as soon as I took a look at the agenda for Career Day. Not only did they start it off with a shady, backhanded mention of Mom's fiasco—"in light of recent updates"—they replaced her presentation with a chat about resolving disputes "the nonviolent way," moderated by ~~my nemesis~~ Nina and her dad, Prescott. *Seriously?*

What's worse is that each session was assigned seating and of course Tatiana and I were nowhere near each other in the auditorium we were stuck in for hours. Sister Gayle explained during the Welcome that our placements had been selected pre–Career Day to ~~prevent us from talking with our friends and shaming her in front of the people who pay our tuition~~ ensure that we got the most from the day's activities. But what really solidified today as the day from hell was when the Voltaires wrapped up their presentation. Nina had insisted on having the largest projector screen possible temporarily installed in the auditorium, where her Mindfulness Moment would take place. Throughout the talk, we were forced to watch clips of various women losing their cool as they tried their hardest to one-up each other and win the affections of a young venture capitalist millionaire named Jake. Each lesson in conflict negotiation and anger management was interspersed with a horrible demonstration by Nina and her father on the "right" way to handle whatever squabble had presented itself on *Will You Be Mine?* It was super weird to watch from my dead-center seat in the front row. I would twist around to make eye contact with Tatiana from where she sat in the crowd behind me at each strange reenactment.

Finally, we had suffered through the last scenario when Mr. Voltaire dismissed us for lunch.

Just as we started gathering up our things to leave, another scene popped up onto the projector. It was my mom on the set of *Sunday Politicos*, seated across from Senator Andres Venegas. My stomach tightened as my mom's outburst played in front of the entire senior class of St. Catherine de' Ricci Academy. The world slowed down as I felt the gaze of my peers fall on me and heard the buzzing of their whispers and cackles thunder like a shaken beehive. As if watching it once wasn't traumatic enough, my mom slapped Venegas over and over again on a continuous loop. Nina must've enlisted the help of one of our more tech-savvy classmates, because Mom's eyes grew larger with each smack, her face turning red as a tomato, steam pushing out of her ears like a too-hot teakettle.

"And this is how you *don't* solve interpersonal conflict," Nina shouted over the steam train engine sound that I could only guess was coming from my mom's head. "Isn't that right, Alaine?"

A hundred sets of eyes kept their focus on me while my own lasered in on Nina. My classmates' laughter echoed throughout the auditorium, drowning out the locomotion noises. Just as I opened my mouth to reply, Mr. Voltaire stepped in.

"All right, all right. That's quite enough," he said, hardly trying to conceal the smirk on his face as he pressed some buttons on a small remote. "How do I turn this thing off, Nina?"

"You'll miss the grand finale, Dad!" she replied, snatching the remote from his hand.

Suddenly, the steam engine noise grew so loud that even my classmates' laughter couldn't be heard. Mom's face had turned an alarming shade of magenta, the smoke from her ears shifting from milky white to black. A countdown appeared on the screen—5…4…3…2…1—*BOOM*. My mom exploded into a cartoony burst of fireworks and perfectly pressed hair.

I imagine that Mr. Voltaire finally grabbed the remote back from Nina and turned off the projector. But I was already gone, pushing roughly past my classmates as I made my way to the bathroom. As I left, I could hear Tatiana shouting after me to wait, but I didn't care. I was plotting. I didn't usually stoop to high school level antics, but Nina Voltaire had chosen the wrong person to mess with.

Saturday, December 12

The Life and Times of Alaine Beauparlant

One of the perks of our expensive private school was "free" access to the local college library. Tatiana and I were supposed to be spending our Saturday finishing up our final safety school applications, but instead I had spent the last thirty minutes whisper-raging about the ~~passive~~ aggressive shade spectacle that was Career Day. It wasn't until I looked up from my computer that I noticed Tatiana sleeping with her eyes open.

"Dude! Did you hear a word I just said?" I waved my hand in front of her face. She started suddenly.

"Sorry. What were you saying?"

"I *said* this is worse than when Nina had everyone calling you 'Tatiana *la Haitiana*' after your mom came to Mr. Berger's class freshman year. It actually had a nice ring to it. But the fact that we *know* she was saying it in a derogatory way just made it so nasty. Anyway, sorry I didn't turn around when you called after me when all of this went down. If I had stuck around, it would've definitely been Celeste Beauparlant Smackdown 2.0 and I couldn't let that happen. Besides, I've already got an idea—"

Tatiana snored loudly and startled herself awake.

"Girl. What is going on?" I asked, annoyed. "Why can't you keep your eyes open?"

"I fell asleep again? Ugh. I'm sorry. Church got out later than usual last night," she yawned. "*Cri de minuit*, more like *cri de* four o'clock in the morning."

"Jesus Christ—is God even awake to hear you then?" I loved hearing about Tatiana's holy ghost stories.

She rolled her eyes. "We were in the homestretch. The pastor was winding down when some lady jumped up from her seat and began convulsing. Of course, he needed to exorcise her and the congregation started singing and my mom had taken my phone, so I couldn't even record the thing."

A college boy sitting behind a tall stack of GMAT prep books and a venti coffee looked up from his laptop and frowned over at where we sat in the corner of the library reserved for groups.

"And then! He started to preach *again* to round out the night with positive energy or whatever and went into this tirade about evil people who do vodou and split their souls into pieces and hide them in jelly bean jars so they can't die."

"You mean Horcruxes?"

"Puh-leez. We had all that before JKR wrote about it."

"But is all vodou evil though?" I asked. "I feel like that particular instance would fall under the 'bad' branch of the spirit tree, but there are good uses too, right?"

Tatiana laughed. "Not at my church," she said simply. "There's no difference to us."

"So if I went to church with you on Sunday like your mom has been hounding me about for the past four years and they found out I had a family curse, would they try to pray it away?"

"What?!"

College Boy growled.

"How have you never mentioned a family *curse* to me?" Tatiana hissed.

"There's not much to mention. Whenever anything bad happens, my aunt says our family's cursed and my mom tells me to ignore her." I chuckled.

"Wow. Cursed how? I'm surprised you believe in all that."

"I never said I did. And my mom doesn't let my aunt get into the details. Mom always brushes it off as silly Haitian superstitions, but my aunt seems pretty adamant that it exists."

"You're always chatting with your aunt though," Tatiana said. She tried to lower her voice when College Boy gave an exaggerated sigh. "She's never explained what it is?"

"Whenever I bring it up and try to get her to tell me more, she says she can't out of respect for my mom. Personally, I feel like it's something my aunt made up to scare me into behaving as a child, and it just stuck around."

"Hmm. That's nothing to joke about," Tatiana said. "Either way, don't *ever* mention this to my parents, because they'd have me stop hanging out with you in a heartbeat."

I nodded. "I promise I won't."

College Boy sighed heavily and started throwing his books into his bag to leave.

"You can find the quiet zone upstairs," I said in a sticky-sweet voice when he was close enough to our table. I pointed to the Study Rooms Level 3 sign by the elevators right across from where we sat and watched as he looked between me and the sign and grumbled thanks as he walked away. He stepped into the elevator and I waved at him until the doors closed.

"You're so annoying," Tatiana giggled. "You've got to learn to let stuff go."

"Or people can learn to use their words in a productive way instead of huffing and puffing like the big bad wolf."

"Your curse has to be being a smart-ass," Tatiana smirked. "In all seriousness, do you think maybe that's what's behind what happened with your mom on air?"

"What?" I asked.

"Your family curse. Maybe that's what caused your mom to flip out on that senator."

"Ha!" I fake laughed. "She flipped out because he put his hand on her when he had no business doing so."

"You're right," she said. "It was just a thought."

Tatiana turned to the computer in front of her so that she could put the finishing touches on her applications. I stared at my laptop screen but couldn't get to work. I'd never seriously considered our family curse as anything more than a tall tale. Yet for some reason, I couldn't totally shake the feeling that Tatiana might be onto something.

Friday, December 25

The Life and Times of Alaine Beauparlant

I'm trying to be mature, but I just want to scream.

Your mom's in Haiti, Alaine, which means she can't be in Miami.

She's trying to feel better, Alaine.

So what if it's been, like, a month? It'll take the time it'll take.

Playing "Jingle Bells" on repeat is supremely annoying but one of your dad's Christmas traditions, Alaine. No need to rock the boat there and bum him out.

Those stupid kids in class don't know anything, Alaine. Even if your mom basically instructed them to tune in and watch her professional demise. ~~Don't sink to their level.~~

Even though it's very, very, very, very, very, very, very, very, very, very, very, very, very, very hard not to.

Just smile and be thankful for your new DSLR camera and bookstore gift cards. Yippee.

Merry Christmas. Bah humbug.

From: Alaine Beauparlant
To: Estelle Dubois
Subject: Oh, look, it's me, checking in

Dear *Tati*,

Greetings from sunny South Florida! How are you doing on this glorious morning? Let me give you an update on my life, it won't take long: ~~Like my good friend Harry Potter, I've been in my room, making no noise, and pretending that I don't exist.~~ You break curfew one time... (And the worst part is, I was late coming home from a party I didn't even want to go to in the first, second, or thirty-third place. My friend Tatiana recently graduated to the level of mutually indifferent nodding between her and this meathead she has a crush on. She was ready to up the stakes by having one of those conversations that can only happen in a corner of someone's damp basement over loud music and grinding. I was stuck snapping at and ignoring comments about Mom's...situation...by the food table. Tatiana's little tryst took longer than she thought it would, and since her older brother was our ride, I couldn't just leave without her. Dad was not impressed with my explanation. These are the best years of my life, right here.)

I can hear you telling me to "quit being so dramatic" so I'll stop.

What's going on in your neck of the woods? By woods, I mean the ruggedly deforested and mountainous lands of my ancestors. And at the risk of burying the lead, how's my mom? What's she doing all day? Is she going up the wall without any sketchy politicians to interrogate? Oh wait...

Sincerely yours truly forever and ever Amen,
Alaine

P.S. Don't think I forgot that it's a special day for my people. Independence Day. Boy, would I kill for some (pun intended). I'll send over my paper on the very subject as soon as I'm done with it. It'll blow your socks off.

Chérie,

It's been ages. I hope you weren't referring to me as one of those sketchy politicians! To answer your questions in order—

I'm doing very well. Another round of funding for PATRON PAL was successful and I couldn't be happier. Our new intern Jason is already putting out fires. The app was accidentally double charging some PATRONS and he fixed it in record time! We sent out a statement and most of the feedback from our users was they hadn't even noticed. We're helping so many underserved kids.

As for your mother...you know how she is. We might be twins but we're like night and day. She doesn't come with an off switch (or even a place to remove her batteries) and hasn't been doing much relaxing. The last time I saw her eyes unglued from her phone was when we had a blackout a few days ago and the battery died. She was forced to go outside and fraternize with her relatives, poor thing. I may or may not have been behind said blackout. ;)

P.S. Our Haitian ancestors did what they needed to do to win their freedom and become the first Black republic in history. I am proud to descend from them, as I know you are too. Your mother made the most delicious soup *joumou* to celebrate the holiday.

P.P.S. The issue of deforestation in Haiti is much more complex than a pithy line in an email. Don't tell me your school is saying that Haitian children eat trees too.

Bisous,
Estelle
——
Estelle Dubois
Haitian Minister of Tourism
CEO of PATRON PAL
L'Union Fait La Force

Wednesday, January 6

Alaine Beauparlant
Latin American History/Creative Writing
Sister Wagner

PART 1: THE LIST
DUE - WEDNESDAY, JANUARY 6...... 10% OF FINAL PROJECT GRADE

Instructions: Create a list of notable individuals in your chosen country's revolution. Include the defining moments of five or more principal actors (at least one should be from your prominent family) and describe his or her claim to fame. Use the List as a framework for both the Presentation and Story sections of your project. Be sure to also include a short paragraph describing your presentation plans.

Who's Who: The Major Players of the Haitian Revolution

History wasn't made for the folks who "win" participation ribbons. There were a lot of people who were instrumental to the eventual formation of Haiti as an autonomous state. Just being there as a Conscious Observer or having the smallest part in the making of a country is admirable—and more than I've done in these past seventeen years. Sadly, we don't know the name of the woman who might have watered Toussaint Louverture's horse and allowed him to keep riding into the night to warn my people that the French were coming, the French were coming. History has left us with only a few names to attribute to Haiti's inception and, unsurprisingly, they're all men. These are the guys who would win superlatives in the high school yearbook of antiquity. They were operating at the end of the eighteenth and beginning of the nineteenth centuries, which explains the lack of a strong female presence in their freedom fighting. I'll cut them some slack, I guess.

Who am I kidding? I won't.

Without further ado, a sneak peek of some of the "Who's Who" of the Haitian Revolution (1791–1804):

Vincent Ogé: Freeman known for sparking a two-month rebellion against French colonials near Cap-Français (now known as Cap-Haïtien) in 1790, which was considered a precursor to the 1791 revolt that began the Haitian Revolution. Ogé was rich, educated, and what people in the olden days called a quadroon, which sounds like a type of pirate but is a person who's of one-quarter African and three-quarters European ancestry and also an offensive word. He was in favor of giving other free men of color in the colony the right to vote, but nothing too outrageous like the women or slaves. Ogé and his fellow free supporters were able to overthrow numerous white colonial militiamen before eventually being captured. He was executed on the Catherine wheel, which entails tying the offending party's limbs onto the spokes of a large wooden wheel and hitting him with something hard and heavy to break his bones while the wheel turns. Don't worry, it's named after St. Catherine of Alexandria, no relation to our school namesake, St. Catherine de' Ricci. I checked.

Jean François Papillon: An African slave who worked on the Papillon Plantation. *Papillon* means "butterfly" in French and that's exactly what he wanted to be. Papillon yearned to escape that horrible cocoon of slavery and morph into a free butterfly. He was also a maroon until the 1791 slave rebellion he helped lead. And although *maroon* sounds curiously similar to something pirate-related, it refers to African slaves who ran away and set up settlements separate from their bondage systems. Think of 1791 as the Big Bang of the Haitian Revolution.

Léger-Félicité Sonthonax: French commissioner in charge of the free people of Saint-Domingue (aka modern-day Haiti). Sonthonax also had ties to the Society of the Friends of the Blacks, a group of French abolitionists. In fact, on August 29, 1793, the day he announced the emancipation of slaves in the colony, Sonthonax said he had "a white skin but the soul of a black man"—which I guess is the closest the eighteenth century ever got to meeting Justin Timberlake.

André Rigaud: So-called mulatto military leader who became the mentor of future presidents Jean-Pierre Boyer and Alexandre Pétion. He liked to wear a wig with straight brown hair to look whiter. No comment. Even though we can clearly see why that's problematic. Something else that's problematic? The word *mulatto*.

Dutty Boukman: A slave who was born in Jamaica who eventually became an early leader of the Haitian Revolution. On August 14, 1791, Boukman (along with a vodou priestess named Cécile Fatiman) led the religious ceremony at Bois Caïman that served as the catalyst for the Haitian Revolution. To show their loyalty, attendees of the ceremony had to drink the blood of a pig. There's really no going back from that.

Cécile Fatiman: One of the few women in Haitian history that you can find a bit of info on. (A bit = not much, but more than the others.) Cécile was the *mambo*, or vodou high priestess, who co-led the kick-off to the Haitian Revolution at Bois Caïman. In fact, she was the one who slit the throat of the pig whose blood the attendees supposedly had to drink. Some scholars believe that she died at 112 years old. She's probably still alive to this day.

Alexandre Pétion: The first president of Haiti. The John Adams to Henri Christophe's Thomas Jefferson.[1] Pétion and Christophe were such ideological enemies, they split Haiti into two separate countries. Pétion took the south with the *gens de couleurs* (mixed-race free people) and Christophe established his kingdom in the north with a predominantly black population. Rumor has it Oprah was inspired to produce her documentaries about colorism on OWN after traveling back to 1806 in her time machine and visiting Haiti during this tenuous period.

Like Jefferson and Adams, Pétion and Christophe died within hours of each other on the fiftieth anniversary of the country they helped create.[2]

---

1   Or John Adams to Alexander Hamilton/Alexander Hamilton to Thomas Jefferson/Thomas Jefferson to Aaron Burr/Aaron Burr to Alexander Hamilton... I suppose all founding fathers were incredibly messy.

2   Not really. But wouldn't that have been amazing?

Henri Christophe: Built the Citadelle Laferrière in Milot. To avoid an attempt by the southern government to steal his throne, Christophe killed himself at fifty-three years old after falling ill, leaving the crown to his son Jacques-Victor...who was assassinated ten days afterward by enemies of his father's reign. Historians aren't sure, but Christophe was likely buried in the Citadelle, or the location for the most adorable meet-cute ever. #shoutouttomymomanddad

Jean-Jacques Dessalines: Called for the massacre of Haiti's white minority, which resulted in several thousand deaths. He became emperor of Haiti in 1804 and was assassinated in 1806. Fun fact: Haiti's theme song (that is, national anthem), *La Dessalinienne*, is named after him.

Toussaint Louverture: The real OG.

Marie-Madeleine Lachenais: Mistress to Pétion and his successor, Jean-Pierre Boyer. The brains of the entire operation?

Marie-Louise Coidavid: Henri Christophe's wife. She spent almost a decade in exile in Europe after Christophe's suicide before returning to Haiti.

TL;DR: Folks fought for freedom, a lot of them died.

~~~~~~~~~~~~~~~~~~~~~~~~~~~~~~~~~~~~~~~

****Presentation update*: I'm still working on the details for that side of things and have no new developments to report, other than the fact that I'm no longer making a PowerPoint. I'd like to keep it a surprise, but believe me, it'll be worth it. Just you wait.****

~~~~~~~~~~~~~~~~~~~~~~~~~~~~~~~~~~~~~~~

Alaine,

Your write-up on the major actors in your chosen country's formation was very tongue-in-cheek. It had that singular voice of yours that I've come to know well. I would even say that the voice surpassed the content in development, and your tangents and personal opinions distracted me from the substance of the work. Did you have any rhyme or reason as to why you chose to highlight the contributions of the individuals you summarized?

You devoted just a line and a half to Lachenais after complaining about the lack of women recognized in history and mentioned Marie-Louise only in the context of her husband. Your explanations broke down along the way and I was completely unable to follow the chronology of the important historical moments. What is a "meet-cute"? And what does that have to do with the Citadelle? You gave an extensive portrait of Vincent Ogé but completely glazed over arguably the most important historical figure, Toussaint Louverture. And distilling Dessalines to three sentences? You know better than that.

I'd like to give you a challenge. Switch it up. Take this project as seriously as it should be taken. Not just for the grades component (although don't neglect that this assignment is worth 10 percent of your final project grade), or because your aunt would want you to because of her very public role in Haiti as the Minister of Tourism. Take it seriously because you take *yourself* seriously. This class is about growth, and in your case, growth will mean your ability to showcase your skills in taking directions and feedback. My feedback for this submission:

less is more. Save the creativity for Assignment 2 and the creative writing workshop. You should've given me what I asked for, which is relevant information, sans the unnecessary side comments. Just think of what your mother used to do each day for work. Her stories were supposed to be objective and absent of editorializing, right? (Some would argue that they were not...but do what she was supposed to.)

For this reason, you earned a C- on this assignment. Don't fret! You're a wonderful writer and, with a lot of discipline, you'll ace the paper and hit the upcoming in-person presentation portion of the project out of the park. Don't you love unintentional alliteration? But you know something I don't love? Surprises. I implore you, do NOT go overboard on Tuesday, January 12.

Please let me know if you have questions.

I'm praying for you,
Sister Wagner

-----------Message-----------

From: Alaine Beauparlant
To: Sister Patricia Wagner
Subject: Re: Re: Alaine Beauparlant - Part I Assignment

Hi Sister Wagner,

I've read your critiques and I agree—focusing on the women behind the scenes would be an interesting story. It'll require some digging, but I'm up for the task. And I would argue that editorializing is what sets me apart from others.

Also, a C-? Don't you think that's a bit harsh? I have a 3.8 GPA to uphold!

Your favorite student,

Alaine

They're really not going to let this go, are they?

What's Next for the Reigning Queen of Sunday Talk?

By Colt Rivers, *The Capitol Post*

Has Celeste Beauparlant left TV news for good? The beleaguered host of *Sunday Politicos* has yet to emerge from the safe cocoon that is her family home in Haiti weeks after an unexpected face-off with Florida senator Andres Venegas. Sources very close to the situation at GNN have said that they aren't even sure if Beauparlant will ever return to television.

"Everyone's still discussing possibilities at the network, but she's clearly damaged goods. There's an enormous risk of losing a segment of our viewer base," one source familiar with the dealings said on condition of anonymity.

Beauparlant, who made headlines six years ago for signing a $10 million contract to stay on as host of the surprising ratings hit *Sunday Politicos*, caught the attention of the public for another reason last December.

"She's got a sizable deal and the management definitely wants its money's worth," the source said. "But slapping a senator on live television has to be some sort of breach of contract, even if he chose not to press charges."

Viewers are still in the dark about what caused the violent outburst from the political journalist, but sources have said that the network intends to get to the bottom of it before making any long-term decisions. With the end of her contract on the horizon, network executives may choose to cut their losses and start over with a new host. Internal speculation points to midday anchor Keith Donahue, husband of *Sunday Politicos*'s executive producer, William Donahue, as a strong contender for the job.

The receiving end of Beauparlant's attack, Venegas, is not without his own negative publicity. The former rising star of the Republican Party is facing calls to resign in the wake of questions regarding his use of party funds for personal use. Venegas's stop on the show was widely considered the first leg of a non-apology tour to salvage any future political ambitions.

Celeste Beauparlant is the Latest Victim of the Racist Mainstream Media

By Tricia Jenkins, *Beautiful Brown*

Celeste Beauparlant is an award-winning journalist. She has five Emmys and three Peabodys sitting on her shelf. She consistently serves face and keeps her hair in an impeccable blowout while she's out grilling our nation's most powerful individuals. But that's not what we're talking about this week. We're not discussing how she's the first Black woman to solely anchor a network news channel's flagship Sunday morning political show and kill it.

A show, I might add, that was essentially a *sinking* ship that was relegated to her care after, rumor has it, her bosses knew they had to promote her to keep her at the network. The only stipulation: they didn't want to give her anything "too big." Instead, Celeste saw that Titanic for what it was and somehow fit the show's entire production team on her wooden plank before they all died of hypothermia. Ratings hell is surprisingly cold. She demanded a new set that didn't scream, "Our heyday was 1987!" and brought in panelists who weren't all old white guys who *were* eighty-seven. She expanded the discussion topics, encouraged viewer feedback via social media, and actually implemented suggestions when they made sense.

I was never one to spend my Sunday mornings couched in front of a television screen. I wasn't raised that way. But I still flipped to GNN six years ago because I wanted to see how Celeste would do in the new gig and ended up staying for the content. Yet here we are. Too busy pondering the fate of a woman who has done nothing wrong but fall victim to the angry Black woman stereotype.

The press is just about ready to skewer Celeste's career without getting her side of the story. I'm sure she had a legitimate reason for lashing out at Andres Venegas the way she did. Maybe it was his touch. What made him think he could lay a hand on her, besides male privilege? I tried to contact Celeste, but her reps say she isn't taking any interviews, which is her right; a right so often stripped from our hands as Black women in America. But that isn't the point. Let's not pretend that Venegas is the most popular politician in DC anyway. If that were the case, we wouldn't be looking into his suspicious spending, hmm? Show me the receipts, Senator.

No one asked what I thought about this whole debacle, but that's never stopped me from giving my opinion before. GNN doesn't deserve Celeste, and if they have her step down, they don't deserve us as an audience.

Don't just take my word for it. I leave you with an email I received from a GNN producer with proof that the show's management is undermining Celeste:

From: ▮▮▮▮▮▮▮▮
To: Tricia Jenkins
Subject: You didn't get this from me

Thought you and your readers would like to know.

-----------Forwarded Message-----------

From: William Donahue
To: Michael Sanders
Subject: Slap-Gate

Mike,

I've taken the liberty of reiterating my reservations here regarding the future trajectory of *Sunday Politicos*. Our viewers expect to enjoy an hour and a half of stimulating intellectual analysis of the week's political events, not watch a full-on brawl. Another freak-out like the one we witnessed in December would be most undesirable.

I remember watching *Sunday Politicos* growing up in rural Michigan. I don't know if my parents would have allowed me to if they feared I'd encounter such violence on a show that should be promoting compromise and diplomacy among polarized groups. Imagine if parents around the country stop watching with their children. Those young people will never learn to love *Sunday Politicos* the way I did. She's a huge liability because she could cause us to lose an entire demographic.

I'm happy to discuss this further in your office.

Sincerely,
William Donahue III

Executive Producer, *GNN Sunday Politicos*
Two-time Emmy Award winner

------------Message------------

From: Michael Sanders
To: William Donahue
Cc: GNN-SP-LISTSERV
Subject: Re: Slap-Gate

Will,
As long as the viewers love her, she stays. Please don't take the liberty again.

Mike
GNN President

An Imagined Email Exchange Between
Mom and Her Boss After Those Less Than Flattering
Articles About GNN Came Out

From: Michael Sanders
To: Celeste Beauparlant
Subject: Taking a break

Greetings from the Concrete Jungle,

I hope you're enjoying your time off to reset and recharge in the Real Jungle. As per our earlier chat with your agent, stay out of the spotlight as we conduct yet another focus group to make sure our audiences still react positively to you.

Mike

P.S. Please don't do anything else that will add to my stress load. I can't afford to lose any more hair.

-----------Message-----------
From: Celeste Beauparlant
To: Michael Sanders
Subject: Re: Taking a break

Haiti is not a jungle.
C

Monday, January 11

~~~~~~

TEXT MESSAGES FROM ME TO DAD

Daddy-O

ALAINE 2:07pm:
What career do you think Mom should try next?

ALAINE 2:13pm:
Okay I'll start.

ALAINE 2:14pm:
Pottery smasher.

DAD 2:15pm:
Not funny.

ALAINE 2:16pm:
MMA fighter's more her speed.

DAD 2:17pm:
Alaine...

ALAINE 2:18pm:
You're right.
She should hang up her fighting gloves for good.
Puppy petter.

DAD 2:18pm:
Chef.

ALAINE 2:19pm:
Rhythmic gymnast.

DAD 2:20pm:
Reality TV star.

ALAINE 2:21pm:
Yes! Contestant on "The Bachelor."

DAD 2:21pm:
(...)

ALAINE 2:34pm:
Dad????

~~~~~~

Tuesday, January 12

LETTER FOUND IN OPEN ENVELOPE

At the top of Dad's "Read" pile on the kitchen island

ST. CATHERINE DE' RICCI ACADEMY
1865 CARROLL LANE
MIAMI, FL
305-111-2222

Tuesday, January 12

Same Day Delivery Expedited Correspondence
Formal follow-up letter from initial phone call

Dear Dr. Beauparlant:

I will never forget the moment St. Catherine appeared to me in a vision while waiting in that CVS Pharmacy line thirty years ago. Imagine: the patron saint of the sick revealing herself to a woman picking up Tamiflu! It was in that haze of congestion that she called me to head a school of vivacious youngsters and transform myself from prematurely retired dentist to proud principal. It is this precious memory I turn to during trying times. Having to write this letter is one of those times.

All of us at St. Catherine's have *truly* admired you and Ms. Beauparlant's compassion and long-standing patronage to this illustrious institution. I repeat, we have appreciated every gift—financial or otherwise—to furthering our goal of educating Florida's gifted youth. We will be forever grateful to you. In addition, St. Catherine de' Ricci Academy is an institution that holds *all* its students in the *highest* regard and that is all I've ever wanted. There's no one else quite like Alaine in our student body and we've enjoyed having your daughter bring her unique sense of humor to our classrooms.

That being said, in light of a recent incident caused by Alaine's insistence to exercise that special brand of humor despite requests from her teacher Sister Wagner to rein in the theatrics, I have no choice but to suspend her through the end of the school year. It is my understanding that Alaine intentionally deviated from a more traditional presentation in favor of a distasteful demonstration that was never officially approved. Suspension is a very serious repercussion I feel is appropriate in this circumstance. Upon her return I strongly encourage a disciplinary hearing to address the future of Alaine at St. Catherine's.

All the blessings,

Sister Gayle Pollack

Sister Gayle Pollack
PRINCIPAL AND FOUNDER, ST. CATHERINE'S

Found in the refrigerator next to the almond milk

Alaine,

I am <u>very</u> disappointed in you.

I'm sure you aren't happy to read this note from me. Well, let me tell you, it is <u>not</u> a great feeling to come home and find a letter from your principal rehashing the terrible phone call we had. Your mother and I do not work <u>this hard</u> to have you act out in school. Is there an underlying cause for your actions that you would like to discuss with me? If so, you must use your words. You are equipped with the tools to make yourself heard.

I will work on getting you back into school. You will <u>ace</u> your remaining assignments and submit something respectable.

Love (but still disappointed),

Dad

P.S. PLEASE FIND MY BREAD MAKER. I KNOW YOU MOVED IT LAST.

P.P.S. WHAT WERE YOU THINKING?

Wednesday, January 13

The Life and Times of Alaine Beauparlant

My dad is making good on his threat to ship me off to Haiti. While this is definitely the go-to reprimand given by *all* immigrant parents when they're upset with their kids, Dad has never, ever used that with me. He's always going on about how "going to the homeland is a privilege, not a punishment." But here I am packing my bags.

I texted Tatiana and (even though she keeps saying that I "might've gone too far this time") she still couldn't believe that I was actually leaving the country. Considering the fact that her parents say this to her brothers ("Oh, and to me too, if I ever got pregnant before I was married and had a degree") at least once a week but never go through with it, she didn't have any advice to offer.

I sucked my teeth with each balled-up shirt I threw into my suitcase. Obviously, I wanted to go to Haiti. I'd never been before. I just didn't want to go under these circumstances. Why did it have to be wielded over me like some sort of prison sentence? Be good or the *Tontons Macoutes* will get you. They're waiting for you on the left side of Hispaniola. I emptied my shelf of hair care products into my suitcase. I didn't know what kind of humidity I would encounter in Haiti, but I wasn't about to let my twist-out suffer.

Maybe Dad's playing a weird mind game where he'll buy me a plane ticket, drive all the way to the airport, check in my luggage, and right when I'm about to head through security he'll say, "Just kidding! Get back over here, kiddo. You have a few months left of high school. Just don't screw it up and we'll all be okay."

But you want to know what's freaking me out the most? I spent the day looking up what a suspension will mean for my college applications and am officially starting to hyperventilate… What have I done?

Tati,

Don't listen to a word my dad says. He's already called and filled you and Mom in but here's the thing: he's *wrong*. Dad always believes Sister Pollack and all the other ladies at that godforsaken school over me. His only child and pride and joy.

Because I know you're much more reasonable, let me tell you the truth about The Incident. I've had about a week out of school to think it through. The day it happened, I burned my polka-dot dress while I was ironing it. Even though I could hear you screeching, "Bad luck! Bad luck!" in my ear, and despite being fully aware of how much of an "ill omen" you say it is, I still put it on because you really couldn't tell it was burned.

So really, all they can blame me for is making the terrible choice of wearing an unlucky dress despite knowing better.

In the interest of disclosure, I present to you a ~~biased~~ recollection of The Incident in question. Tatiana sent me screenshots of the conversation for posterity. Do they seem like innocent bystanders to you? Methinks not!

Alaine

SCREENSHOTS FROM STUDY GROUP CHAT ABOUT "THE INCIDENT"

LAT.AM/C.W. STUNNAZ

Tuesday 4:37 PM

Nina Voltaire:
So…she's insane…

Kaylee Johnson:
It's not even funny anymore 👎

Nina Voltaire:
Seriously

Tatiana Hippolyte:
Cut it out guys

Renata Balvin:
What happened??? I stayed home today

Nina Voltaire:
Lil Miss Waltina Cronkite finally cracked just like her mom

Renata Balvin:
NO

Kaylee Johnson:
YES. She *literally* strolls into class late in a full length dress with an enormous hoop skirt. Doesn't say a word to anyone until she gets up to do her oral presentation.

Nina Voltaire:
As soon as she's up there, she turns on a recording of drumbeats and starts going on and on about this creepy voodoo ceremony in Haiti. Then, all of a sudden, she runs out of the classroom and pushes in this cart carrying a cake shaped like a pig. It's covered in black fondant and everything!

Renata Balvin:
Did it taste good?

Nina Voltaire:
...That's like not even the point of the story -_____-

Renata Balvin:
I'm just saying! I don't really like fondant. It's pretty but too sweet and tastes super fake 😬

Nina Voltaire:
ANYWAY she takes out a knife from the big pocket of her dress and slices open the neck of the pig cake and blood LITERALLY SPRAYS EVERYWHERE

Renata Balvin:
NO 😨

Nina Voltaire:
YES. The first two rows were dripping with it and the red food coloring stained all the desks and the whiteboard and Sister Wagner's computer and the ceiling and MY TOP which I'm definitely gonna make her pay for

Kaylee Johnson:
And who would be sitting smack dab in the line of fire but Peter Logan

Renata Balvin:
Omg he's allergic to everything

Kaylee Johnson:
Including gelatin apparently which she had put in her gross little mixture

Nina Voltaire:
Yup. Wagner's screaming, Peter starts wheezing and going into anaphylactic shock. Alaine is *still* holding the knife and freaking out until she finally dumps out his bag and stabs him with his EpiPen so he doesn't DIE

Renata Balvin:
Wow! Yeah she's def a psycho... And isn't Peter's dad like a judge?? How much trouble will she be in?

Nina Voltaire:
Mmhmm. I heard that he's trying to get her dumb ass expelled

Tatiana Hippolyte:
NOT COOL EVERYONE

Alaine Beauparlant:
Y'all. I. Can. See. Everything. You're. Saying. 😃

Nina Voltaire:
Kaylee you were supposed to remove her 👎

Alaine Beauparlant removed herself from
LAT.AM/C.W. STUNNAZ.

*Annotated transcript of what I heard when I
listened in on the second house phone
(yup, we still have those) during Dad's
(pointless) conversation with Mom*

DAD: How are you, Celeste?
*Translation: I may not have grown up with a
summer home in Pétion-Ville, but I have manners too.*

MOM: Fine. You?
*Translation: I'm not going to spill my guts to
you.*

DAD: Alaine and I are fine.
*Translation: EVERYTHING IS FINE. I have every-
thing under control. By the way, you have a
daughter.*

MOM: I was getting to that.
Translation: You idiot.

DAD: I can't believe she got herself suspended
over a stupid class presentation.
*Translation: Alaine is dismantling everything
we've worked to put together for her future.*

MOM: Well-behaved women rarely make history.

Translation: I feel the need to be antagonistic with you by habit, but I agree.

DAD: Well, Constantine Logan *rarely* doesn't get what he wants. And right now, what he wants is Alaine out of school for almost killing his son! What if they press charges?
Translation: I'm spiraling, woman!

MOM: Okay, take a deep breath. We'll figure this out.
Translation: Chiiiiillllllll.

DAD: [*takes a shaky breath and clears throat*] Thanks. So… How's Haiti treating you? How's Estelle?
Translation: Ugh. Maybe she won't notice my change in subject.

MOM: It's Haiti. Estelle's…Estelle.
Translation: I'm not going to make this easy for you.

DAD: …
Translation: Well, then.

MOM: …
Translation: Ugh.

DAD: …
Translation: I'm a psychiatrist and very com-

fortable with extended periods of silence when I speak with reticent patients.

MOM: …
Translation: I'm a journalist and very comfortable with extended periods of silence during interviews with reticent politicians.

ALAINE: Hey, everyone! Can this conversation get any more uncomfortable?
No translation needed.

DAD: Oh! Hey, honey.
Translation: Oh, thank God.

MOM: How are you doing?
Translation: This is a thing that mothers ask their children, yes?

ALAINE: Fine, fine. I've started a new skin regimen and my pores have really embraced this rosewater face wash. How are you?
Translation: Will I finally be visiting you soon? Do you miss me? Have I adequately distracted you from the larger issue at hand?

DAD: I'll let you two have some mother-daughter time.
Translation: Because you're never available for any real mother-daughter time.

MOM: I actually have to get going. Jules, tell her.
Translation: I'm very busy and perhaps terrified to speak to my daughter alone.

ALAINE: That's okay! Talk later?
Translation: What a surprise. Psych.

MOM: [*hangs up*]
Translation: Probably not.

The Life and Times of Alaine Beauparlant

After that horrifically unpleasant phone call, I sat patiently in my room, waiting for Dad to explain himself. Just as I'd anticipated, I heard a soft knock on my door.

"Come in."

My dad drifted into the room and paused just past the threshold. He walked over to my desk chair and sat down before getting up to gingerly perch himself at the foot of my bed instead. He was using his "concerned shrink" face. I knew something was wrong before he said a word.

I remember when he sat down at the same corner of a much smaller bed and sighed before announcing to seven-year-old me that our family hamster, Flavia, had died. The tears fell almost instantly and he was ready with a box of tissues and a spoon for the pint of chocolate chunk ice cream he held behind his back. He enveloped me in a hug and kissed the top of my puffy hair.

"It's okay, Aly. These things happen. It's life."

"But...it's...not...*fair!*" I'd said between sniffles and gulps.

"I know. The best we can do is appreciate our memories and move forward."

With my short attention span, coping had been easy. We got a replacement parakeet, Flavio, after deeming three weeks a respectful period of mourning.

I was driving myself insane with thoughts of dead pets and cut through his silence.

"Dad."

"Alaine..."

My dad is a human ellipsis. He's always pausing...and pondering...and dragging...and trying not to stutter like he used to as a child. He always thinks before he says anything and I'm sure that's part of why he couldn't make it work with my mom. She probably figured she got enough hemming and hawing from the politicians she interviewed for work and didn't need it from her husband too. But this faltering wasn't because of his usual lulls. Something was different.

I couldn't stand the quiet.

"Just tell me whatever it is! Are you sick? Did somebody die? Did Mom smack another senator?"

He flinched.

"Your mother has Alzheimer's."

The room stood still. "I don't understand what you're saying… She's barely forty."

"You're right. It's early onset." My dad mouthed the words to himself silently, as if to make himself believe them. I didn't. My brain was on fire and couldn't, wouldn't make sense of what he was saying. *No. That can't be right. No.*

"How can that even happen?"

"Scientists aren't sure. There appears to be a genetic link, but she doesn't seem to have many relatives who had it. Maybe her grandmother when she was old."

Does that mean that I'm at risk? Am I terrible for having my first instinct be to wonder whether I could get sick too?

I tamped down my guilt and fought back the involuntary sensation of tears forming behind my eyes.

"When did she find out?"

"She confirmed the diagnosis with the doctor today."

"Confirmed?"

"I…recommended she see a neurologist."

I closed my eyes and the dam broke. A warm trail of salty tears slid down my cheeks as I held my face in my hands, shaking my head left and right, trying my hardest to not let what my father said sink in. And then something dawned on me.

"So you knew about this…this whole time…" I wiped roughly at the tears that wouldn't stop streaming down. "I didn't even know you spoke to each other enough to be handing out doctor recommendations! Why didn't anyone tell me?"

"She called me when she became concerned… I think this is something she needs to discuss with you herself."

"When? If she remembers to call in another week?"

I regretted my words as soon as they tumbled out of my mouth. My dad stood up.

"This conversation is no longer conducive to sharing information. I'm going to let you process this. We can talk later." He patted my leg and, because I know he had no idea what else to do, placed a pint of ice cream and a spoon on the small nightstand beside my bed. I likened my father's telling me the worst news of my life to the announcement of a rodent's death. But unlike seven-year-old me, I'd attacked him for no reason other than because I was angry.

Alzheimer's.

I looked at the ice cream on my nightstand and my vision blurred as tears threatened to flow again. No amount of chocolate chunk could soften the blow that my dad had just dealt. I crawled under my covers and stared up at the ceiling. How could this be? My mom was still young. She had her whole life ahead of her, a career that would stay on the rise once everyone got over stupid Slap-Gate. But the diagnosis explained her moment of confusion from a few months ago. A brain fart, I had called it. Her more recent outburst must have been because of this too… I didn't even want to think about it.

If I was being honest, I felt sorry for myself. I'd always imagined that I would get to know my mom when I got older. She might not have the super nurturing mother gene, whatever that was, but I'd hoped that we could have a different kind of relationship later on. One where she was more friend than parent, since the latter hadn't worked out so well. I would've been more than happy with that. But now it seemed that would never happen.

My gut clenched as I sank deeper into my sheets. That night, in my restless dreams, I watched my mother's face sag into wrinkles and folds belonging to a woman with blank eyes I didn't recognize.

PART II

AYITI CHERI, AYITI WTF

Wednesday, January 20
From: Estelle Dubois
To: Alaine Beauparlant
Subject: READ ME

Alaine, you have no idea how busy I am with PATRON PAL.
This news of your behavior comes at a very inopportune time.
I want you to listen to everything that I am saying (without
interruption) so I'm sending you this email. And to be clear,
this is about more than "The Incident" as you are calling it,
Alaine. In the past two years alone, there has been:

• A Situation: The time you said you couldn't attend your
  physics class because you thought the feng shui was
  "off" and messed up your "chakra alignment"—which was,
  frankly, offensive

• That Occurrence: When you staged a sit-in at the beauty
  supply store since you "no longer cared to subscribe to
  European standards of beauty"

• An Overblown Fracas: The instance during your sopho-
  more year when you decided that after fifteen years of private school education, it was no longer becoming of you
  to wear a uniform because it stifled individuality

  And you've had an excuse for each. It's never your fault
and always a misunderstanding propelled by a force beyond
your control.
  Darling, you know I love you and think you're quite special
but you make it very hard for others to see what I see. (And if I
had reviewed the paper you promised to send me, I would've
told you what a terrible idea this whole thing was and stopped
this chain of events before it even got started.) Principal Pol-

lack doesn't get to chat with you about your favorite sketches from *Saturday Night Live* or hear your thoughts on the merits of standardized testing. Your teachers, despite their good intentions, will never understand what it's like to live your life.

BUT that doesn't mean that you throw away your good sense and refuse to take responsibility for your actions. People are watching you, Alaine. You can't go around joking about Haitian history when you're the daughter of a very powerful journalist and the niece of the Minister of Tourism *in Haiti*. Your father sent us your assignment and I was disappointed. Again, why didn't you come to me? Why do you insist on doing things the hard way? There is no dishonor in asking for help, Alaine. I promise it does not diminish your genius to do so.

All things aside, you must know the important role Marie-Louise Coidavid and Marie-Madeleine Lachenais played in our very existence. I understand that finding information on them might have been difficult because they are relatively unknown in the larger scope of Haitian history, but as descendants of Marie-Louise Coidavid, we have access to letters that if included in your assignment would have elevated the quality of your paper. Instead, you wrote about these women as if they were simply the wives of powerful men. How inaccurate! They changed the course of my country and ensured this family's survival. Were it not for an agreement between these two women, you wouldn't even be around to string together those four weak sentences about them.

You have a lot to learn.

With that said, you are indeed coming to Haiti. Your flight leaves tomorrow. This is not a request, nor is it a vacation. It is a dose of reality. Your father says that you have already packed your bags for a lengthy stay. Thanks to his tireless efforts (and your parents' donations) you will not be expelled. Instead, you will spend two months in what the school is calling a Spring Volunteer Immersion Project working under the watchful eye of both myself and your mother on all things PATRON PAL. And your other teachers have been gracious enough to allow you to finish up your coursework online. You will also be working closely with Jason, the intern that I mentioned to you a while back. He is responsible and should be a positive influence on you. I have been quite busy with some behind-the-scenes happenings and trust me when I say that I don't need any more headaches than I've already got. Even if it's coming from my very imaginative niece. You've been warned.

Tati Estelle

P.S. I'll have roasted *labapin* waiting for you when you arrive if you promise not to get into any more trouble in the next 48 hours. If you do, I will have *ble*. The decision is in your hands. You have a lot to think about.

The Life and Times of Alaine Beauparlant

My initial reaction after seeing my aunt's email: okay. Did *Tati* Estelle not get the memo or does she need my dad to send a copy of one of his emotional intelligence pamphlets? And if she mentions that stupid intern One. More. Time! Responsible and a positive influence? Psh. He's just trying to get a nice letter of recommendation at the end of his little internship. He's the last thing I'm worried about. Him, and how my actions have come at an "inopportune" time for *her*. Not when her twin sister—my *mother*—is battling Alzheimer's. ALZHEIMER'S.

I can't stop reading about it online. You slip away little by little...or in a split second. That might be the scariest part. You don't know what's happening until it happens. And there isn't much out there in terms of treatment. You're sitting there, filing your nails, waiting for your brain to melt. I hate not being able to do anything.

"You can always do something." My mom said that to me once when I was seven and complaining about some bully who kept messing with the quietest kid in class. It's stayed with me my whole life. It's part of why I want to be a journalist, to at the very least share information with the world so that more people can choose to act. But dreams can't fix this. I can't imagine how powerless Mom feels and this has cracked my heart in two.

But that was my initial reaction. Anger and frustration. How predictable of me.

Then I realized that my aunt is going to lose the person who knows her the best in the world. I might hide behind my ~~hilarious jokes~~ snark when I can, but everyone's got their shields. Hers just happens to be putting on airs and going on like nothing's wrong. If she wanted to chastise me about my project, she could join the club. Besides, she was right: the internet isn't exactly teeming with information on Marie-Louise Coidavid and Marie-Madeleine Lachenais. And don't even try searching only their first names. It's *Marie*. That's like the Haitian equivalent of Maria in Miami. They're everywhere.

And even though me freaking out on my classmates seems even more justified now…I'll take the get-out-of-jail-free card that is this volunteer experience.

My dad's face was contorted into a terrifying grin as we sat across the panel of nuns who decided my fate. He was doing his best to remain calm as they handed down their judgment. When they finally said that I had to make up for my behavior by volunteering, my dad's smile had only tightened as he said, "I have just the place for her to do this."

Peter Logan's dad gave in and stopped pressing for more punishment when he learned I would be away from his son for a couple of months. And that I was a huge reason why he wouldn't have to repeat calc. (Again.) Not to mention, Peter's life was saved because only *I* thought to give him his EpiPen shot. ~~Let's ignore the fact it was my fault his life was in dan~~

~~ger to begin with~~. I suspect Dad told Sister Pollack privately about Mom's diagnosis and she didn't have the guts to kick out the girl who was already losing her mother. But she's not lost yet. I may be doing community service for PATRON PAL, but I'll also get to spend time with my mom, who still isn't ready to come back to the States. That isn't a penalty. It's a gift. I gave Tatiana a heads-up that I wouldn't be able to chat as much because my dad was giving me something called a "text messaging allowance" that was only for emergencies and part of my punishment.

The next afternoon when we arrived at the airport, my dad was silent as he helped me unload my luggage from the back of the car. My feelings about the trip hadn't changed overnight and that was clearly etched on my face. My dad sighed deeply and pulled me in for a hug. He was always the first to cave. But when he did, I was soon to follow.

"I love you, Alaine," he said as he held me tight.

"I love you too," I grumbled, the remaining anger I had slowly deflating as my shoulders dropped. "I don't mean to be a disappointment."

"You could never be a disappointment, although your actions are sometimes disappointing," my dad said with a small smile as he tilted my head up to look at him. "But you really need to learn to use your powers for good and not chaos."

"I'll try," I said. I gave him one last tight squeeze before I gathered my things. "Check my closet."

"Huh?"

"Your bread maker's in my closet."

I shrugged.

"Goodbye, Alaine!" he shouted as I headed into the airport. "Please don't do anything stupid."

The Life and Times of Alaine Beauparlant

My dad's words were still swirling in my head as the plane eased to a stop on the runway. I was in Haiti. *Ayiti*. The Motherland. Would you believe me if I said that I instantly felt a connection to the people? I could feel the blood of my ancestors coursing powerfully through my veins. Intense pride swelled within my chest as I realized that I had returned to the country of my forefathersmothers.

I kid. I scurried off the plane, weaving in between a youth group full of white teens wearing HOPE FOR HAITI shirts, desperate to find someone I recognized. I wondered briefly why it was always HOPE we wanted for Haiti and not other alliterative choices, like HIPPOS or HALLOWEEN. I couldn't help but be paranoid as I remembered the warnings my aunt had given me during our quick call that morning as I waited to board my flight.

Don't wear big jewelry.

Hide your phone.

And your camera.

Only ask for help from someone in uniform.

Actually, don't.

Actually, if you have to, make sure they have a badge.

By the end of our conversation, I was almost too scared to look the flight attendant in the eye. My thoughts wandered to the first time I was ever in an airport alone. I was eleven years old. As the child of divorced parents, it was my duty to make the yearly pilgrimages that kids with parents in different parts of the country made during alternating vacations and holidays. I had insisted that my parents let me travel alone this time.

"I can do it!" I had whined, convinced that showing my maturity by chasing my dad around the house would get him to concede. "Besides, our next-door neighbor Ashley does it. And she's only nine and a half!"

I like to think that my eleven-year-old persuasion skills were above par, but as a form of insurance, I did what any smart child of a broken home would do. I complained to my mom.

Mom has always been an…interesting parent. Her entire life was work. She'd seemed surprised when I gave her a call, interrupting her go-getter, unattached, twenty-first-century-woman bubble. It fascinated me even then that she could be so single-minded.

"What? Alaine who?"

"Alaine…your daughter."

"Oh! Yes! How can I help you, Alaine?"

"I wanted to remind you that I'll be visiting you this summer and—"

"Okay! Thanks for calling—"

"And! I wanted to fly to you…by myself."

"By yourself?"

"Yes."

"Have you ever done this before?"

"No."

"So why now?"

"Because I can do it."

"Hmm. Well. I don't see why not, then."

"Great! I'll just need you to tell Daddy and I'll be good to go!"

"Does he not want you to come visit me?"

"He does. But not alone. He just thinks that I'm a little girl and little girls shouldn't be traveling alone."

Hook. *Lie*. And sinker.

The easiest way to get my mother on my side was to summarize any argument as an attack against her feminist ideals. And because my dad thought of himself as a progressive man, (and more important, he loved to prove my mother wrong) he agreed to let me travel to Washington, DC, alone.

Two months later, I was on a plane from MIA to DCA. The ride was a smooth one and I made it through security without a problem. I walked confidently to the baggage claim section where my mom said she'd be waiting for me. As I settled into the plastic seats where I would meet her, after checking in with my dad via text, I felt like I was a mini–Celeste Beauparlant, looking at all the interesting faces of potential new stories headed to retrieve their luggage.

"That suitcase might be laced with anthrax. The resurgent perils of domestic traveling and the congressional gridlock preventing us from doing anything about it."

"Should babies crying midflight subject their parents to fines? A North Carolina lawmaker sure thinks so."

"Compression socks may be doing more harm than good. And we're not just talking about your outfit. Details coming up on Sunday Politicos's *'General Buzz.'"*

Two hundred headlines and three hours later, I was still waiting for my mom. My dad's phone calls were now increasing in frequency from one every half hour to one every five minutes.

Was I waiting in the wrong place? Had something happened to her along the way? The longer I waited, the more the friendly faces of the potential *Sunday Politicos* guests morphed into potential perps from *Law & Order: SVU*.

Finally, after what seemed like 525,600 minutes, I got a phone call.

"Alaine! There's breaking news and I've been held up. I have a flight to catch, but I'm sending my driver, James Richmond, to stay with you until your father gets there. James will have a sign with your name, my cell phone number on the back of it, and he'll be wearing a GNN shirt. Do you have any questions?"

"What—what's going on?"

"There's been a major earthquake in Port-au-Prince. I have to go to Haiti."

She was gone before I could ask a follow-up. I walked to where rows of television screens were blasting images and sounds of rubble and sirens. "We have no hope," cried one woman. Tucked in my oblivious world of excitement over getting to see my mother, I had missed the news.

Not long after, a very round man in shades ("Call me Jimmy"), carrying a cardboard sign with my name (Alayne B.), arrived to hang out with me. He held snacks in a grease-soaked wrinkled paper bag. My mom didn't have time to stop at baggage claim to say goodbye. Her flight was taking off. My father had already called to say he was on his way. Meanwhile, Jimmy and I played cards and ate sour straws and salt-and-vinegar chips that stung our mouths until Dad rushed over to where we sat and gave me a hug.

"Hey! Are you okay?"

"Yeah, just disappointed. Are you?"

"She'll make it up to you, Aly. Haiti needs her today…to let everyone know what's going on over there."

Dad used my emergency pair of keys to enter Mom's apartment and we stayed there for the weekend, visiting the Newseum and all the Smithsonians. He was a great guide, but my heart wasn't in it. I could tell my dad was distracted with the news of the earthquake as well.

When I became less self-centered a few days later, I squeezed his hand and mustered up my gravest face.

"Tell me how you're *really* feeling."

He hesitated for a second, then said his best friend growing up had died. Dad blinked back tears.

"I hadn't seen him in years... You always think you have time to do these things."

The Life and Times of Alaine Beauparlant

Seven years later, here I was in the Hugo Chávez International Airport in Cap-Haïtien ("Au Cap" if you're nasty), following the other passengers of my flight as we exited the aircraft. I clambered down the steps, whipping off my round sunglasses, a gasp escaping my lips at the sight of never-ending green mountains rolling into the distance. That and the dense fog made me look over my shoulder for dinosaurs, certain I had been transported into *Jurassic Park*. But soon I could hear the banging of *tanbou* and was quickly brought back to the present. Five men stood side by side as they beat their drums, while an older man with milky-white eyes sang a song about the beauty of Haiti as he strummed a tiny guitar. They all wore matching, bedraggled shirts and looked hopeful that someone would leave a little something in their hat. I mentally kicked myself for not having cash.

I hummed along to the music as we moved into single file and waited to be called by the agent. The people around me were from all walks of life, some looking bored as they waded through the mundane bureaucracy of returning home, while a group of people wearing the same mission trip shirts buzzed excitedly about the village they were headed to. A man a few places behind me tapped his foot impatiently. He wore a black-and-gold coordinated outfit: expensive-looking black sneakers, shining gold belt buckle, black sunglasses with metallic gold lining, and a large cross hanging from a chain on his neck. The oversize jewelry must've been freshly polished, because it gleamed in the light, whispering, "Come snatch me," with every twinkle. *He must not have an aunt who cares about him*, I thought as the customs agent finally called me to approach his stand.

"Name and business," he said with a thick Haitian accent.

"Alaine Beauparlant and to visit family," I replied in Creole.

"And where will you be staying, *Alaine*?" He spoke in English again, lingering on my name like he was trying to memorize it. I hesitated but gave him my aunt's address. There would be no escaping him now.

The agent frowned and switched to Creole. "Carrefour 54? Are you the niece of Estelle Dubois?"

"Y-y-yes?"

He sat up straighter in his chair. "*Bienvenue!* Right through these doors you will find your bags on carousel number two." He waved forward a man in a black shirt, the telltale insignia of an airport worker sewed onto the shoulders of his button-up. "Please show Mademoiselle Beauparlant to her luggage. Her family will be waiting outside to greet her."

Sometimes I forgot just how important my aunt was to the Haitian community. It was easy to be disconnected from all that when most of our conversations were congenial updates via email or phone. I nodded in thanks to the customs agent and followed the worker to the carousel. The airport was painted in shades of blue and large photos of grain, mangoes, and random landscapes from around the island hung on the walls. Colorful daisies accented each picture, rounding out the Caribbean decor. The busy airport terminal teemed with life as travelers on the day's final afternoon flight claimed their luggage and drivers sought passengers for their taxis. As I moved to take my own bags, the airport worker reached out and grabbed them before I could.

"*Merci*," I said with a tight smile.

"*Pa gen pwoblem*," he responded in Creole. While the

worker grappled with my three suitcases (he refused to let me hold even one), I shook my head at the memory of Dad insisting I pack one last bag full of my mom's favorite snacks.

ACTUAL SHOPPING LIST OF ITEMS DAD
MADE ME BRING TO DAZZLE FOODIE MOM

Blueberry rice cakes
Cinnamon-swirl gluten-free bread
Gluten-enriched chocolate raisin-stuffed muffins
The organic strawberry preserves that weren't on sale
last week
Grass-fed veal
Plain Greek yogurt
Almond milk
Vanilla almond milk
Almond butter
Chocolate muesli
Wine
Cherry madeleines
Two baguettes from that French bakery in Wynwood
that's closed Thursday to Sunday
Wheel of Parmigiano-Reggiano
~~Dozen free-range quail eggs~~

*(removed at the last minute because I convinced him it
wouldn't travel well)*

Dried kale chips
Quinoa

The Life and Times of Alaine Beauparlant

As we headed outside to meet my mom and aunt, I suddenly felt uncharacteristically shy. The palms of my hands were clammy as I gripped my purse, still unsure of how I would greet my mother.

I'd done my homework and looked up symptoms and tips on how to come to grips with The News, but none of that was enough prep to make me confident that I wouldn't mess up this reunion. She was such a proud woman. I knew my mom wouldn't want me to treat her any differently. But we were hardly close even before the diagnosis. What would she be like now?

It didn't help that this was my first time in Haiti. Some of my oldest memories were of my parents arguing in hushed voices, a never-ending debate about taking the family on a trip to our home country. My dad would be so earnest in his suggestion, "It'll be a good bonding moment! It'll bring us closer together!" My mom would vehemently refuse, "I will *never* go back. And neither will my daughter." And that would be the end of that conversation. Yet here I was, just a daughter, standing in a Haitian airport, searching for my fractured family and attempting to drown out the hurried clips of conversations happening around me.

"Alaine!"

I held my breath.

"Hi, Mom. Hi, *Tati* Estelle," I said tentatively as I approached them.

Suddenly, I was wrapped in a bear hug from both sides, my mom and aunt circling me with pleasantly dry arms that contrasted with my own sweaty limbs. My nerves dissipated, chased away by the relief I felt from seeing the two women I admired most in the world. It had been too long since we were all together.

"Welcome to the land of your people!" my aunt said, extending her arms in a grand gesture and nearly hitting the man handling my bags. (Clearly, you see who inspires my flair for the dramatic.)

Tati Estelle stopped to thank the airport worker as she stealthily slipped a tightly fisted wad of cash into his hands. We stepped out of the airport and there waited hordes of people hoping to make a little cash by carrying suitcases or giving a ride. Others stood with their hands extended, simply hoping to receive a few dollars just because. My mom quickly ushered us into the idling car where my aunt's driver, introduced as Fernand, was waiting and soon we were on our way. Lush palm trees with colorful flags tied around them dotted our path out of the airport and onto the country roads, the mountains rising and falling in the background as we drove along. The concrete wall that separated the airport from the surrounding community was covered in murals of Haitian people, spray-painted messages of hope and justice, and island scenery. We continued through the countryside and eventually came upon a monument depicting what looked like three men dressed in soldier uniforms, swords hanging from their sides, a bicorne hat planted firmly on the head of the man in the center.

"This is a statue commemorating the Battle of Vertières," my mom said, noticing the direction of my gaze. "It was the last battle before Haiti gained its independence."

"Of course!" I said a little too enthusiastically. The last thing I wanted was to crack open the possibility of her asking about my own botched tribute to Haitian independence... I changed the subject by asking a question I knew the answer to. "Is Henri Christophe shown too?"

"Not in this one. Henri Christophe is our ancestor…the one who built the Sans-Souci Palace and Citadelle Laferri-ère," Mom answered, her voice lowering slightly as if she were trying to recall an old memory. The right side of her face was awash in sunlight, accentuating her bottom lip, which she bit in concentration. "Jules left the field trip early with us… I could tell he didn't want to, but he came along anyway."

"Do you mean Dad?" I asked. I had heard their meet-cute story a ton of times. For the record, always from him. He conveniently never mentioned this sneaking away part when he told me of the day they'd shared their lunches. I filed the new fact away in my mental comeback drawer by habit, even as I realized my mom's mind had taken her somewhere else.

"Papa?" Mom spat. "That man is going to get what is head-ing his way any minute."

"Mom… Celeste… You there?"

She barely glanced my way before murmuring to herself, "He thanked me for saving him, you know. Andres shouldn't have been messing with him."

"Celeste?" my aunt said gently, placing her hand on Mom's arm.

My mom gave her head a slight shake and smiled sheep-ishly. "Sorry. That happens sometimes."

I nodded, for once at a loss for words. She looked as put together, as beautiful, as proud as ever. But that was a mi-rage. The walls of the car abruptly closed in on me. I couldn't escape this new reality, no matter how much I wanted to. We continued on our way to the house in silence, each of us avoiding eye contact with the others, staring ahead or out the window as we drove up yet another small hill. I swallowed the knot in my throat.

Papa. That man. Did she mean her own father? I wondered what he could have done to make her react that way. My grandfather had died years before I was born, but I sensed that whatever wound he'd inflicted was still fresh. The sting in her words confirmed it. I retraced our conversation in my mind in an effort to find a trigger. A distraction to keep the unexpected tears that were forming unshed. Dad. The Citadelle. Sans-Souci. Henri Christophe…

"Hey, *Tati* Estelle?"

"Hmm?"

"What did you mean when you said I wouldn't even be around to write those 'four weak sentences' if it wasn't for Henri Christophe's wife?"

Tati Estelle glanced at my mother, who had gone still.

"Well. Marie-Louise Coidavid is the matriarch of our family. She lived long after Henri Christophe—even her own children—had died. She was exiled for many years yet still made her way back to Haiti with the help of another first lady, Marie-Madeleine Lachenais—"

"Oh, look, we're here!"

My mother pointed out the imposing estate as we drove through a gate that had swung open. *Tati* Estelle sighed in what could only be described as frustration. I swept my gaze over the exterior of the house, which was painted a light yellow with white accents along the balconies, window frames, and front doors. A dark blue sedan and light gray SUV were parked in the driveway to the left. A large mango tree cast a long shadow over the cars, the first signs of the sweet fruit peeking through its curtain of leaves.

"This is our family home. Your grandmother moved to

Pétion-Ville years ago, so I moved back here," my aunt said as we climbed out of the car. Fernand was already rolling my luggage into the house.

"Snazzier than what you expected, eh?" my mom said. She glanced at my surprised expression. "Haiti isn't just dusty roads and impoverished people."

"Not if you go with what they show us on TV, anyway," I countered. Plus, we did have to zoom past dusty roads and impoverished people before we got to the more impressive homes with wide spaces in between. The same could be said of neighborhoods in Miami or anywhere else, of course. But this was to an exponential degree.

The foyer was lined in white tile and, a few steps ahead, the living room was on an elevated dais. Toward the back, white couches and mahogany fixtures rounded out the seating area with a flat-screen TV hanging on a far wall and an elaborate chandelier dangling from the center of the ceiling. Island Airbnb chic. Mom and I walked up the stairs, following *Tati* Estelle as she led me to where I would stay.

"This used to be my old bedroom," Mom said as I entered.

There was a large bed with a blue patterned quilt laid out on it. A lamp stood on a table on either side of the headboard and a dark cedar ottoman chest sat at the foot of the bed. Directly across from the bed, a wide archway marked the entrance to the bathroom with twin sinks and matching mirrors on the wall above them. Tucked into a corner was a sliding glass door that led to the balcony.

I stepped outside and gasped. The entire house was filled with tall windows that let in plenty of light, but even they hadn't prepared me for this view. It was like the whole country was stretched out before me. To the right, green mountains lay in the distance, clusters of houses peeking through the brush. And to the left, the Atlantic Ocean sparkled like a Caribbean diamond.

"Alaine, can you come here?" my mom asked, returning my attention to her. She was standing beside the bed, her arms folded. *Tati* Estelle was doing the best that she could to quietly sneak out of the room. "We need to talk about your behavior."

The bedroom door slammed as my aunt disappeared behind it.

"Sorry!" she shouted. "So much for a muted exit!"

And there we were. Me and Mom. Staring at each other as we stood in the room that was once hers, that I would now be sleeping in. She sat on the edge of the bed and patted the space beside her. *Straight from Dad's I'm-going-to-be-a-parent-now playbook.* I promised myself that I wouldn't speak first about The Incident and, by the looks of it, she had made the same vow.

We had a familiar mother-disciplining-daughter dance. The Celeste-Alaine two-step. I anticipated her next moves: break eye contact, shake head, smooth clothes when standing up in ~~defeat~~ retreat. Sure, I got into the occasional shenanigan, but it never affected my grades—until now, anyway. My mom wasn't around often, and when she was, she didn't have much of a say in my day-to-day actions. This fact hung silently in the air whenever we reached this impasse. What she *would* say was, in a very serious tone, "Alaine, you can't keep up this behavior," and then she'd back away from me slowly, inching toward the doorway, racing down the hall like an escaped prisoner as soon as she crossed the threshold.

This time was different.

"Alaine," my mom said after she was done clearing her throat for the third time. "I have to be frank with you. This is all my fault."

I picked up my eyes from where they'd fallen out of their now-bulging sockets. Was my mom ~~admitting that she had screwed up as a parent~~ making it easier for me to back out of my unavoidable punishment? Yes, yes, she was.

"How so?" I asked.

"I understand why you act out the way you do. When your father and I divorced, we decided it was in your best interest to live with him in a more stable home with someone who would be there regularly."

"How about we stop pretending that being away from me wasn't in your best interest too."

My mom paused.

"It has been admittedly…easier on my career to not have to deal with conventional parenting—"

"Please stop."

I could've easily let her continue to wallow in her guilt, but I knew that for all of my mother's faults, I had gotten into this particular trouble myself.

"Your actions have been a cry for my attention," she continued.

I tried to memorize her brown eyes and pointy nose the way they were right then. I volunteered in a nursing home and had seen older residents with Alzheimer's only in passing. Her skin was still so smooth and youthful, nothing like them or the version of her that I'd seen in my dream the night I'd found out. I wondered if she would even get the chance to grow old. I read online that the life expectancy after diagnosis was four to eight years on average but could be decades longer. Celeste Beauparlant was nothing if not above average… But just in case, I didn't want to spend the time we had left fighting about a stupid, immature thing that she wouldn't remember.

"You can't take *all* the blame," I said. I groaned inwardly as I pulled up the screenshots from my study group chat about The Incident for her to read herself.

My mom sat quietly as she skimmed through all the messages. When she was done, she handed the phone back to me and said nothing for a moment.

Finally, she spoke. "Your father told me something happened, but I didn't think it was as bad as he was making it out to be."

"Oh...it was bad."

"And this Peter? Is he okay?"

"He had to be taken to the hospital, but he's a trouper. Sometimes there are casualties of war."

"This isn't funny, Alaine. He could've gotten really sick."

"But he didn't. And I wasn't aiming for him. He knew that. I helped him study for calc last semester."

She rubbed her forehead.

"What is wrong with you?"

"Look. I had every intention of redeeming myself in class and taking the assignment more seriously. We each got to choose one major moment in history and of course I decided to write and present on the Haitian Revolution. Then Sister Wagner—"

"Sister Wagner?"

"History and creative writing teacher. She had us rehearse the presentation portion of our project in groups during class a few weeks ago. As soon as I started reciting from the Emancipation Decree of 1794, I heard snickering. Some of the students were calling out that I should make my presentation... on..."

Now, I know what you're thinking. Will I ever get the secret to this bomb twist-out? But what you should really be wondering is: Why the hesitation? What could the students have said that would be so bad as to warrant you acting out in such a way that would get you suspended? And if you weren't thinking that, you should be. Because that's exactly what my mom asked.

"You know how you were supposed to present during Career Day?" I continued when my mom nodded. "Well, Nina Voltaire and her father thought that it would be a great idea for their presentation to focus on conflict negotiation and anger management on the set of *Will You Be Mine?* in light of…recent events. I stuck through the presentation even though I could tell that it was going to be a load of—"

"Alaine."

"Crap. Finally, they came to what I thought was the end of their presentation. But I was wrong, because there you were on the projector in front of my entire senior class, slapping Senator Venegas on an endless loop. And then there was a countdown with smoke coming out of your ears and your eyes bulging out of their sockets…and you exploded.

"As I explain this to you now, of course it sounds like a stupid high school prank that I should've just ignored. But I couldn't let it go. That's when I got my bright idea to use my class presentation to demonstrate a moment of epic retaliation and get Nina back."

"Do *not* let your aunt hear you describing the kickoff of the Haitian Revolution at Bois Caïman as a moment of epic retaliation."

"I was just joking."

"Not everything's a joke, Alaine!"

"I understand that. And I tried to ignore the stupid 'jokes' from almost everyone in my classes—including teachers—

and that only worked for so long. Sue me for not wanting to deal with them bad-mouthing you anymore.

"And now I have to spend my first trip to Haiti making up for it by doing community service for the next two months. Dad handled it, and I won't be run out of school by a mob. It's fine."

"No, Alaine. You don't understand. Peter could've been seriously hurt. Luckily, you had the wherewithal to find his EpiPen, but what if you hadn't? Would you be prepared to face those consequences? You tell me that you watch every single episode of *Sunday Politicos*. Do you remember when I brought Donna Lewis on to discuss discipline disparities in the school system? By and large, children of color are punished more harshly for their actions. Yes, this was supposed to be your way of getting back at Nina, but look at how many other people were caught in the cross fire. You're focused on the fact that you were able to dodge expulsion, but all your father and I can think about is how this would've turned out if Peter had been seriously injured or, worse, died. Alaine, the decisions you make, even if they're well-meaning, can impact the rest of your life. And I need you to remember that your father and I will not always be here to get you out of trouble."

I was looking down at my lap as Mom spoke, but when her voice caught, I lifted my head. She was staring at me so intently, her expression pleading with me to hear what she was saying and not forget it. But I couldn't bring myself to think about the day my parents would no longer be around.

"I'm really sorry, Mom."

My mom smoothed down the front of her pants and got up. Instead of slinking out the door like she normally would whenever she had to have a stern talk with me, she stepped in front of me and took my hands in hers.

"Thank you for trying to stick up for me. I know you meant well. But next time, let's think things through a little bit before we act."

"I'll try harder," I muttered.

"That's all I ask," she said as she stroked my hair like she used to do when I was younger. One of my sharpest memories from around the time of my parents' divorce is my mother sitting me down and showing me how to massage my scalp and twist my hair so I wouldn't have to depend on Dad's embarrassing pigtails when she moved to DC.

I smiled at my mother as I realized this was the first time in a long while that we had had a meaningful conversation. Why hadn't it always been this way? It would've been great to have more mother-daughter moments like this instead of all those endured awkward silences on the phone. But as we sat here wordlessly, I could tell there was something more she wanted to say. She hadn't brought up her diagnosis or that strange moment in the car and I realized then that I was avoiding mentioning them too. And although we had so much opening up to do in an unknown period of time, I still wasn't ready to hear it from her. My mom must've sensed my ambivalence, because she leaned over and hugged me tightly. There was something about the way she held me now that made me feel like she was holding on for more than just a quick embrace.

"Are you all right, Mom?"

She leaned back, her sad brown eyes peering straight into my heart. "Yes...yes. I'm fine."

But I knew that she wasn't.

Research Following My Convo with Mom

The American Association of Alzheimer's Awareness (AAAA)

What to Do if Your Loved One is Diagnosed with Alzheimer's Disease (B.R.E.A.T.H.E.)

Believe that your loved one is still in there. Alzheimer's is a disease that lies to its sufferers and their family and friends by saying they're gone. That is not the case. You will always have the memories and moments that make up the experiences you share with each other.

Research. It's important to be informed after learning of this diagnosis. The weight of all the details may appear insurmountable, but they will start making more sense, little by little. Join support groups to have morale boosters in place in the most trying times, as well as the special moments that lead to smiles.

Eat. With so many other things going on, it might be hard to prioritize.

Advocate. You want the best for your loved one and so does their doctor. But if something doesn't feel right, don't be afraid to speak up for them.

Take five. Every so often, evaluate the relationship between patient and doctor and confirm the schedules, medications, and general treatment plans are still working.

Have a life. Make some time for yourself and keep up hobbies that make you happy. Go on a cruise. Practice meditation. Write letters to your loved one that you can share when they're having a bad day.

Empathize. It's easy to get frustrated, but imagine what it must feel like to actually have Alzheimer's and experience the changes in personality, judgment, and cognitive ability firsthand. When those emotions bottle up, take a breath and a step back to put things into perspective.

The American Association of Alzheimer's Awareness (AAAA) is a national organization devoted to increasing public knowledge of a form of dementia that affects over five million Americans. Please consult with a physician if you suspect you or a loved one has Alzheimer's. The AAAA does not replace expert medical opinion.

Bomb Twist-Out Instructions:
A water and leave-in conditioner mixture with a glob of aloe vera are your best friends when attempting a twist-out. Spray a small section of your hair until it's slightly damp and separate into two individual sections. Rub some mango butter on your hands and twist the two individual sections around each other. Do this across your whole head. For a stretched twist-out, start off each section as a flat twist and then two-strand twist to the ends. Leave overnight so that it can dry completely and rub some mango butter on your fingers as you untwist to keep things sleek. You're welcome.

Friday, January 22
From: Tatiana Hippolyte
To: Alaine Beauparlant
Subject: Hey Girl!

Hey, hey!

How is the motherland treating you? I know you can't be on your phone like that, but I still thought I'd check in. I'm already missing you! And you're so lucky that you don't have to endure the rest of these presentations. After your...mishap... Sister Wagner stopped all the presentations for a week. We're just getting started with them again because she had each person submit a line-by-line agenda of what they would cover and all props being used for review. It goes without saying that the rest of the presentations are stale AF.

    Anyway, talk to you when you get a chance!

Your bestie,
Tatiana

P.S. Oh! Almost forgot. Peter says that he forgives you. That boy's got it bad.

-----------Message-----------

From: Alaine Beauparlant
To: Tatiana Hippolyte
Subject: Re: Hey Girl! (Unsent Draft)

How's the motherland treating me? Pretty terribly. Why, you ask? Well, because my mom has Alzheimer's. I know. It doesn't make any sense to me either. That's why she slapped that senator (not that he didn't deserve it). But she definitely wouldn't have reacted that way otherwise. I'm sorry to spring this on you... I'm just so lost. What do I do, Tatiana? How can I help her? I'm trying to research to better understand this disease and it's all so scary. How am I supposed to focus on this immersion project *and* try to redeem myself from The Incident? You don't have any answers? Neither do I, for once. And I don't like it.

Scared, sad, and sleepless,

- A

Monday, January 25

PATRON PAL: The Digital Age's Response to Charitable Gifting

By Henry Boulder, *Techable*

PATRON PAL is single-handedly changing the way millennials and Gen Z donate.

Created by Estelle Dubois, Haiti's Minister of Tourism, the app allows users to connect directly to a child in Haiti who is in need and shows how their donations impact the lives of its recipients. For instance, donors can view photographs of their "Pal" with their brand-new book bag for school or eating a warm meal at dinnertime.

"I'm so happy to be able to give back to my community," Dubois told *Techable*. "Haiti still has not fully recovered since the earthquake and this is one way that we can all help get this country back on its feet."

PATRON PAL appeals to young people through its gamification of charitable giving. The app's interface is user-friendly, and users receive notifications if they haven't logged on to their account for more than a week to check on the progress of their Pal. While Patrons can be from all over the world, Pals are currently limited to Haiti. There are talks to expand the app to other countries as well.

"When you make donations to certain charities, sometimes it's hard to pinpoint exactly how your contribution is impacting someone. PATRON PAL allows you to see firsthand how your monetary donations are being used in Haiti and, very soon, throughout the world," says Dubois.

PATRON PAL isn't without its controversies. Some critics believe that the app reduces the suffering of the children showcased to no more than a human version of the once-popular Tamagotchi game.

"Apps like this are just a fad. Once people move on to the next craze, the kids that are serviced on the platform will return to a life overrun with hardship," said Haitian-born activist Michelle Charrier. "Who will explain to the child when they inevitably stop receiving support? They aren't Pokémon. We shouldn't put the Haitian people or any other group through this."

Dubois's role as Minister of Tourism is already under a microscope. The line between public service and private company blurs as PATRON PAL grows into more of a force.

While the merits of the app can be debated, Dubois's efforts as a political official in Haiti have unquestionably increased Haiti's GDP through tourism and the creation of PATRON PAL. The app's future is still uncertain, but one thing is apparent: it's not going anywhere anytime soon.

Hi there PP Team!

I hope you're prepared for another awesome week of changing lives and having fun doing it. We are on track to meet our biweekly goal for subscribers but not quite there so let's kick it into overdrive, Sales.

Engineers: even *one* email from a Patron having issues with accessing the donate button is a problem. It may be $10 for us but that's the difference between missing school or a week's food to our Pals.

Let's give the Marketing team a cyber round of applause for setting up the latest interview singing the praises of PATRON PAL. Next time, we'll be even clearer in the objectives of this company and preempt any questions of misconduct. I can't reiterate how delighted I feel knowing that I can have a vision one day and that my loyal team of movers and shakers will execute it the next. Don't let the haters hijack the narrative!

And finally, I'd like to take the opportunity while I have you all here to introduce you to my wonderful niece, Alaine. She will be joining the team for the next few weeks and I expect everyone to teach her something new—and to assign her plenty of work! Make her earn that A, as she is doing this as part of a spring immersion project for her school in Miami and I'll be giving her teacher regular updates. ;)

Alaine was the coeditor in chief at her school's online newspaper before taking a leave of absence to explore the world of nonprofit app development. Her series on gang members using online social media platforms to plan attacks and illegal activities won her the Gumshoe, the National Student

Press Association's leading scholastic award. She's volunteered at the Miramar Assisted Living Facility for the Elderly as a bingo caller for the past two years and was a candy striper at Aventura Hospital for a year before that until she decided she hated children (joking). To say I'm a proud aunt is an understatement.

Also, please stop by the kitchen and help yourselves to some of Tony's famous peanut butter. I grabbed a few jars earlier and decided to share. Yes, it is true—I am the best.

ED
Your fearless leader
— —
Estelle Dubois
Haitian Minister of Tourism
CEO of PATRON PAL
L'Union Fait La Force

P.S. I can't wait for our company-wide volunteer day!

From: Florence Jean-Pierre
To: Alaine Beauparlant
Subject: Re: Company Updates

BIENVENUE, Alaine! Estelle gushes about you and your amazing accomplishments all the time. I'm so happy to formally make your acquaintance at the afternoon meeting. Bring your ideas!

FJP

From: Thierry Dieudonne
To: Alaine Beauparlant
Subject: Re: Company Updates

New kid. Bring snacks.
TD

From: Antoine Rochelle
To: Alaine Beauparlant
Subject: Re: Company Updates

Hey.
AR

From: Jason Williams
To: Alaine Beauparlant
Subject: Re: Company Updates

Finally another intern in the house! I'm excited to have someone lower than me on the office hierarchy. Don't worry, I'll be
gracious in my ascent.

Best,
Jason

From: Alaine Beauparlant
To: Jason Williams
Subject: Re: Re: Company Updates

Ah. How quickly you've forgotten a key fact: you're not Our
Fearless Leader's niece, are you?

Best,
Alaine
P.S. I can't promise grace or anything else to you.

From: Jason Williams
To: Alaine Beauparlant
Subject: Re: Re: Re: Company Updates

True. True. Well, I'll be your faithful servant then. Let me know if you need anything and I'll be sure to show you the best food truck that comes to the plaza at lunch. (It's the only food truck so it really is the best.)

Best,
Jason

From: Alaine Beauparlant
To: Jason Williams
Subject: Re: Re: Re: Re: Company Updates

And technically also the worst. I'll take a rain check but thanks.

Wednesday, January 27

SENT ON BEHALF OF: Jeremie Francois
To: Alaine Beauparlant

Welcome to the world of your Pal, Alaine!

PATRON PAL was created to give the young people of Haiti a chance at success. The inhabitants of our small island nation don't just see "the poorest country in the western hemisphere." They see home. The truth is, even though they'd like to make their home better, they can't with what little they have. That's where you come in, Alaine. With your minimum weekly donation of $10, less than the price of some streaming service subscriptions, you're helping support the brightest children in our country on their quest to change its landscape. You'll be a Patron to a burgeoning talent and gain a new Pal in the process. Get it? Good.

Without further ado, check out this handwritten note from your new Pal!

PAL NAME:

Jeremie F.

AGE:

9

LOCATION:

Plaisance, Haiti

FUTURE ASPIRATIONS:

I want be lawyer for my country.

A LITTLE ABOUT YOUR PAL:

I am oldest brother of 3 with 2 sisters. I play futbol. I love the beach. My favrit food is *griot* and *bunon*.

PAL SINCE:

January 27

Howdy.

You're probably overwhelmed by my avalanche of calls, emails, smoke signals, and pigeon-carried messages but I want to exhaust all forms of communication with you so you can't say "YOU NEVER CALL" or "WHAT HAVE YOU BEEN UP TO?" or "I'M ALL ALONE IN MIAMI AND COULD HAVE DIED TWO WEEKS AGO AND NO ONE WOULD KNOW UNTIL MY BODY GOT WARM ENOUGH TO MAKE A STINK."

And I would inevitably respond,

"UH, I CALLED THIS MORNING" and

"I'VE BEEN ENRICHING THE LIVES OF HAITI'S CHILDREN, ITS MOST PRECIOUS RESOURCE" and

"IF YOU DIDN'T SHOW UP AT MY SCHOOL FOR YOUR MONTHLY DELIVERY OF BAKED GOODS AT 9:00 A.M. ON THE DOT LIKE YOU ALWAYS DO, NURSE KELLEY AND THE REST OF THE OFFICE WOULD SEND OUT A SEARCH TEAM BY 9:15 A.M."

Oh darn. I've run out of space. — *Aly*

Speaking of places of employment, let me tell you a little about mine (if you can call working for free, employment... Educational employment?). It's awesome!

Mostly. PATRON PAL took off seemingly out of nowhere and it's exciting to be experiencing the start-up culture at a place that creepily takes all your personal data and financial information for good and not evil. There are only ten full-time employees (plus another intern) in the Cap-Haïtien office (and a small team in Palo Alto) and everyone is so passionate about the Pals. Oh yeah, they're super strict about referring to their users as "PATRONS" and the kids as "PALS." It's kinda weird.

—Aly

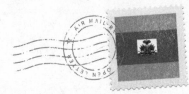

The Dubois's ancestral home is absolutely breathtaking. I have my own room, which is so critical for us teens and our angsty feelings. It used to be Mom's, who's now in another even fancier suite nearby. It's strange to be up close and personal with her stuff here, especially considering how I can barely even point out where her bathroom is in her apartment in DC.

I tried to brush my hair with the brush she kept on the dresser and broke its handle right off. Mia Thermopolis–style. Ultimate fail.

—Aly

Oh! And her closet. It's amazing.
I've decided to take up the vintage
'80s—'90s look for the time I'm here
because it'd be wrong to stay in that
room and not wear those skirts.
You wouldn't approve of the length,
which makes them even more perfect.
I really hope Mom and I click.
I want us to stop the charade and
start being ourselves while we still can.
Whoa. That got pretty #HEAVY
for a postcard. My bad.

Love you, mean it.

—Aly

POSTCARD TO TATIANA

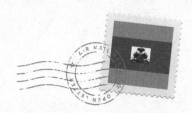

Hey girl hey!

How quaint is it that I'm sending you a postcard? Isn't it nuts that they still make these things even though we can just text and email one another? I know. It doesn't make any sense to me either. Speaking of email, sorry I haven't replied to yours. Things have been hectic since I got here.

But I'm loving the motherland!

Eating all the fritay and tablet that my stomach can handle.

Anyway, miss you.

Talk soon!

Alaine

Thursday, January 28

The Life and Times of Alaine Beauparlant

I know, I know. I wasn't being honest with Tatiana. While I was definitely eating all the amazing treats that Haiti could offer, I wasn't on some wonderful vacation. Although it did sometimes feel that way whenever my aunt's driver, Fernand, pulled over to buy freshly cut coconuts for us to drink on the side of the road. It was disconcerting how many men walked around with machetes in hand like they were briefcases. In the few days that I'd been here, we'd already started a little ritual. Once a day, we'd sit out on the second-floor balcony and look down the hill that *Tati* Estelle's house was perched on, watching the crowded streets below as people went about their daily lives. Colorful tap taps, obnoxiously painted school buses or pickup trucks repurposed into share taxis, were decorated with images of Michael Jackson and Bible verses. They zoomed down the road, loaded with more people than was safe, a random person on Rollerblades grabbing ahold of some part of the truck to help them glide through the crazy traffic a little faster. Just when I'd settle into a nice rhythm of people-watching, I would suddenly remember that I wasn't there for a getaway—I was missing school because I let stupid Nina get under my skin. And even worse than that was the fact that my mom was suffering from something that I still didn't fully understand. I didn't know how to feel about everything and the thought of sharing that with Tatiana gave me a major headache.

And I wasn't completely truthful in my postcard to Dad (#2 that is). PATRON PAL may be doing amazing work, but I'm *def* not a part of making that happen. What did I expect, that I'd waltz into an office with powder-blue-and-pink-striped wallpaper and glass cubicles and a not-so-ironically-declared Fearless Leader and change everything up? Don't fix what ain't broke, as they like to say, and it looked like PATRON PAL was a well-oiled machine running at peak levels. But I knew that if I waited any longer to get into the mix of things, *Tati* Estelle would just dump me on her favorite intern, ★Jason★, and have me figure out my place from there. Yes, he had been pretty nice so far. But what did I look like, becoming the intern of an intern? Not gonna happen. ~~Even if he was distractingly cute…with a quick smile, warm brown eyes, smooth light brown skin, and wavy dark hair that looked like he cared for it but not in a douchebag way.~~ I quickly realized that the only way that I'd be able to make any impact was if I put myself out there and asked how I could be of service. But let me tell you, it hasn't been an easy task to show how useful I am to what I've dubbed "Estelle's Trifecta." In fact, they've all rebuffed my advances in varying degrees of politeness:

FLORENCE, CHIEF MARKETING OFFICER

Florence was a tall, thin woman who wore all red and had the splotches of discoloration on her face usually associated with people who used harsh creams to lighten their skin. I remember making eye contact once with a young woman who walked out of my dad's office while I was waiting for him to get dinner. She must've also used those lotions. The center of her face was as yellow as her arms were black and she shrugged on her sweater protectively when she noticed where my gaze had naturally trailed. I tried to smile at her in what I hope was solidarity. My mom was fair-skinned, and I shared the same deep brown complexion as my father. They never made me feel like one shade was more valuable than another...but one time, Tatiana did spend the morning crying in my car on the way to school because her mother had thrown a tube of the skin lightener Peau-Clair at her.

With all these garbled ideas of colorism swirling in my mind, I'd sent Florence an email asking if she needed help with anything and tacked on the darkest fist emoji for good measure. Her response was sufficiently shady.

From: Florence Jean-Pierre
To: Alaine Beauparlant
Subject: Re: Greetings from the Intern

Hi Alaine,

So happy you're a part of the team but I'm good for now. I'll be sure to reach out as soon as I think of something.

FJP

P.S. Professional tip! Work emails aren't the best place to use smiley faces and the like. Thanks again!

ANTOINE, CHIEF TECHNOLOGY OFFICER

Antoine was apparently based in Palo Alto with the rest of the nerds (*Tati* Estelle's words, not mine) and was in Haiti for meetings the day I started. He left soon after the Trifecta met up in my aunt's corner office. I took the liberty of shooting him an email and never heard back.

From: Alaine Beauparlant
To: Antoine Rochelle
Subject: Greetings from the Intern

Hi Antoine,

I'm Alaine, the new intern. I wanted to introduce myself virtually. I've just gotten set up with some of the accounts and I noticed an email from a Patron hoping to meet her Pal. What if we set up individual or group visits between our users? And maybe we could have virtual hangouts where we schedule times to get Pals without internet access to our offices? We could even go to them and make a trip of it! I'd love to get your feedback and look forward to working together.

Best,
Alaine Beauparlant

THIERRY, CHIEF FINANCIAL OFFICER

The most noteworthy aspect of Thierry's appearance was
his rings. He wore two thick silver bands on each hand (pinkie, ring finger, duh) and a diamond ring on a chain around
his beefy neck. I wondered if he was going for menacing, as
well as tacky. Thierry was inaudible through the glass walls
of his office, but I could clearly see the long, throbbing veins
bulging out of his neck whenever he was particularly aggravated. I refused to get close enough to confirm for myself,
but I suspected the murky, smeared clouds on the otherwise
transparent cubicle had accumulated from the spittle spraying
from his mouth as he stood up to survey the small office from

behind the clear wall. He'd pace a few steps before stopping, legs spread in a power pose that would make Amy Cuddy proud. The way he shouted into the phone when discussing something as simple as probably a budget report made me think he wasn't above striking the person on the other end of the receiver with a bejeweled backhand.

"Thierry is a gentle giant," *Tati* Estelle said when I asked about his…er…passionate outbursts. "He means well but isn't afraid to get his point across."

I walked up to his office on my second day and took a deep breath before tapping firmly. He intimidated me, but I was the daughter of Celeste Beauparlant (who once went viral after grilling the country's most prominent "men's rights" advocates on her show during a contentious interview. "Men's rights— It's redundant, Jerry!" trended on Twitter for a full twenty-four hours and several Etsy shops popped up selling mugs and hats with lines like "You have a superfluity problem" and "Trust me, it's you." She later went on *Late Night with Seth Meyers* and he surprised her with a sweatshirt that read "Crawl back to your mother's basement"). So I wasn't going to let anyone stop me from doing my job—even if that job was just asking if I had one, and that answer was probably "no."

Thierry lounged with his legs crossed on the desk, his computer resting precariously beside his feet. He motioned for me to come in.

"Hi there! I'm Alaine, the new intern. Do you need anything at the moment?"

"Yeah…" My heart soared. "I'll take one of those *Cubanos* at the truck." It sank.

Tati Estelle strolled by on her cell phone and gave us a thumbs-up.

From: Alaine Beauparlant
To: Jason Williams
Subject: I concede.

Seems like I'll take you up on that food truck offer after all.

Alaine

-----------Message-----------

From: Jason Williams
To: Alaine Beauparlant
Subject: Re: I concede.

Awesome! You'll love it (either that or you'll starve lol)
JW

Google Search History

» Jason Williams

» Jason Williams +Haiti

» Jason Williams +PATRON PAL

» Who is Jason Williams
  -football player -basketball player

» Is it cheesy to say "it's a date"

» Food trucks in Haiti

» Dating in the workplace yay or nay

Aly,

Greetings from the NE 29TH Street bodega!

I was unaware that our neighbors down the street
   sold postcards but a prophet isn't without honor
   except in his own town.

I'm glad you're having fun but I must say dear,
   I briefly experienced angina when you called the
late-eighties and nineties vintage. This sounds cliché,
but that era seems like it was just yesterday.
   I don't think you expected to have your paternal
   death awareness theory tested out so early.

Love you (and of course I mean it),
        DAD

        P.S. Knowing you and your mother,
                you'll be bonding faster than you think

Monday, February 1
From: Tatiana Hippolyte
To: Alaine Beauparlant
Subject: Re: Hey Girl!

Hi Alaine,

I got your postcard—my first time getting one! It was actually kind of cool. Anyway, I completely understand being busy. They must have you running around all over to meet family and see the sights. And I'm so jealous that you're eating all that yummy food. Ugh! You should def try and bring me some goodies back from your trip. I want all the coconut-filled *kassav* that you can stuff in your suitcase! Please and thank you.

So...um...I don't know how to say this, but there are rumors that something's happening with your mom. Is she okay? It might just be gossip but I wanted to check in and let you know that I'm thinking about you and hope everything is all right. I know that you're on punishment, but if you're able to sneak away for a quick call, email, text message, whatever—I'm here!

Love ya,
Tatiana

Wednesday, February 3

The Life and Times of Alaine Beauparlant

~~~~~~~~~~~~~

Today was a good day. Until it wasn't.

"It's important to stay intimately connected with our Pals," *Tati* Estelle intoned in a meeting yesterday. The whole office was going to sign up new Pals at a village barbecue, and she'd invited Mom to join us and "get out of that old house." My research on the best way to approach life with someone with Alzheimer's was never ending. I read a blog series from a woman who would wake up at 5:00 a.m. to go running with her mother because she knew how much she loved it. The running shifted to walking, and then they eventually stopped once her mother's body couldn't take the strain on her muscles. That was a surprise to me. I'd always imagined Alzheimer's to be a curse reserved strictly for the mind. I spent so little time with my own mom that I wasn't sure what she would want me to wake her up at five in the morning to do. Luckily, she got up that morning on her own with a mission, which was making breakfast.

Mom. Threw. Down. French toast with fried eggs, loaded with tomatoes, chives, and onions. I'm not sure it's possible for Haitians to eat if there isn't a side of plantains with every meal, so she boiled a couple of those too.

Any fears of awkward silences were unfounded. Mom and *Tati* Estelle took turns sharing stories of growing up. Mom and *Tati* Estelle at fifteen stealing the neighbor's cat Mimi as payback for telling their parents how late they had stayed out one Friday night. Mom and *Tati* Estelle stealing their mother's convertible that same Friday their parents were away. Mom and *Tati* Estelle forced to undergo *pinisyon* and locked in their rooms for a month. I was impressed.

"Roseline had to sneak us books so we didn't go crazy," my mom said.

"Who's Roseline?" I asked curiously. The air shifted in the room.

"She was our *restavek*," *Tati* Estelle said quickly. "A house girl. She stayed with us."

"Why?"

She just shrugged. Her eyes begged me to say no more. Our easy conversation sputtered to a stop at the mention of Roseline, whoever she was. But before that, I watched in fascination as my mother and aunt teased each other and finished each other's sentences.

Mom rarely visited Haiti and *Tati* Estelle was living her own life, giving Haiti's image a face-lift, so she didn't fly out to DC much. Yet they'd fallen into the rhythm that comes so easily for twins. I loved how close Dad and I were ("The *dos amigos*," he liked to joke) and I wasn't obsessed with the idea of having another sibling…but growing up, I would sometimes imagine having a built-in friend on retainer, ready to spend time with me on the days he would work late. I wondered how *Tati* Estelle felt, knowing that there would come a time when their twin-tuition would no longer be the same, a day when she would look into the mirror that was her sister's face and not recognize the person who stared back at her.

"Tell her the story of when you first met Andres," my mom said between sips of orange juice.

"That was such a long time ago," my aunt said quietly.

I glanced uneasily between *Tati* Estelle and my mom. I didn't know much about how their paths crossed with Senator Venegas when they were younger. And while I was curious, I could tell my mother was not thinking of the last time she had interacted with him.

"Come on. It's hilarious!" Mom pressed.

"All right, all right." My aunt cleared her throat. "Once upon a time—"

"No! You're saying it wrong."

"Dammit. I must've forgotten. Oh well, we've got to get going."

I gathered the plates and cups and moved to the sink, where I turned on the faucet to rinse them off before scrubbing.

"Bon Dieu!" Mom said.

I nearly dropped a plate.

"What is it?"

She wordlessly lifted up a watch from the refrigerator and slipped it on.

"I thought I lost this forever ago and it's been here this whole time. At least it still works."

I smiled tightly and turned to my washing.

I'm not sure how long the ride to Limbé was, but I thought I would never get out of that car. Fernand drove like he was auditioning for *Fast & Furious 14: Haitian Cliff*. He would've gotten the lead. *"Ti Ameriken,"* he said when I yelped at a particularly sharp right turn. "This is nothing compared to how the rest of the country drives." I was never one to be carsick, but I kept my mouth firmly shut in case the plantains made their way back up. I reckoned my nausea here surpassed any of the discomfort my dad had claimed to have when he taught me how to drive two years ago. The road to the northern village we were visiting was a winding one with sections loosely blockaded from a steep ledge by wooden stakes. I obsessively inspected the gravel and dirt roads we sped on until I noticed the thick spikes were gone. I groaned. One overshot turn and we would tumble to a bloody death on the jagged rocks resting below. I shut my eyes to avoid them looking up at us.

We made it to our destination, technically in one piece. PATRON PAL was adopting a new school into its program. L'Institution de St. Dominique LaCroix taught boys and girls in *École Première*, which would be the Haitian equivalent of grade school.

"The vast majority of schools in Haiti are private," *Tati* Estelle said, getting out of the car. "A solid ninety percent."

"Why?" I asked.

She sucked her teeth. "Why do you think?"

"Money," my mom and I said together. She winked at me.

The company had chosen this school because it was one of the few public ones in the area, and in the second most important northern region after Au Cap. The private schools taught mainly in French because of the stigma of teaching Haitian Creole in the classroom. French had been Haiti's official language for decades before Creole gained the same status. The fact remained that French was the language of the elite and some people used it to segregate themselves from the bulk of

Haitians who couldn't speak it. *"Li pale franse"* (s/he speaks French) was a favorite saying my dad would use when complaining about a colleague of his being deceitful. That was my cue to remind him that he also spoke it.

"Alaine, there's Jason. Go check in with him," *Tati* Estelle said, pointing to where he stood in front of a table lined with name tags. "Your mom and I are going to make the rounds."

I thought we'd be early, but the front yard of the building was already bustling with activity. Clusters of children ran around in their blue uniforms, shrieking excitedly, playing a game that only they knew the rules of. Another group looked on enviously as its members waited in line to take their Pal portrait. The PATRON PAL team stood at various posts, manning the grill and tables with snacks and even small carnival games. The parents of these children must have dropped them off and gone on their way.

Mom pursed her lips. "I could've stayed in DC if I wanted to endure insufferable schmoozing."

"Yes, well, pretend that you're in DC, then," *Tati* Estelle said with a wry smile.

I left my mom and aunt to bicker among themselves and made my way over to where Jason stood shuffling the cards.

"Need any help?"

He looked up and smiled. My stomach squirmed.

"Actually...yes. Could you get me a taco from—"

I gave him a playful shove. "Ha ha."

"But seriously, I'll take any assistance I can get right now," he said. "I had one job. One. Staple the pictures of the kids to their intro bios so they can be transferred into the system later."

"And?"

He sighed. "And I mixed them all up. Thierry took the pictures and Florence asked the questions."

We turned to where Thierry, clad in a ribbed tank and vest, was taking pictures of the remaining children. His rings flashed as much as any camera could. Florence stood beside him in a wide-brimmed straw hat to block out the harsh sun.

"Stay still," he barked to the child seated to be photographed.

I slid half of the cards on the table into my hand and looked down at the top name-tag bio.

"I take it the kids already interviewed are the ones currently terrorizing each other until their parents return for them?"

"Yep."

"Let's do this."

"You're a lifesaver."

We fell into a comfortable silence as Jason picked the first card, CLEMENCE I., 8.

"Hmm...let's try that one," I said.

"The girl with the glasses?"

I walked over and plopped myself beside the little girl sitting on a bench alone with a book. The tattered yellow-and-brown cover was partly obstructed by her hand, but I saw *DERLAND* and took a guess.

"I love that story," I said.

She looked at me uncertainly. "Alice?"

"Alice was one of my favorite people growing up."

"That's my sister's name. *Men avèk yon y pa yon i.*"

"I think I like that spelling more," I replied in Creole. "Do you want to be a writer when you grow up?"

"Yes," she said shyly.

"Ahh. Then you must be Clemence." She nodded. Jason

sifted through the small stack of snapshots he pulled from his pocket and stapled her picture to the index card that read:

PAL NAME:

Clemence I.

AGE:

8

LOCATION:

Limbé, Haiti

FUTURE ASPIRATIONS:

I want to write stories.

A LITTLE ABOUT YOUR PAL:

Alyce is my little sister. She is 4. I like reading and writing.

"*Merci, Clemence.* Keep reading, it gets wild," I said.

Jason whistled as we set out to find NELSON V., 7. "Impressive. Are you, like, a child whisperer?"

I laughed. "No. Just observant. She reminded me of myself."

"You're not a timid bespectacled girl."

"No, but I do know a book nerd when I see one."

"Nice. Do you want to be a writer too?"

"Yeah…a reporter. Having Celeste Beauparlant as a mother definitely complicates things though."

"I'm sure you're an amazing writer."

"You don't know that," I said, suppressing a smile as I glanced at him from the corner of my eye. "I mean, I *am* but there's nothing that suggests to you that that's true. I'm really more concerned with whether I want to live in her shadow by stepping onto her turf."

"That's a fair concern." Jason nodded. "But something tells me that even the shadow of the great Celeste Beauparlant will become too small for you one day."

I couldn't have stopped the grin that sprouted on my face even if I'd tried.

"For the record, I'm #TeamCeleste all day. Especially after watching what happened on *Sunday Politicos*. I've hated Venegas since he tried introducing that bill that would've made it easier for corporations to not disclose all of their overseas accounts."

"Wow. How do you even pretend that there's nothing sketchy behind coming up with that idea?"

"You'd be surprised. Some of these politicians are really skilled at making their terrible proposals seem as if they're for the greater good. Especially since Venegas was suggesting that not passing this particular bill was a national security risk… Something about not wanting rogue hackers to gain access to financial accounts and use the money to fund acts of terror."

"Well, when he positions it that way, it almost sounds reasonable," I said.

"It does," Jason said, shaking his head. "I wish your mom had gotten the chance to grill him about it when he was on her show…before things went left. How's she been since then? Is she okay?"

Dammit. "There've been better days," I said cautiously.

"I can imagine. Well, *Sunday Politicos* hasn't been the same without her these last few weeks. No one cuts through the bullshit the way your mom does. And have you heard how they're trying to make it appear like she's taking medical leave—"

I cut him off before he could continue.

"No offense, but I'm officially *Sunday Politico*'ed out for the foreseeable future."

"Oh," Jason said in surprise. "Of course. You must've re-hashed this a million times by now. My bad."

"No worries!" I chirped. Like a *bird.* "I'll start on this stack. We'll go faster. Cool?"

"Yeah. Sure."

I enjoyed hanging out with Jason, but I wasn't ready to talk about my mother with anyone, even though I was the one who'd brought her up for discussion. What was I supposed to say? I walked away with my cards and pictures and settled on a little boy with a fade haircut and a scar on his chin. I'd find him and ask him what he wanted to be when he grew up and keep it moving. Hopefully it wouldn't take much longer to plow through the rest of the cards and I could get out of there.

Just as I was opening my mouth to get his name, a scream erupted. I jerked my head in *Tati* Estelle's direction.

"Celeste! *KOTE OU YE?*"

I ran to my aunt, who had her arms wrapped around herself as she fought back tears. I didn't need her to say what I'd already deduced.

Mom was gone.

PART III

TELL ME A STORY

Wednesday, February 3

The Life and Times of Alaine Beauparlant

I'm way too young and reckless to even envision life as a mother, but in the twenty-three minutes it took me and *Tati* Estelle to find my mom, I decided that this was what it must feel like when parents lose their kids. One second you're scolding them for sneaking a package of chocolate chip cookies into the shopping cart at the grocery store and the next you're freaking out when you realize they've somehow disappeared. As you're running through aisles and toward the customer service station to make an announcement, you're praying that they're already there, waiting impatiently, just like you instructed them to do if you were ever separated. Then you can breathe.

There is no customer service for wandering mothers in the middle of a Limbé forest. My aunt, the person I expected to have it all together, was paralyzed.

"Where is she? How could this have happened?" She muttered curses under her breath as she pulled her phone from her pocket and went to her call log. My mother's name was the most recent and she pressed it to redial. The ring went on and on with no answer and my stomach clenched.

I grabbed her shoulders. "When did you realize she was missing?"

"Just now. I stepped away for a moment to grab a plate of *akra* for her because she said she was hungry. She was sitting on that bench! I told her to stay," *Tati* Estelle said.

"What's around here?"

"I—I—" My aunt pressed on her closed eyes in a poor attempt to block the tears that were now streaming down her face.

"Everyone!" I shouted. "We need to look for Celeste. She looks just like Estelle."

Of course they knew that, but I didn't know what else to say. Some of the children stopped midplay and stared. *Tati* Estelle snapped out of her reverie and gave direct orders to her PATRON PAL employees, telling them to split up and search the surrounding area. There were trees big enough to hide her from view and the land was wide and lush with other vegetation. She shouldn't have gotten far if *Tati* Estelle had walked away for just a second, but we couldn't be sure. Even in my stressful hunt, I recognized the twinge of annoyance that invaded my thoughts. We both knew that wandering was a potential risk for Alzheimer's patients. My aunt shouldn't have left her alone in this unsecured area. She had never wandered off before, but we should've been prepared. It's a major concern for loved ones with Alzheimer's, and this was yet another example of how new this was for us and how much this diagnosis was changing our worlds. I was bothered by myself as well. My mom had slipped away and could have been who knows where by now, and at the same time I had been abruptly cutting off conversation with an attractive college boy to avoid discussing her because it would inevitably mean talking about her condition. Her sickness could no longer be ignored.

With Thierry left with the children to scare them into behaving, and the rest of her team in pursuit mode, *Tati* Estelle grabbed me and slid into the car where Fernand was already waiting.

"Where are we going?" I protested.

"I may have an idea where Celeste is," she said.

We rushed up the gravel path, driving away from the direction we came from until we approached a broad, rushing river. I barely blinked as my gaze roamed the land, convinced I would see her tumble down one of those steep cliffs and get carried away by the water any minute.

"Stop here!"

Fernand turned off the engine and my aunt leaped out of her seat.

"I'll be here," he said simply. "Good luck."

She pulled my hand and dragged me down to the bank of the river and stopped. There was my mom, digging a hole into a patch of wildflowers. A growing pile of dirt was beside her, with more soil smeared over her white top and linen pants. She lifted her head when she heard us approach and waved us over. I exhaled. My head throbbed and I pushed aside questions of how she could have made it this far on foot so quickly. But was it really a stretch? Mom's fitness regimen was legendary and had been featured in *Shape* magazine just a year ago. Her body wasn't deteriorating as fast as her mind was.

My mom looked up at us from where she sat on the ground, serene. "This is what she wants."

A Note And An Old Diary *Tati* Estelle
Left On My Bed After We Got Home

Alaine,

I know you might be feeling down or confused right now but hopefully these will help. It's time you knew what stock you come from.

Bisous,
Estelle

Thursday, January 31

From The Desk of Celeste Dubois

Roseline is cursed, or so she says. Of course I don't believe it. But if you hear you're a monster every day of your life, you might start to wonder if there's something to the lies. She's asleep now beside me, but her voice has not yet left my head: *I'm cursed, I'm cursed, I'm cursed.*

I don't correct her with what my mother actually claims: *we're* cursed. This entire family. That woman has the gall to believe that the detestable actions of ~~my father~~ her husband are because of a stupid family *madichon*. Roseline's pretty face and his refusal to accept "no" are simply *Maman*'s heavy crosses to bear. She's promised me and Estelle more than once: *Yours is coming. Your name may be Dubois, but that Christophe blood runs in you too.* Ours could be anything. Infertility like *Tati* Gladys. Going broke like *Tonton* Carle. *Ti* Vin Vin's kid's *ti pwoblem*. Maybe we'll be like her and lose track of reality. Blame spirits that don't exist for every bad thing we've done or allowed into our lives.

I don't think I've hated my parents more.

My hands shake as I write this because Roseline said she didn't want me to barge into their room and raise hell. It wouldn't be my first time, but she refused to have me getting in trouble "on account" of her. This would be righteous trouble, I argued. It's not right, what he did. I wanted to know why my mother could hiss such venom at Roseline and remain the doting spouse of a monster. I don't care if he's my father. He deserves to rot in hell. I have to do something. Say something. *Something*. Roseline just shook her head, her bloodshot eyes pleading with me to go against everything in my nature and stay silent. Pretend that my mother was right to call her a *malediksyon*, believe that she is the problem behind that man's wandering eye and violence. It's unacceptable.

Writing is supposed to contain my anger, but I feel it growing with each scratch on this page. I need to breathe…bottle this up and distill my rage into a plan that leads to real consequences. I still haven't figured that part out. How do you take down the most powerful man you know? How do you escape?

Thursday, February 7

From the Desk of Celeste Dubois

You rebound a curse with an oath. I don't usually encourage this kind of talk, but those are the first words Roseline has spoken to me since the incident. I didn't want to scare her away, so I sat quietly as she explained. The only way to coax the spirits into untying you is to have them tie you to something else.

Nothing is free, but we can make new rules under our own terms. Better terms.

I pushed back: *Why do you want to do this, Roseline? This isn't your mess to clean up. It isn't real.*

The eyes that bored into mine were long dried and resolute when she replied: *Yes, it is. So long as I'm here, it is.*

I didn't remind her that I don't buy this nonsense. That I want nothing to do with my family and their moans of curses and evil. Terrible things happen to terrible and good people, I wanted to say. We need a better justice system that acknowledges the horrors women experience in their homes… or the closest they have to it. Not more calls for *maji*. Instead, I squeezed her hands and said I would talk to Estelle when she sneaks back home from cavorting with Andres tonight. I still haven't created a viable solution, so we will do this ceremony tomorrow to release my family from its "curse" and appease her. Roseline deserves that at least.

Friday, February 8

From the Desk of Celeste Dubois

I'll start from the beginning so I can order my thoughts. We had a field trip today visiting Citadelle Laferrière. We all stood around the guide as he made his presentation. Estelle and I had already been taken on a private tour with our parents a few weeks earlier by *Tonton* Gideon, the Minister of Culture. I was hardly paying attention as the guide droned on about cannon size and concrete. I'd learned it all before. The things our parents cared about in order: their lineage, their assets, their children. When all three swirled together into one bouillon like they did at the Citadelle, *Maman* and *Papi* made sure we paid attention. *Papi* was already back in Port-au-Prince, his role as Minister of Communication keeping him busy. When I was young enough to still love him, I'd watch as he would lean back in his chair and spin food shortages and riots into "slight agricultural setbacks" and "passionate gatherings." No one in the country believed a word that came out of his office, but he kept the press releases coming, convinced that his time to lead would come soon. After all, he was a potential successor of the current president the way all Haitian cabinet members were. Now I could not think of him without thinking of Roseline.

"Does anyone know what year the Citadelle was completed?" the guide asked. There was a slight pause and then—

"Ei-ei-eight—"

I turned around to see a student about my age wearing the standard uniform colors of the all-boys private school a few miles down from our all-girls academy. He had smooth brown skin and a square jaw that vibrated with each attempt to spit out his words. The sun gleamed off the close crop of his dark hair. His gaze darted left and right as he struggled through his response.

"C-c-c-come on!" one of his classmates heckled. I knew which one.

"Nobody c-c-c-cares!"

"We don't have all day, J-J-J-Jules!"

"Shut up! None of you even know the answer and it's not like you have anything better to do at the moment. Let. Him. Finish," I said, raising my voice above the taunting. They finally quieted down and I gave this Jules a reassuring nod as he finished. The answer was 1820.

At the end of the tour, we were dismissed for lunch. Even in the shuffle of students breaking into their respective cliques, I felt his gaze on me. I sat on the thick roots of a tree surrounded by grass, in the shade cast by the side of the towering fortress. It was the same tree Estelle had carved an obnoxious heart into when we had visited earlier.

He was halfway through his peanut butter sandwich by the looks of it when he worked up the nerve to tap me on the shoulder.

"Can I sit here?" he asked.

I shrugged and he lowered himself beside me.

I felt silly as I opened up my lunch bag next to his meager meal. He had another peanut butter sandwich and a water canister, while I had a conch salad, a potato salad sandwich, and sliced apples slathered in American peanut butter courtesy of our chef, Jacques. That morning, I'd had the same fruitless argument that I always did with my mother: *Let Rose-line come to school with us. Jacques doesn't need her help.*

It would've made it easier for the plan she developed the night before. But no matter. Roseline gave a nod to signal we would still see her at the designated time that afternoon.

"Can I have some of that?" I said, pointing at his second sandwich. "I haven't had any real peanut butter in ages. My parents keep buying this American stuff, but it's way too thick and doesn't taste as good." I pushed my small package of extra peanut butter and apples toward him. "I'll trade you."

He nodded again.

"You can talk, you know."

"N-n-no. I c-c-can't."

"Don't let them get to you like that."

He shrugged.

"Have you ever tried a goat horn? They say if you fill one with water from the ocean and drink from it, it will cure your stutter."

"Wh-who's th-they?"

"It's more of a she," I amended. "My friend Roseline. She has a remedy for most things." *Except my father.* "Anyway," I said, pushing my thoughts far from me. I nudged him play-fully with my shoulder, "those guys should be teasing you for knowing boring facts about this place, not your stutter."

"I l-l-love the Citadelle... And history. It's the m-map to where we're h-headed."

"I don't know what to think of it."

"Wh-why's that?"

I looked at him sideways and, for no reason I can explain, leaned in. "I'm related to Henri Christophe. Plus, I'd rather be anywhere in the world besides Haiti. Redraw my map, if you will."

"What—really? *The* C-Christophe?"

"The very one. I'm Celeste Dubois by the way."

"Jules B-B-Beauparlant."

I groaned, "Your last name literally means 'good talker' and you stutter? You definitely have to try the goat horn."

"M-maybe I w-will. I've tried e-e-everything e-else. What's w-wrong with H-Haiti? You're n-n-not exactly s-s-suffering." He held up the plastic package pointedly.

"No, not exactly... But there are other ways to be unful-filled."

At that moment, I heard Estelle laughing as she made her way to where we sat. She had Andres Venegas in tow and my face let her know that, no, I still wasn't going to "give him a chance." He was the one who had set off the teasing from the other students. I had no idea what Estelle saw in him.

"Hey, sis!" she said to me as she wrapped her arms around Andres's waist. "Andres and I are off to our adventure."

"My guy! I didn't realize you knew Celeste," Andres said. "My bad."

"Apologizing for mocking someone just because he knows your girlfriend's sister isn't a proper apology, Andres," I said.

"It was just a joke about the scholarship kid, *chérie*," Andres responded. "Estelle told me about the ceremony you're doing. I'm down."

I turned my glare onto my twin instead. *Why would you invite Andres to this?*

"B-b-better scholarship than sp-spoiled," Jules said. "And th-that sounds like v-v-vodou to me."

"It's harmless, just our *restavek*, Roseline," Estelle said. "Are you ready, Cel? We gotta go before they start the head count to get back on the bus."

I carefully avoided eye contact with Jules, this stranger I suddenly felt the need to impress.

"She *is* my friend," I interjected. Andres snorted and Estelle had the decency to elbow him in the stomach.

"I'm n-not sure th-th-that's how it works," Jules said evenly.

"You should meet her! She'll probably really give you a goat horn," I said.

Can't you see I'm not like them?

I don't know why he decided to come along, but after looking at his scuffed watch with its raggedy band for a few seconds, he nodded. We stuffed our makeshift picnic items into our bags and walked past the white wall that surrounded the Citadelle. Where we were going wasn't far. We headed toward a small group of homes that stood on the edge of the cobbled road that was on a steeply angled incline. The houses were modest at best, held up by wooden planks for walls and metal sheets for roofs. It was unnervingly quiet and devoid of people.

We stopped when we saw her, sprinkling water over a low fire in front of the smallest home. Roseline grabbed an urn full of what looked like dirt and motioned for us to follow her inside. The door had no locks. It'd been empty since her mother died and the neighbors discovered a ten-year-old girl crying in the middle of the night. They had taken turns caring for her until *Maman*, on her usual self-congratulatory stroll through the Citadelle, heard about the abandoned child down the road and decided to bring her in, earning the praise of rich and poor alike. Roseline had been with us ever since.

Back in the home she'd tried to escape to many times, Roseline glowed. She'd braided her thick black hair into a dozen or so individual plaits and wrapped them into a low bun held in place by a blue-and-red scarf. I opened my mouth to explain Andres's and Jules's presence, but she waved me quiet.

"Everyone who is meant to be here is here," she said. "Sisters and strangers, I know what brings you to my mother's house."

We fidgeted under her gaze. Roseline's mother had been a popular *mambo*. So many people had been willing to help Roseline all those years ago because her mom had healed them or solved their problems. I suspected *Maman* had taken Roseline in hopes of getting some residual *benediksyon*. My parents rarely did anything without calculating potential costs or benefits.

Estelle grabbed Andres's hand and Jules stole another glance at his watch. Roseline motioned for us to come closer and to stand side by side. She stepped in front of each person individually, stopping to flip over our hands, palms up. As she ran a finger down my own hand's life line, I shuddered.

"More than one hundred and fifty years ago, the fates of Celeste and Estelle were sealed," Roseline began. "Not only them—two halves of the same womb—but all the subsequent generations whose lives have sprung from Henri Christophe and Marie-Louise Coidavid's union."

Andres snickered and made crude finger gestures when Roseline mentioned "union." Estelle tutted in disapproval as I met Jules's nervous gaze and rolled my eyes.

"The actions of those long dead leave our friends trapped. They are cursed, you see, and we gather here today to break it," Roseline said. She sounded almost as though she were in a trance, pulsing with all the power she hadn't had when she was crying in my room days ago. Jules's eyes sprang open wide. He looked ready to run as far away from us as he could.

I could see him mentally calculating how far his school bus could be by now.

"Stay," Roseline said simply, looking directly into his eyes. "Celeste may be the cause of our meeting today, but she doesn't have to be the sole reason. I sense what you desire most in the world and I can help you attain it. All I ask for is payment."

"Ugh. A scam," Andres scoffed. "I should've known."

She put up her hand. "Not for me, boy. I can taste what we all want on the tip of my tongue. Money. Power. Love. Success. You can get it—and supersede this family curse—but I need a commitment. We will be tied to each other. I'll guide us here, but it will be your responsibility to see this through."

"What do you want us to do?" Estelle asked nervously.

"I am just a vessel. The spirits will lead you to a site on the island to collect its soil. There must be no delay in this. If the payment is missed, the contract we will enter will be null. If you hesitate too long or fail to do it, there will be painful consequences."

"Wh-wh-what do you use the d-d-dirt for?" stammered Jules.

"Nothing is free," she said. "We must incorporate the earth because it's the earth that grants us these things. *Dakò*?"

We were reckless enough to agree. After a quick glance around with no objections, we nodded. In the moment, I told myself that I expected nothing to come of this besides hopefully putting Roseline in a better mood… But what if… what if she succeeded?

Roseline lit the thick deep red candle that already sat in the urn. The scent of spicy cinnamon and nutmeg filled my nostrils. She turned for the hefty glass bottle of aged amber rum standing on the table behind her that Andres had been eyeing with interest. It was my father's favorite liquor. She untwisted the cap and took a swig, then handed it to me and motioned for me to take a gulp and pass it on to Estelle next as she walked around us, circling like a cat. She lifted Jules's head with her finger and pulled quickly at a hair. Beside the bottle of rum was a wooden mortar and pestle. She handed the mortar to me and the thick stick to Estelle and motioned for us to take turns grinding the green leaves inside. She slid what looked like small blue stones in both Andres's and Jules's palms and directed them to nestle the items into the ground leaves. A blue liquid oozed from their centers.

"Ow!" Estelle yelped, examining her thumb. Roseline grabbed her hand and pulled out the splinter that was lodged shallowly in her finger.

She flicked in the tiny piece of wood, just barely glistening with a hint of her blood.

"Here," Roseline said. She rinsed my sister's hand with a few splashes of Florida water. She stirred the mortar's contents and poured the liquid and paste into the urn. When she pulled out a small knife from beside the urn, we all took a step back. The knife in her hand mirrored the symbol of a dagger plunging through a heart that was drawn with a cornmeal powder on the floor.

"I *definitely* didn't sign up for that," Andres said.

Roseline took the knife and dipped it into the urn. Five drops of the fluid fell onto the candle's flame, a small cloud of smoke rising after each drop made contact. My nose tickled at the citrus scent now wafting around the room. Her irises shone as red as rubies and two faint scars emerged on her face. I blinked twice to adjust my lying eyes.

I held in a gasp as the candle flickered back to life. "Look at the fire and envision what your heart yearns for," she demanded. She stared into the smoke for an eternity before looking up. "The deed is done."

From the Desk of Celeste Dubois

It started with a whisper. An insistent murmuring at the back of my head that I refused to acknowledge. A breath of air passing by my ear until it grew into a restless chatter that was finally too loud to ignore. I still couldn't explain what we'd partaken in yesterday, nor did I fully believe it would change anything. But I told Roseline we would see this through. Without a word, we all knew we would go to Bois Caïman.

Estelle, Jules, and I sat quietly in Andres's car, lost in thought, as we sped toward the ancient forest that was purported to be the start of the Haitian Revolution. Legend maintained that slaves conducted a secret ceremony that eventually led them to defeating their white overlords. As if slitting a pig's throat and not carefully thought-out machinations were behind the people's liberation. *Papi* always said that if the story was true, it was the last time, if not the only, that Haiti was able to come together as one. Roseline would say that they hadn't succeeded in getting rid of all slaves. She was hard at work marinating a Cornish hen when Estelle and I stumbled downstairs with the same idea.

"Go," Roseline said.

Somehow, we instinctively sensed where to head for the collection. An internal compass lodged in our cores directed us as we passed under low-hanging branches and climbed over high-arching roots. We wound deeper and deeper into the forest until finally we stood at a tree with the widest trunk, stretching out on either side farther than I could wrap my arms around. It stood separate from the surrounding trees.

"Well…here we are," I said, breaking the silence.

"What do we do?" asked Estelle, her voice barely above a whisper. I could feel the fear rippling off my sister. I wondered if the others could too.

"We dig," answered Jules in a voice that sounded surer than he looked.

Andres stepped ahead of us to the base of the tree and crouched down. No one had thought to pack a shovel, so we all sat on the ground beside him and used our hands to pile dirt into our respective large containers. I tried not to think of all the dirt lodging under my nails as I cracked through the hard earth.

We worked side by side, falling into silence once again. I shivered in the uncharacteristically brisk evening air and looked up at the sky. The moon was almost fully obstructed by the surrounding clouds. The thin sliver shining through was a sinister grin.

"I think we should stop," Estelle said abruptly. She stood up and wiped her hands on the front of the loose-fitting polka-dot dress she was wearing. She looked older than seventeen when she faced us now, the shadows adding years to her face. "We shouldn't be doing this. It's creepy and I think we're making a mistake. And…I'm scared."

"What are you talking about?" Andres asked. "We said that we wanted to do this."

"Yes," Estelle responded. "But that was before…before…"

"Before what?" He stood up, towering above Estelle as she stared up at him. Her mouth opened and shut as she searched for the words to speak.

"I should have told you earlier. But…I think I'm—" Estelle let out a bloodcurdling scream and fell to the ground, writhing in pain. She wrapped her arms tightly around her midsection, working her jaw again, this time in silent prayer.

"Estelle!" I raced toward my sister. As I reached out to her, she recoiled from me, her body convulsing on the forest floor.

"I didn't drink it. I didn't drink it. I didn't drink it," she kept whispering the phrase like a chant.

"What's wrong? What's happening?!" I said.

Jules pointed at Estelle, his face in shock, and I saw what made him tremble. The front of her dress was red, dark blood seeping through the white dots of fabric at an alarming rate. Andres shouted and ran toward her. Again, an invisible shock leaped through Estelle's body, and she crawled away from him. Her scream carved through my soul, a piece of my being ripped out with her drawn-out breath.

"We have to take her to a doctor," I screamed.

"We c-can't stop," Jules shouted over Estelle's screams. "I think that's wh-what's causing this!"

"Keep going," Estelle gasped out. "Roseline warned us."

The three of us threw ourselves to the ground, clawing the earth into our jars. Estelle lay near us, her breathing now coming in shallow pants as sweat drenched through the parts of her clothes that were not already covered in sticky blood. I gingerly approached my sister and reached out slowly until I cupped her hands to help her fill the rest of her glass jar to the brim. The nighttime clouds dissipated until the moon shone brightly in the clear, red sky. Estelle gave a violent shudder, her eyes rolling to the back of her head, and then she was still. You would almost think that she was asleep. We slowly crept toward her and I held my breath as I placed my hand in front of her nose.

"Oh, thank God. She's still breathing," I cried, a sob escaping my throat. "We need to get her help!"

Andres and Jules sprang up from the ground, each of them grabbing one of Estelle's arms and draping them over their shoulders. She didn't so much as blink as the boys dragged her to the car. We piled into the convertible once more and raced to the hospital with no idea how to explain what happened. *My sister started convulsing, but we kept digging.* When we arrived, Jules ran ahead, shout-stuttering about his friend who was dying.

There was no time for questions as the nurses came to the open car door and quickly collected Estelle. They placed her on a gurney and raced into the building with her, urgency in their voices as they shouted for people to make way. I followed until I was barred from getting closer. They made a sharp turn around a corner, and Estelle's right arm dangled lifelessly over the edge of the moving bed.

Andres, Jules, and I waited for hours. My parents didn't care what we did with our free time as long as we didn't embarrass them, but even they must have been worried about us by now. I couldn't bear the thought of spelling anything out to them, but I called the house anyway. No one answered. I wondered for a moment where Roseline was, but then I was preoccupied with fear for my sister. Was Estelle okay? Was she in pain? Had she made it through the night? The boys and I ambushed each nurse who passed by, asking endless questions about her. But none of them could say a thing and eventually they stayed away from us. Word must've gotten out to avoid the three bloody teenagers if they wanted to get any work done.

Finally, a doctor in black scrubs made his way over to where we huddled. His small, round glasses sat perched on the edge of his wide nose, the legs of the spectacles disappearing into thick white tufts of hair, glaringly different from the shining bald spot that reflected the hospital lights. He held his small surgical cap in both hands, twisting it this way and that as he stood before us. My stomach dropped. Something had gone wrong. I could see it in the way his brown eyes lowered to the ground.

"I'm sorry," the doctor began. "The girl is fine, but I could not save the baby."

"Baby?!" Andres and I exclaimed in unison.

"Yes," the older man answered, staring intently into Andres's eyes. "She was only a few months along… I've never seen anything like this before. It was like someone had ripped the fetus from inside her."

I swayed on my feet. Maybe it was the fact that I hadn't had anything to eat in hours and had been up all night. Or maybe it was the news. Or the crushing realization that Estelle meant that she hadn't drunk the rum. But I could no longer keep myself upright. My knees buckled and in seconds Jules was behind me, lowering me into a seat.

"When can we see her?" Jules asked, placing a protective hand on my shoulder.

"She's resting," the doctor said. "But we'll let you know as soon as she wakes up. The worst has passed."

Jules thanked the doctor while Andres and I sat in stunned silence. He stared at the doctor's retreating back, his jaw clenched so tightly I could see the imprint of his teeth through his cheek.

"Andres—" I began. But I never finished. Tears streamed down his face as he turned and left the hospital. I could hardly lift myself from the chair.

"Let him go," Jules said.

Jules stayed beside me when I eventually tried calling home again. *Maman* was hysterical on the other line, thinking that we had gotten kidnapped for ransom or had been in a bad car accident. I tried to calm her down and explain that we were fine, but once I told her that Estelle was in the hospital, she became incoherent with another round of wails. *Papi* took the phone from her and barked that they would be at the hospital within the hour. I said nothing to him before hanging up. They got there in thirty minutes—food, a change of clothes, toothbrushes, and strong black coffee in tow.

"I don't d-d-drink coffee," Jules said as my mom forced a cup of the hot drink into his hands. His stuttering seemed to be from nerves and not a heavy tongue. My heart thumped in my chest when I realized he'd mostly stopped stuttering since leaving the forest.

"This is not for taste," my mom said as she drank her own. "You must drink strong black coffee when you experience a grave shock."

"Why?"

"Don't ask questions!" she snapped, and Jules hastily took a sip.

A nurse motioned that we could enter Estelle's room. She looked tiny wrapped in the white sheets of the hospital bed. Her eyes were closed and they had pulled her hair out of her face and into a ponytail.

"Estelle?" I said as I sat carefully on the edge of her bed. She opened her eyes and I saw her face flood with emotion. She looked relieved to see me but then started to cry.

I wrapped my arms around her. "It's okay. We're here."

We sat around the room, *Maman* sobbing over her youngest, her favorite. Eventually, *Papi* cleared his throat to address the unspoken and asked Estelle directly what happened.

She didn't mention Roseline and I wouldn't have let her. I interjected with a made-up story of a meeting with a mysterious old woman who could grant wishes and my parents exchanged a look. Jules nodded along, agreeing with everything that we said until then. Estelle plowed through.

"This was my fault. I wanted to stop, but it was too late and—"

Jules fidgeted uncomfortably.

"She was freaking out and she fell. We didn't know what was wrong with her, but she kept screaming until we filled the jars," I cut in firmly. "We took her here as fast as we could. Andres left."

Tears welled in Estelle's eyes again at the sound of his name. "I was pregnant. I had only suspected it for about a month. I didn't know what to do, so I didn't tell anyone. Not even Celeste—" The words I'd tried to conceal tumbled out anyway.

"*Ki sa!*" My father balled his fists and, with no outlet in sight, placed them on his head.

"How could you, Estelle?" *Maman* said, twisting her ring. "What would people say?"

"You and *Papi* somehow survived the shame when you were teenagers," I spat. "*Grand-mère* said that's why you got married in the first place."

"How *dare* you speak to me this way—she was a crazy woman—"

I stood up without waiting for her to finish and signaled for Jules to follow me out the room. As if unsure of what to do, he bowed before exiting.

"Thanks for staying with us," I said when we were alone. "But I think you should probably give your parents a call. I'm sure they're worried sick."

"I'll…just head home." Jules nodded. I walked him to the hospital entrance, and we hugged goodbye as he climbed onto the back of the motorcycle I had hailed. He tried to wave away the money I gave him to pay for the ride until I pressed it into his palm and wouldn't let go. As I watched them leave the driveway, I saw Andres. He was wearing the same dirty clothes from hours before and he held a large vase of flowers. He sauntered up to where I stood frowning at him, swaying like a tree in hurricane winds. His eyes were bloodshot, and when he opened his mouth to say hello, the stench of alcohol revealed what he'd been doing since he left the hospital.

"You better not have driven here," I said.

"No. I have a chauffeur for that," Andres retorted. "Where's Estelle?"

"In her room. *With my parents*," I said pointedly. "You can't go in there like this."

"Watch me," he said.

Andres made a beeline for Estelle's room, shaking his head in a weak attempt to sober up. My parents were walking out with the doctor when *Maman* realized who it was careening toward them. Her eyes bulged and she jerked my father and the doctor in the opposite direction. Her hands shook the way that mine did when I was upset, but she said nothing to him, as I'd known she wouldn't. Anything to avoid a scene. Andres entered the room and stopped short at the door when he realized that Estelle was sleeping. He turned to place the flowers on the edge of the table that stood at the entrance. As he wobbled to stand beside her bed, I raced over and grabbed his arm.

"Leave her alone!" I hissed. "She needs to rest."

"Well, I *need* to speak with her," Andres said, crossing his arms.

"We don't always get what we want."

"That's not what your Roseline promised," Andres said.

Again my mind fluttered to Roseline, who had looked very much at peace this morning. Was this her doing? I didn't know if coincidences would be this strong. I held my ground as Andres tried to maneuver closer to Estelle, refusing to move from where I stood between them.

"You need to go," I insisted.

"I'm not going anywhere," Andres said. He took another step closer to Estelle, tightening the gap. "What I *need* to do is put you in your place."

Suddenly, Andres was on me like a lion locked on its prey. He grabbed me by the arms and pulled me toward him, holding my body against his. I smelled vomit mixed with the alcohol. He was tugging me closer and closer to his lips. I beat against him in panic as I realized what he was trying to do.

"Andres!" I hissed. "Let me go right now! Stop this!"

Andres looked down once more and then he was on me, kissing me roughly as he pressed me even closer into his chest. The liquor on his tongue made me gag as he forced my mouth open with his. I still tried to fight him off, stomping on his feet to no avail. Finally, I bit him on his bottom lip. I tasted blood and retched. He pushed me away from him and I bumped against the side of Estelle's bed. I turned around quickly, hoping that my sister had not awoken to see her worthless boyfriend shoving his tongue down my throat. It was too late.

"Andres?" she asked, her voice small. "What are you doing?"

He stood near the foot of Estelle's bed and his face was marred with shame. He didn't look her in the eyes as he shook his head.

"Get out," Estelle said. She sounded more tired than angry. "I don't want to see you ever again."

"You don't mean that," Andres said, wiping at the blood on his mouth.

"Trust me, I do," Estelle said with more ferocity. "Losing this baby was probably the best thing to happen to me. Now I have nothing tying me to you."

He opened his mouth to speak but closed it and gave a curt nod. Without another word, he left the room and walked right into my father. I looked at them there, one man who had never been denied a thing, and another who was growing up to be just like him. *Papi* opened his mouth to presumably shout at Andres when his eyes bulged forward. His hands clawed at his throat, pulling at the skin to widen its passage for air.

"Gregoire!" My mother ran toward *Papi*, where he had collapsed on the floor. "*Doktè, Doktè!*"

Without getting up, I watched his breathing fade, then stop altogether. He was dead before the doctor rushed back into the room.

My mind flickered to Roseline.

Estelle's face crumpled and she wept. I will never forget how broken she looked. I sat with her on the bed, cradling my twin in my arms and letting her cry until she had no more tears left. I had none to shed myself, but I felt a shadow descend on me, the fear of whatever caused my father to die. Money. Power. Love. Success. It was obvious that Jules, the poor scholarship boy who was embarrassed about his need, would want to be wealthy. Andres planned his entire life to one day exert control over others. Estelle wanted the world to adore her. And I craved to have accomplishments separate from the family I resented. Even as I consoled Estelle and told

her that everything would be fine, I felt like a liar. We had set
a horrible ball in motion and we were plummeting toward
the ground with nothing to cushion our fall.

～～～～～～～～～～～～～～～～～～～～～～～～～～

Friday, February 5

The Life and Times of Alaine Beauparlant

A list of possible reactions my mother could have if she discovered I'd read her innermost thoughts (by degree of likelihood)

- Joyful surprise (Very unlikely)

  » CELESTE: Oh, did Estelle give that to you?

  » ALAINE: Y-yes?

  » CELESTE: How swell! I'd love your opinion on our decades-old familial strife and secrets. What did you think of the part when my father died dramatically on the floor of a hospital? Or that said father was a sexual predator? The heavy allusions to blood magic?

  » ALAINE: Uh…

  » CELESTE: You know what, you need more context. Here, take the rest of my hidden diary entries.

- Vehement outrage (Unlikely)

  » CELESTE: *ROOOAR* I AM SO VERY UPSET

WITH YOU THAT I'M RAISING MY VOICE
TO PROVE MY POINT [*moves to throw chair across
room*]

- Flat-out, absurdist denial (Neither more unlikely/likely)

  » CELESTE: Is nothing sacred? How *dare* you read
  my fan fiction without my permission?

- Feigned ignorance/business as usual (Likely)

  » CELESTE: How is your paper going?

  » ALAINE: Mom, can we talk about what I read in
  the diary *Tati* Estelle gave to me?

  » CELESTE: What diary? What's a *Tati* Estelle? Do
  your homework.

  » ALAINE: Please…?

  » CELESTE: I have to go.

  » ALAINE: Go where?

  » CELESTE: Oh…to the…um— [*runs from room*]

- Stony silence (Very likely)

  » CELESTE:

  » ALAINE:

The Life and Times of Alaine Beauparlant

Tati Estelle said that I needed to know where I came from, but reading my mother's diary only succeeded in making me more lost. "I don't really have a relationship with my mom™" could be the Alaine Beauparlant catchphrase at this point, but I do know her (and the average diarist, i.e., me) well enough to understand how huge of an invasion of privacy reading this was. *Tati* Estelle found the diary when she was moving back in and thought to pass it along as a sort of treat but ended up using it as something to distract me from my whirling thoughts after Mom wandered off. Reading about *Tati* Estelle's miscarriage hurt. I had no idea that she had carried that with her all these years. I wondered if she could even have children after what happened to her. In an alternate universe, I had a cool older cousin who was just as full of life as her (yes, her) mom. Then again, *Tati* Estelle had said she was happy about the miscarriage because it meant she could move on from Andres…so who knows if she would've let that pregnancy result in a baby at all.

I knew my mother had been reacting to more than a skeevy senator's throwaway lines that day on her show. He'd forced himself on her, and his promise, *I'm not going anywhere*, brought her right back to that moment. I sensed that Andres's story with my mother and aunt did not end in that hospital room. But someone who *had* been left there was my grandfather Gregoire. There were no signs of him anywhere in the house, and they never mentioned him. Ever. Now I understood why. I hoped Roseline was okay, wherever she was now. I wondered if my grandmother Jacinthe still harbored those foolish, hostile feelings toward her, even in her home clear across the country in the suburbs of Pétion-Ville. She was a bigger mystery than my own mother was. This was a lot to process.

Is it bad that a part of me thinks that after years of not having a Real Connection™ with my mother, I'm entitled to a level of transparency? Even when her memory is a memory itself…maybe these pages will come to hold something she won't be able to give me. It comforted me that I could see pieces of myself in her writing—how she dug into writing a full story even if it was just for her eyes.

I still hadn't decided what was up with that ceremony and needed answers:

- Where was Roseline?

- Could she have been behind my grandfather's freak death?

- Would I blame her if she were?

- What had she endured living in this house?

- Could Andres Venegas be a more terrible human being?

- And why hadn't I ever heard of any of this until now?

I know My People had spirits and *lwas* and vodou and Jesus, and they were all over the place if you knew where to look, but I had been removed from all of it growing up. I'd read that their spirits were linked with Catholic saints and mysterious entities derived from Africa. That the enslaved and their descendants had worshipped in secret for safety. There were others like the ones at Tatiana's church who considered all those practices to be depraved and demonic. I suspected the truth wasn't so clear-cut. There were folks who called on the spirits to urge their crops to grow, cure sicknesses, find love. The darkness was only a fraction of what these forces could do.

Dad always said science was his savior, and we had just two Sunday rituals: yelling at the screen during football or soccer, then trying out a new restaurant for dinner. I wouldn't be remotely surprised if his attachment to biology and chemistry and physiology—to the mechanisms he could explain—derived from the inexplicable course of events that night decades ago. Our church was Monday morning at breakfast when he would tell me, like some kind of Haitian Ellen DeGeneres, to not be too hard on myself and to be kind to everyone.

The Life and Times of Alaine Beauparlant

〰〰〰〰〰〰〰〰〰〰〰〰〰

What was meant to be a painfully uncomfortable dinner to celebrate my grandmother Jacinthe's birthday with family/close friends tonight upgraded to a painfully uncomfortable *and* depressing dinner for family/close friends. It was a dark and stormy night (like, for real, for real) and I had just started working on the meal with my mom. She insisted that she be the one to prepare everything, even though *Tati* Estelle begged that Jacques, the longtime family chef, handle the feast. After reading her diary, I didn't understand Mom's desire to cook for her mother.

"We *pay* him for this!" my aunt exclaimed as my mom gathered ingredients for the various dishes. "It's *Maman's* birthday, for heaven's sake."

"Well, you can pay him for the time if it makes you feel better. But I'll be the one to make it," she said in that final tone of hers that had cut off many an interview.

My aunt left the kitchen in a huff, muttering, "Celeste always gets her way."

I had volunteered to help my mom so that I could try to

get info on the people coming to dinner. We stood in the large kitchen, sunlight streaming through the open windows above the sink that overlooked the pool area. We worked together to prep the ingredients, my mom interjecting with tips along the way. We chopped onions into tiny pieces *(But not too small so that my cousin Jean can pick them out)*, seasoned grilled chicken with our homemade spices *(This* epis *will make any meal delicious. The secret is to wash the meat with water, lime, and a tiny bit of vinegar first)*, and sprinkled just enough shredded cheddar cheese on top of the macaroni before popping it into the oven *(It's much better than that box stuff)*.

"How do you know how to cook all this food?" I had yet to bring up the diaries to her, and I had a feeling the answer was Roseline.

"Classes… A friend."

"How do you feel?" I asked as I finished peeling the beets and potatoes we would be using for the *salade russe*. I didn't press her, painfully aware that I had no trouble squeezing info from anyone except her. "The internet is going crazy over that leaked GNN memo firing you from the network."

My mom shook her head as she scooped mayo into the bowl that I'd placed the vegetables in. "They didn't fire me—I quit. They were going to let me go anyway. I just beat them to the punch. With William swimming around like some maniacal piranha, I'm surprised Mike's note wasn't released the same day I sent in my resignation."

"William must've used that time to celebrate with his hubby, Keith," I said. I had gone to only one of my mom's company holiday parties, but even at the age of eleven, I noticed how contentious her relationship with her EP was.

MY HAZY RECOLLECTION OF THE ONE TIME
I MET WILLIAM DONAHUE, MOM'S EX-EP

Setting: We find William Donahue and Celeste Beauparlant at an impasse, standing beside the sole remaining mini ceviche taco at the hors d'oeuvres table of GNN's non-denominational company holiday party.

WILLIAM: Take it. Please.

CELESTE: No, it's fine.

WILLIAM: I know how little you cook. This must be lunch and dinner for you. I insist.

CELESTE: Actually, there are these new places called restaurants, so I never have to starve anymore. The things people come up with.

Enter the star of the show, Alaine Beauparlant, dragging along Celeste's driver, Jimmy Richmond, to settle a disagreement. Cue audience applause.

ALAINE: Mo-*om*! Jimmy says that he doesn't believe I can get straight As with "my mouth."

CELESTE: Where are your manners? Say hello to Mr. Donahue.

WILLIAM: Hello there, Alaine. Tell me. Are you as bossy as your mom?

ALAINE: *[pauses to think]* No, probably more.

Scene.

From: Celeste Beauparlant
To: Michael Sanders
Subject: I quit.

Michael,

In light of recent events, I must submit my resignation, effective immediately. Of course, our representatives are in touch, but I wanted to state personally that I have enjoyed my time at GNN and grown so much throughout my years with the network, even with a bloodthirsty vampire like William Donahue as my EP. Entrusting me with *Sunday Politicos* was considered a "risk," but you took the chance—because you had no choice if you wanted to avoid the wrath of what you so lovingly called the "PC Police." And in the six years since I've held the role, the program has flourished. I will always remember the amazing team that has been beside me through the ups, downs, and sideways. I would not have been able to reach such heights without their expertise and support. Thanks for giving me the opportunity to create a platform that has engaged an audience so ripe for stimulating discussion. I will cherish this experience always. I hope they stop watching.

Celeste

From: Michael Sanders
To: Celeste Beauparlant

Subject: Re: I quit.

Thank GOD. Now I don't have to fire you.

Mike

Press Release From GNN Announcing
Mom's Departure A Few Days Ago

Friday, February 5

GNN CORRESPONDENCE
For immediate release:

From the Office of Michael Sanders

It is with great regret that GNN ends our professional relationship with Celeste Beauparlant. In her time anchoring *Sunday Politicos*, she made great strides for the program and the network as a whole. Effective immediately, Keith Donahue will serve as Celeste's permanent replacement and lead anchor for the show. Keith has done a superb job standing in for Celeste since her departure at the end of December. We are excited to see where he will lead the program.

Celeste will be missed and we wish her the absolute best.

Michael Sanders
GNN President

SIGN THIS PETITION

REINSTATE CELESTE BEAUPARLANT AS HOST OF 'SUNDAY POLITICOS'

TRICIA JENKINS, ATLANTA, GA

Greetings. I run a successful blog about the intersection of race, gender, and culture in America. Something I have in common with many of my readers is an admiration for Celeste Beauparlant. She's a wonderful role model who had a minor lapse of judgment.

Politicians themselves have been forgiven for much worse and, as Solange has reminded us, Celeste deserves her seat at the table. We still haven't heard her side of the story! Please join me in demanding GNN reinstate her as host of *Sunday Politicos*.

If the allegations are true regarding her health, the least they can do is allow her the dignity of a proper resignation, signing off the air in her own way.

Sincerely,
Tricia Jenkins, *Beautiful Brown*

Sunday, February 7

The Life and Times of Alaine Beauparlant

Soon, everything was in the oven, on the stove, or cooling in the fridge as we wrapped up our prep. I stood at the sink with my mother and we washed up in silence. We were all gossiped out about GNN drama. I poked her arm after drying my hands.

"Will you be okay tonight?"

The water was still running over her fingers as she absentmindedly rubbed her hands together. She shook her head to clear it, then looked at me. "We're late. Let's go change our clothes for dinner."

I showered and quickly slipped into a high-neck floral dress I'd been dying to wear since I'd seen it in my mother's closet. The hem reached a couple inches above my knee, the lightweight fabric floating out as I twirled in front of the mirror. My hair was styled in my signature twist-out, the fluffy strands coiled into themselves in a curly 'fro. I had already sent Tatiana a picture of my outfit, to which she responded, Fieeerce! I inspected my reflection one last time before heading downstairs, the buzz of conversation already rising up to where I stood at the top of the landing. There were at least a dozen people in the foyer greeting one another. Kisses planted on cheeks. Hands slapped on backs. I suddenly felt like an outsider intruding on an intimate family moment. I decided to quietly sneak back into my room, never to be seen again.

This uncharacteristic shyness wasn't me, but a houseful of relatives was foreign territory. I navigated easily enough when I was hanging out at Tatiana's. They weren't *my* people. I maintained a polite yet aloof distance in my mind even as I charmed them with my glowing personality. It was almost anthropological. *Watch as the younger brother playfully grabs the remote from his sister. After a period of short observation, the sage maternal grandmother intercedes on her granddaughter's behalf and calmly demands the item be returned.*

But this was different. I was as much a part of them as they were a part of me, whether we liked it or not. They were strangers—I would walk by them in a room without a trace of recognition—but our DNA tied us together. I came across an article during my research about a family in Colombia who all shared a mutated gene that caused Alzheimer's. I doubted that was the case for us; I would've heard about it already. But reading about them reminded me that we didn't have to know each other to share the same fate. Blood is blood.

As I turned to leave, I spotted a photograph of an older woman placed above a hallway vase. I'd never noticed it before. She was tall, her bony shoulders held back with pride. Her gray-streaked hair cascaded to her shoulders and her lips were tilted in a knowing smile. Even with the gorgeous sapphire gown that she wore, I was drawn to her eyes; one was brown and the other green.

I jumped when someone placed a hand on my back.

"I didn't mean to startle you. But I did mean to stop you

from escaping," my mom said with a laugh. She looked like a modern replica of the woman in the photograph. Wavy bob tucked behind an ear, navy wrap dress. Her long neck was accented with a simple diamond necklace.

"Mom, you look amazing!" I gushed.

"Cute dress," she said, playfully tugging my neckline.

"It's yours."

"I have good style, then."

She linked her arm through mine as she guided me down the stairs. "That was my grandmother Natacha," she said, referring to the photo. "She was...like me."

I nodded in understanding, recalling Mom's own mother calling her "crazy." I had yet to hear Mom verbalize her condition. But I guess she still had some coping to do. We made our rounds, my mother introducing me to the relatives who had come together for dinner, before stopping at a tall girl with bone-straight shoulder-length hair who looked my age.

"This is your second cousin Félicité. Her mother, Bianca, and I are first cousins and grew up together. I'm sure you'll be great friends while you're both here." My mother bent her cheek to receive Félicité's kiss and went on her way to the kitchen.

"Alaine, is it?" Félicité gave me the universal once-over, its meaning clear: *unimpressed*.

"It's my mom's," I said defensively, refusing to ignore the nonverbal slight.

"I can tell. Very late eighties." Her own dress was a white body-conscious midi. It was the kind of outfit I avoided if I were tucking in for a big, messy meal. I said as much.

"I trust myself," she said.

Eye. Roll.

The guest of honor had yet to arrive and everyone else had

made their dramatic entrances earlier that evening. So when the doorbell rang one more time, the crowd hushed instinctively and turned to welcome the famed Jacinthe and her second husband, Yves. But the woman to walk in was not my grandmother. It was a very pregnant Roseline. I could sense it in the frosty reception she received, and from the look on my mother's face where she stood in the family room. She had seen a ghost. I gasped.

"I *know*," Félicité said. "Come on, let's get this over with."

I followed Félicité as she strolled over to the man who stood with Roseline, his hand clasped in hers. Roseline shook her wet umbrella near the front door before wiping her shoes carefully on the mat, as though to avoid making a mess for someone else to clean up.

Though she wore an expensive floral maxi dress that confidently accentuated every curve, baby bump or otherwise, up close the sheen of sweat on her forehead and bottom lip she bit told another part of the story.

"*Ton* Pierrot," Félicité said to the man beside Roseline as she gave the air beside his face a quick peck and bumped his cheek with hers. "Roseline. Have you met *Tati* Celeste's daughter? Annabelle, was it?"

He barely noticed when I greeted him; nothing could tear his gaze away from Roseline for more than a moment at a time. I held my breath when I kissed Roseline's cheeks and smiled tightly as her staring went on longer than was polite. Félicité, who had not kissed her, excused herself and made a beeline for the door, which had just opened again. I didn't move. I couldn't.

"You must visit my home, Alaine. Oh yes, I know your name," Roseline said softly before briefly rummaging through her purse and pressing a neatly folded piece of paper into my palm. "Please come. Soon."

I looked down and saw the beginnings of an address and slipped it into my bra to peruse later, since I had nowhere else to put it. ~~Then I looked straight into the eyes of Medusa and turned to stone.~~ Jacinthe, with a thick halo of silvery curls that circled her head like snakes, stretched her lips into a smile that didn't reach her eyes. The physical similarities my mom and *Tati* Estelle shared with her were powerful: her bright skin, sharp nose, and wide lips. I wondered if they held any resemblance to Gregoire. I hadn't found any pictures of him around the house; it was as if he'd never been there at all.

"Is that my granddaughter over there with the help?"

My jaw dropped while the adoring crowd of relatives around her roared as though she were the world's best stand-up comedian.

"Is that a real question?" I asked.

"You're too pretty to look so serious," she said disapprovingly. "That's how we joke here. And she's family now. What a blessing." My grandmother looked meaningfully at Roseline's stomach.

Roseline's hand went to her middle. She opened her mouth as if to say something but apparently thought better of it and drifted away to the kitchen, where *Tati* Estelle stood, instead.

"Do you remember me, Alaine?" Yves, my step-grandfather who had watched our verbal tennis match wordlessly, saw his opening to defuse the situation and took it. I had met him and Jacinthe two short times before, on their visits to the States. Each meeting had been perfunctory and awkward.

"Ah, yes, she was always more comfortable in the kitchen," Jacinthe said lightly. ~~Cruella de Vil the Wicked Witch of the West, East, North, and South Regina George~~ She refused to back down. Goose bumps sprang up all along my arms. Was this lady for real?

"Time for dinner!" The twin voices of my mother and aunt rang throughout the tense room. They glanced at each other as if not quite surprised but grateful they'd had the same thought.

I made my way to the dining room, where there were already thick place cards on the long mahogany table for each guest. I suddenly yearned for the simple meals my dad and I shared in front of the television, yelling out answers to *Wheel of Fortune* and *Jeopardy*. (We pretty much yelled at the television whenever we watched it together.) I was unsurprised to find myself assigned to one end of the table, with Félicité to my right and a middle-aged man with very dark leathery skin to my left. I mused about how rude it would be to ignore my cousin when—

"I'm bored. I'm going to get you up to speed on CFG," she said.

"CFG?"

"Christophe Family Gossip." She grinned. "None of us have that last name anymore, but that's who we've all got in common."

By the time we got to dessert, I was well versed in the juiciest happenings of House Christophe. A cousin Jean-Paul was dating a Dominican girl ("Out of *all* the women in Haiti…"). A great-aunt Cléophanie remained unmarried in her sixty-third year but lived with a longtime female "companion." A *Tonton* Ronel (who wasn't really an uncle, anyway) was on to bride four and baby ten ("Total…how do you say…creep?"). Félicité was diving into her world of *zuzu* girls (glamorous young women who lived in Pétion-Ville and relied on family wealth to fund their expensive habits) when the man to my left gently tapped me on the shoulder.

"Excuse me, *mademoiselle*," he said. "I don't mean to interrupt, but can you please pass me the butter?"

Félicité must have decided that he was too beneath her to interact with, because she was already chatting with the young man who sat on the other side of her.

"Don't worry," I said as I handed him the dish. "You've actually saved my ears from falling off."

He smiled politely and looked over to my cousin as she talked and talked. And talked. The poor guy was already looking around for an escape.

"What did you do wrong to get placed at the 'kids' end of the table?" I asked.

"Wrong?" He laughed. "I'm happy to have been invited at all! I've been selling peanut butter to this family for as long as I can remember. It's an honor to be here."

"Wait… Selling peanut butter? Are you *the* Tony Juste?"

His chest puffed up with pride.

"I almost killed a boy at school because of you!"

"Um…excuse me?" he said, his delight quickly turning into confusion.

"I mean, I was eating a delicious sandwich that my dad made with your peanut butter. It just so happened that a boy in my class is allergic. He's fine now," I added.

Tony let out a sigh of relief. "I'm happy to hear that he's okay. And that you enjoyed the peanut butter."

"Definitely! I'm probably your biggest customer. I'm Alaine by the way."

"Alaine! Estelle's niece. I should've known. I can see your family resemblance."

Just as I started to respond, Yves cleared his throat to get the room's attention. He stood at the head of the table, while my grandmother Jacinthe sat to the right of him with a small tiara *Tati* Estelle had presented to her upon reaching the dining room.

"I'd like to wish my beautiful wife a happy birthday," Yves said to applause. "Thanks to our hard work and dedication, we've had everything we've ever dreamed of. Now we can enjoy watching our darling Estelle follow in our footsteps building this country up…and Celeste as well."

I gripped my silverware and glanced at my mother, seated a few seats away, who had either ignored or hadn't heard the clumsy declaration. She appeared to be almost in a trance. *Cousines* Emilie and Rebecca sat across from me and cheered. They were a few years older and, according to Félicité, the epitome of *zuzu* girls. They spoke Creole in the singsong lilt of women who liked to pretend they were speaking French even when they weren't: *meeerci beaucoooup* instead of *mèsi anpil*. My mom's uncle Emmanuel, notable for wearing more jewelry than even Thierry, rapped his knuckles on the table. He'd kissed my hand when he met me, eyes twinkling as brightly as his bedazzled wrists and neck.

The only other person to not react was Roseline.

I was still staring at her intently when Félicité caught my gaze. She told me that Roseline had started working at Pierrot's family's house for money soon after she'd left the Dubois home. Jacinthe had gone to her cousin Farah, Pierrot's mom, and begged her to fire her, but because Roseline's work ethic was "legendary," Farah kept her on anyway. The joke was on Farah though because her son and Roseline fell in love. And when the family refused to approve their relationship, they got hitched anyway. They were the happiest people at the table.

"Now she's pregnant at a million years old," Félicité sneered. I glanced over at my mom and *Tati* Estelle, who were in deep conversation. Mom shook her head again.

"What a blessing," Tony said with a smile even when it was clear that he didn't approve of Félicité's endless gossiping. There was no ignoring her when she spoke, since she insisted on talking so loudly. "My family isn't as large, so I love to see how this one continues to grow. We should appreciate such things, no matter how they come."

Félicité opened her mouth to make what I was sure would be a snide remark. The last thing I wanted was to get her started again, so I cut her off. "I'm actually new to the big family thing myself," I said. "And I'd kill to look half as good when I'm a million."

Finally, the cake was brought out, one candle placed on top. It was my aunt's turn to tap the side of her glass and draw everyone's attention to her. She stood, pulling my mom up with her for a toast.

"To our mother," she began. "*Maman*, you are the epitome of class and an amazing woman. We wish you many more years of happiness and good health."

Everyone cheered in agreement, but my mom wavered. She placed both hands on the table for support, her head hanging low.

She must've had one too many. I smirked at the thought of my mother letting loose after a few drinks. I wouldn't have blamed her either, with these relatives. But when she looked up from where she'd been staring at the place mat, the smile slid from my face faster than the champagne flute she smashed on the floor. Glass tinkled and clattered at her feet.

"I hate it here!" my mom shouted, silencing everyone. "All you people and your fake smiles and empty well-wishes. Watch, I'm going to leave this stupid place and you'll never see me again!" She trained her gaze on each person in the room and stopped at Roseline a beat longer than anyone else. When she turned to me, I stood up. But her gaze moved on.

"And *you*," she spat at my grandmother. "How could you let him stay here after learning what he did to her?"

Jacinthe let out a sob. "Stop!"

"Mom!" I shouted as I rushed to her side and placed my hand firmly on her arm. Mom's shoulders sagged, and she started coming to as she looked around at our shocked expressions.

"Enjoy the *tarte*," she said and ran from the table.

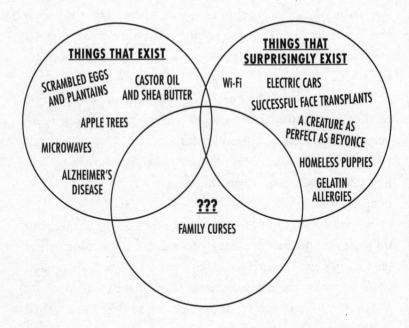

In the age of microwaves and Wi-Fi, electric cars and face transplants, my rational side told me that we didn't have space for family curses to exist. Still, my grandmother's words from the diary had stayed with me and I could not forget what I'd read: *Yours is coming. Your name may be Dubois, but that Christophe blood runs in you too.* Maybe my mom's had arrived in the form of "amyloid plaques" depositing in the gaps between nerve cells and "neurofibrillary tangles" folding into themselves in those very same neurons. What researchers called a "genetic predisposition for Alzheimer's" could really just be a promise that had lain dormant in her until something, anything, called it out to be fulfilled. While those brains cells would eventually stop communicating with each other and die, the *madichon* spoke clearly through Mom's outburst at dinner: I've got her.

If I waited, "mine" would creep up one way or another as well. It just needed time. I hated myself for starting to believe it. Throughout the night, the snippets of conversation I heard stayed on this shared family curse. Nancy can't have dairy because the curse is sooo far-reaching. Jean dropped the fork on the floor and it stubbed his toe? The curse was to blame. Bianca's car accident? *C-u-r-s-e.*

That ceremony. It didn't seem like they had done it right… In the forest, *Tati* Estelle had hesitated. She hadn't really drunk from the bottle of rum either. Maybe the family needed a do-over… In my mother's diary entry, Roseline had said that a curse could be countered with something else, like taking over another person's mortgage and putting it under a different name. I had nothing to lose meeting with Roseline. I needed to learn more about what had caused this supposed curse in the first place and what it really meant for us centuries later.

I decided then. I was going to look into taking over my mom's debt.

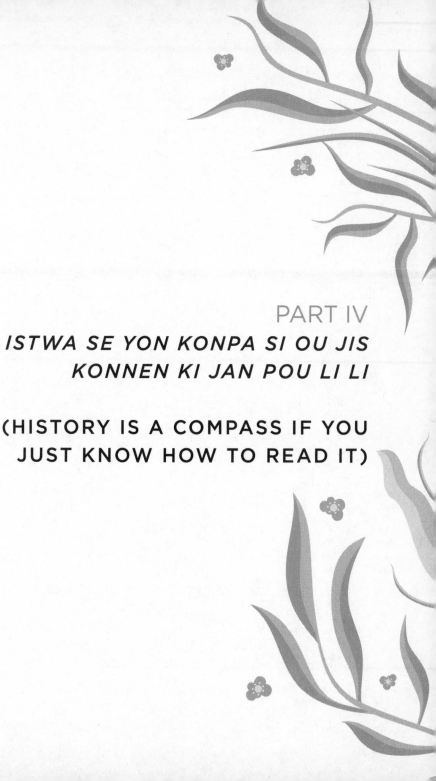

PART IV

ISTWA SE YON KONPA SI OU JIS KONNEN KI JAN POU LI LI

(HISTORY IS A COMPASS IF YOU JUST KNOW HOW TO READ IT)

Monday, February 8

The Life and Times of Alaine Beauparlant

Dear Sister Wagner,

Shhh. Don't speak. I know just what you're thinking.

(It's a gift.

And a curse.)

Which leads me to what's on your mind, and I'll be honest, what was on my mind at first too: Alaine, are you seriously pursuing this whole curse angle? Do you, like, really, really, *really* have nothing better to do with your time? Do not enough people think you're certifiably insane[1]? What's next, investigating the moon landing?

If I may. You're not asking the right questions. What have I got to lose? The sad truth is that I'm already losing my mother. Whether I sit down and accept her diagnosis or not, each day that goes by is one less with her. That terrifies me. She's not perfect but she's mine, and she's all I've ever wanted to be. I dream of being as passionate about

---

1 Self-imposed disclaimer courtesy of my dad, the shrink: terms such as blanket insanity, "nuts," "loony," "cuckoo," and "bonkerzzz" are not found in the Diagnostic and Statistical Manual of Mental Disorders (DSM-V) and are not legitimate attributions to one's mental health status.

something as she is about her work. These days, I cry into my pillow, imagining a future where I won't have her around to disappoint. I always figured we would get closer when I got older and more mature. Now I'm not sure she'll be around to see me hit thirty (the age when presumably all juvenile problems melt away and peak human-hood is reached).

When all I've got to look back on are some letters from a time when my mom was unbridled enough to put aside her doubts and reservations for the sake of a friend, I want to be able to say I tried it all. Even the ideas that seemed crazy. I don't feel qualified to declare unequivocally that certain events that are unexplainable in the natural sense but easily explainable in the supernatural realm are straight-up wrong. (No shade, but you're a nun, so wouldn't you agree?)

So I did a little digging. I'm not saying I have all the answers now, but I did what any good journalist would do when embarking on a highly sensitive story. I thought of all the people in my family—and heck, this country—who believed that *madichon* was a real power that moved and shaped lives. I checked the archives from the time that this supposed curse would have taken seed.[2] I found a few things that swayed me enough to investigate this curse business for real.

Consider this my Hail ~~Mary~~ Marie.

---

2 Thanks, *Tati* Estelle. I guess I should've checked in with you before turning in my Who's Who assignment after all.

Twenty-Five-Year-Old Letter From Mom To *Tati* Estelle In The Dossier *Tati* Estelle Gave Me

SUNDAY, SEPTEMBER 15

Chère Estelle,

I have yet to perfect the gait of a New Yorker. I keep my head up high, face straight ahead, and walk like I'm in an unwinnable race as I resist the urge to yell at each person who bumps into me on the sidewalk. I don't know if I'll ever get that casual confidence down because I refuse to step out into the street with the pedestrian signal on the red stop sign. How can you trust that the drivers will stop every time for you? The risk is too great. And the drivers. You think Port-au-Prince is bad?

Well, Port-au-Prince traffic *is* absolutely terrible. But that's the point! At least you know to expect the unexpected there. There are no rules. New York City is worse for creating all these lights and sidewalks and bike lanes to just ignore them. An utter waste of time making the signs and printing out the DMV books. I could go on for pages about the shared faults of Manhattan pedestrians and drivers but I'll spare you.

How are things back home? How are you and *Maman* holding up? I've thrown myself into my studies to avoid thinking of…everything. But even that can't stop the dreams. Just last night I dreamed that I was wandering around in Citadelle Laferrière. But it wasn't the Citadelle as we now know it. The halls were lit with candles but they did nothing to chase away the darkness that seemed to seep into my bones as I walked through the fortress. I could hear someone wailing in agony. And as I walked toward the screams, I found a woman cradling a man on the floor in her arms, his blood growing in a pool around her as her cries echoed through the halls. Maybe it was Marie-Louise. I didn't see them, but I sensed there were servants tucked away in the shadows watching as she grieved. I could always tell when Roseline was around.

I woke up and couldn't go back to sleep after that. It's such a strange thing to be able to speak my mind without a second thought but to be simultaneously reluctant to express what's in my heart. But I will try to put into words here what I could not say with my lips the last time we were together in person. I had to go. Even before *Papi*'s death. But I can't deny that him dying was the sign that I needed to leave. A terrible chapter in our lives—in Roseline's life—is over. I didn't need to protect her from anyone anymore and I hated myself because I hadn't been doing that good of a job, to be frank. I wanted to get as far away from what he had done as possible. Coming to school here allowed me to do that... I took it as my opportunity to be free and move on. I hope you can understand.

Love always,
Celeste

Scanned Letters I Found In Online Academic
Caribbean Journal Archives From Henri Christophe's
Widow, Marie-Louise Coidavid, To Christophe's
Successor, Jean-Pierre Boyer

Friday, August 17, 1821
Dear Mr. President,

The princesses and I have arrived safely in London with the
kind assistance of Sir Popham. It has been a trying time for
the family since the deaths of Henri and Jacques-Victor.
Though I am cautiously optimistic of the quality of our stay,
I am anxious to return to my countryland soon. I pray that
my husband's enemies have appeased themselves with the
blood that they have shed.

Yours truly,
Marie-Louise I,
former Queen Consort of Haiti

Thursday, October 11, 1821
Dear Mr. President,

Your Excellency, the first anniversary of my widowhood has
come and gone. I have recalled our conversation countless
times over these many months and have not forgotten your
promise to bring me and my daughters home before long. I,

above others, understand the fickleness of the sea and suspect my first letter never reached you. Alas, I persevere by sending this in its stead.

Yours truly,
Marie-Louise I,
fmr. Queen Consort of Haiti

Tuesday, June 11, 1822
Dear Mr. President,

I follow the affairs of our beloved country closely and rejoice in our periods of triumph and mourn in our times of grief. I hope I do not overstep my bounds as a humble widow to congratulate the successful unification of Hispaniola. The third time is truly the charm. Saint-Domingue and Santo Domingo will finally be two stunning hemispheres to the singular pearl that is our island. I do pray this letter finds you well and in good health and that you deem it appropriate to return my family to our grand nation.

Yours truly,
Marie-Louise I,
fmr. Queen Consort of Haiti

Wednesday, March 26, 1823
Your Excellency,

As I acknowledge this March 26, the day I was first crowned Queen, I take a moment to ponder your silence. I understand the delay. Running a nascent country requires much effort and time—more than one person can provide. It isn't surprising if there are other pressing issues that come before answering a weary dowager.

Please know that I do not demand special treatment from you because I deserve it, but I beg you for it because I have nowhere else to turn. I am a Haitian first and foremost and my heart yearns to be in the land my husband helped build. I do not require a royal entourage, money, or fame. I don't even need this title of queen in a land of presidents. I simply ask that my children and I can spend our remaining days in the country we love.

Yours truly,
Marie-Louise Coidavid

Sunday, July 4, 1824
Your Excellency,

I saw it fitting to send this note on the day of American independence. It is widely known you enjoy satirical plays and I'm sure the irony of the six thousand black Americans leaving the alleged "land of the free" to seek their true liberty in Haiti is not lost upon you, as it is not lost on me, even all the way in Pisa, Italy. If you recall from our conversation at the final state banquet Henri and I hosted, I was born of free blacks. I suspect my ancestors would have never conceived a descendant of theirs would reach such distances as

Europe. Despite it all, I desire nothing more than to get back to Nord with my last remaining child. It is urgent.

Yours,
Marie-Louise Coidavid

Wednesday, March 23, 1825
Marie-Madeleine,

Forgive me for the delay in reaching out to you. Even after all these years, I knew I didn't dare come empty-handed. I finally have something important to share, much too delicate to send to Boyer and pray for a reply that will never come...

I spend every Wednesday at confession and this very morning I overheard a white man of evident stature and means confessing to the priest of having an illicit family in Saint-Domingue. He feared God was going to punish him by killing his mistress there and his wife back in France. I think he believed the cathedral empty but the two of them and sobbed loudly, revealing his biggest, selfish fear of losing his own life when he would soon lead an extensive fleet to Saint-Domingue to demand reparations for the loss of income from their slaves. Typically, I would not divulge something so personal as a religious confession but my allegiance to Haiti forced my hand.

I'm sure you've seen the letters to Jean-Pierre. I have always been polite and sanguine in tone with him but I am desperate. My last remaining child is dead. No mother should be so cursed to witness all four of her children reach the grave before her. I have not fully absorbed the shock of

Améthyste's sudden illness but Athénaïre had taken our family's change in circumstances worse than any of us. The hatred that festered in her soul must have overtaken her body when she became with child and she slipped away in labor. She had come to blame me for our life and rarely deigned to speak to me. She became taken by an Italian boy who promised her the moon at the paltry price of her family fortune. What that *pisano* didn't know when he began to court her was that our world-famous fortune was dwindling and he disappeared the moment he discovered his Athénaïre and her money were gone. I would give up and live the rest of my life near my daughters' mausoleum but I have a granddaughter now that I can't look after here in Pisa.

You and I know what Henri and Alexandre would say if they knew of this letter. You and I also know that it doesn't matter because _we_ are the ones who've survived. I implore you, think of our stolen moments of commiseration in the early days of the country, before our men ripped it in half. Is there anyone you can sit and drink with who does not have an ulterior motive? At least I am transparent with my request and you above all know I have no desire to reach the pinnacle of our government again. I've seen the mountaintop and much prefer the view from the valley. You, yes, you, the mind behind two presidents, know my heart. I am simply the sane, aging woman behind an unhinged king. From one first lady to another, please bring me home.

Your faithful servant if you so choose,
Marie-Louise

Tuesday, July 12, 1825
Marie Louise,

Do not insult my or your intelligence by suggesting this "important" information you have is exclusive to you. There have been whispers of such a crisis for years now. It was never a question of what was possible with the French but _when_ they would assemble themselves to publicly gripe about the absurd slight of claiming one's freedom. How dare we.

Nevertheless, I will help you. Nothing is free in this life (as the French so menacingly reminded me with a fleet of ships at our shores not a fortnight ago) and I will need you to do something for me in return. I can offer you safe passage and resources to your precious Nord but you will not return as Henri Christophe's heartbroken widow. You will be a red-blooded Le Cap woman who is ready to move on to a powerful new man. Charles Rivière-Hérard has never been able to hide his affection for you, and speaks of you even now. He's had a notoriously small circle since the beginning but there are even fewer people he allows to get close to him since his rapid, decorated ascent in the military. You will be one of them.

There is something afoot in my husband's ranks and I know Rivière-Hérard is behind it. I urged Jean-Pierre to reject the French's demand for 150 million gold francs. Rivière-Hérard was a snake at his temple, hissing for him to accept the "deal." At first glance there appeared no choice but to agree to their terms, what with their warships and guns waiting at the Port-au-Prince harbor. But the people will revolt over this further bondage. We don't need whips and chains to be slaves if we're expected to sign over ten times our gross domestic product to the very slave-owners we claim to have escaped. Rivière-Hérard knows this fact and will twist it to his advantage. I can hear the cries now; *tear down that mulatto from his ivory tower.* Jean-Pierre turns a blind eye.

You will keep your eyes, ears, and legs open for anything "important" you hear of and from Rivière-Hérard. Pass along to me what you learn and do your part to silence his faction's dissent so then you can live your days in peace in the land you claim to love. Ultimately, I want Rivière-Hérard to be dust in my hands. In every sense of the word.

Jean-Pierre is president for life and it is my intention to keep it this way. I believe he will do what Alexandre and your Henri could not and stay alive long enough to do some good under my counsel. Only embark on this journey if you are willing to follow through to the end. I swear with every breath within me that if you do not fulfill your obligation, you and your children's children will come to curse the day you entered this arrangement.

Letter From Mom To *Tati* Estelle
In The Dossier *Tati* Estelle Gave Me

SUNDAY, OCTOBER 20

Estelle,

I miss you. Please answer me. Don't think I haven't noticed how quickly you pass the phone to *Maman* if you happen to be home when I call on Sundays, or the fact you don't call at all. I know you're upset but we've never gone this long without speaking, even after I accidentally burned your favorite wrap dress when I was ironing. I'm not trivializing this, but you did love that dress.

You know I couldn't stay there. I was suffocating and that was when I realized that there was never going to be a good time to leave. I was never passionate about what life would offer me if I stayed in Haiti. I'm not cut out to marry some politician, have children, and stay home and watch my servants clean things all day. I didn't want to deal with the hypocrisy of summering on a hill that looked down on the abject poverty just a few miles below.

So when Roseline said she wanted to try lifting—exchanging—this curse for something better for us all…I took a chance and allowed myself the luxury of believing that this *madichon* that has plagued us our whole lives was real and agreed to perform the ritual. And if it wasn't, I prayed that this ritual would somehow clean our hands of what *Papi* did. But I was wrong. It didn't make living with his actions any easier. I felt guilty looking at Roseline, watching her stay home to cook and clean when we would go to school or a party. I know you sometimes felt that I picked Roseline over you, that I spent all my free time with her because I wished she was my sister instead, but the truth is, I knew she was safe with me. When Roseline left after he died and I got *Maman* to promise she wouldn't try to get her back…and when you reunited with Andres…I decided that if I was going to be selfish and attempt to build a new life from of all this history, it would have to be then.

Do you know, that *very* night I'd made up my mind, Andres's father mentioned the American student visa program at dinner and *Maman* didn't immediately change the subject? That's when I realized I could actually make this happen. I filled out the application and wrote my essays, and when I got that acceptance letter three weeks later, I cried.

This country isn't paradise. It's draining to sift through everything someone tells me, wondering if it's an unintentional verbal jab or if there are other underlying meanings. I was running to catch a bus, and as the white driver shut the door on me, he said, "Don't be hatin'. There's another bus coming." I was floored. And I was so proud of my English in high school. I flinch a little each time a classmate frowns and says, "What?" when I speak.

But I'm challenged here. There are shops and Broadway shows and parks to explore. I write essays in class and hear feedback from my new column in the newspaper. I'm auditioning to be an anchor on the student-run television station next semester. I'm hurtling toward my purpose. I can feel it.

I miss you. Are you happy? Did you get what you wanted?

Clearly Unsent Letter From
Tati Estelle To Mom

Tuesday, November 19
Celeste,

Allow me to state the obvious, but I miss you. I'm also very, very angry with you. I hated keeping up that wall between us but I was betrayed. By you, my best friend, my mirror. That's never happened before. You've always sworn to "leave this stupid town" and talked incessantly about its flaws (it was a downer at parties) but I thought it was just chatter. I never thought you'd actually go, let alone with our family in pieces. I had no desire to leave Haiti before this and I assumed you wouldn't want to either. I felt stupid for wanting to stay.

I don't know what I hoped to accomplish with the freeze-out but I'm thawing now. Every Sunday, I read all your letters, cry a little, and then stash them in that clunky chest you kept in your room for your books. I took it with me to school.

Port-au-Prince is not Cap-Haïtien. It's not New York either. It probably wouldn't have been enough for you but I feel independent and urbane enough here in college. Jules still asks about you when he sees me on campus. L'Université d'État d'Haïti may not be Columbia but it's just as instructive… But I'm a science politique student with connections. I'm doing most of my learning in the palace anyway. And things down in Palais National are all over the place since Baby Doc left. We've had three presidents since you've been gone. Three.

Maman has found herself a "gentleman friend" already and he spends sixty percent of his time complaining about missing his domino buddies. I wonder how many of them landed in New York with you to escape this mess. Yves (that's his name) can't believe a retired priest was president before he was ("Who would trust a priest who quits the priesthood?!").

For the record...I knew Roseline needed you more than I did. But I still needed you. After she left, I thought I'd get you back. As for those magical wishes, I lost you and Andres but have gained reoccurring nightmares of a pregnant girl dying in labor on the floor of a room I don't recognize. I guess you can rest well knowing you made it to New York on your own.

Yours,
Estelle

Tuesday, February 9

The Life and Times of Alaine Beauparlant

Last night, no matter how hard I tried, I couldn't get myself to fall asleep. I would wake up in fits and starts, my mind drifting to the letters that my aunt had given me and the ones I'd found online. Even Fernand commented on my constant yawning as he drove me and *Tati* Estelle to Tony's peanut farm in Novion, where we would film a segment for our PATRON PAL YouTube page.

"Ou gen yon ti chouchou, Alaine?" he asked.

"Ti chouchou?" I said incredulously. "Nope, no love interest here! What makes you say that?" I looked at *Tati* Estelle, who suddenly seemed very engrossed in her phone.

Fernand chuckled, "That's the only reason why someone your age should be yawning so much first thing in the morning! Late-night phone calls, writing love letters, young love."

I rolled my eyes. I wish the case of my sleepless night was nearly as scandalous and interesting, but instead I had stayed up to think about the curse and what it meant for my mother. I had hardly thought about the curse while I was in Miami, so much so that it hadn't even come up in conversation with

Tatiana until a few weeks ago. This pervasive way of viewing *madichon* was all so new to me. Growing up with my dad, I hadn't been exposed to the Family Curse in the way that everyone on my mother's side talked about so freely (among themselves, anyway). Even my aunt, who seemed to believe in its existence, hadn't pressed the matter and talked about it with me, because my mom was adamant against even bringing it up. And I knew that superstition wasn't limited to just my family from all the times that Tatiana had to cancel plans with me simply because her mother had had "a dream." This was always synonymous with: *if you leave this house, something terrible is sure to happen. You've been warned.* Tatiana and I would always grumble and groan, but she would never push back. I could tell a part of her believed.

My family was no different, no matter how highly regarded they were. Politicians, socialites, doctors, lawyers, executives, masked caped crusaders. It was no secret that people envied them because of the status they held, but no one was above the fear of *madichon.* We were all capable of letting ourselves believe in superstition.

It wasn't just once that I had heard someone blame even minor misfortune on this supposed family curse. It was a way of life for the *tatis* and *tontons* and *kouzen* as they moved through life, a cop-out that allowed them to leave responsibility for their actions in the hands of someone or something else. Maybe it was too unpleasant to explain away more painful tragedy as meaningless chance.

But even though listening to my family drone on and on about this imagined *madichon* was pretty unbelievable, the main thing that I couldn't shake was the idea of my mother and aunt fighting, especially after knowing what they'd gone through. I had never seen the two of them argue in any substantial way—ever. They were so in tune with one another that sometimes it felt like speaking to my aunt was enough to inform my mom through some twin-induced osmosis. I depended on it during those moments my mom couldn't answer her phone or email. But reading that she and *Tati* Estelle had spent weeks without speaking to one another let me know that their relationship wasn't always sunny.

And funnily enough, I could do what they couldn't all those years ago and understand both sides of the argument. My aunt must've felt like she was losing my mom first to Roseline and then to the land of baseball and apple pie. My mother's leaving so soon after their father's death didn't help any. And I could only imagine how *Tati* Estelle felt knowing that her big sister wouldn't be there to help her cope with the memory of Bois Caïman. Any doubt that I had about how real this curse was always wavered when I thought about that moment.

My mom had wanted to get away from the very beginning. And I couldn't even begin to think about what Gregoire had done to Roseline. That sealed the deal for her and she had no choice but to leave. What he did was horrible, a violation that I wouldn't wish on anyone. I hated to think that a part of him was alive in me, my mom, and my aunt. It made me sick to my stomach. And the idea that Roseline was my grandmother's curse to bear was insanity. What a luxury it must be to cast the blame of another's transgressions on an unseen force that you could neither prove nor deny.

Meanwhile, as I headed to work, I was fighting back yawns, because I had eventually ditched the idea of getting any sleep and had stayed up all night rereading the letters that *Tati* Estelle had given me and researching online archives for any information on Henri Christophe's widow, Marie-Louise. If she was the origin of all of my family's misfortune, then it was only right that I find out as much as I could about her. Though everything in my mind told me that there was no logical reason to believe in this curse, there was something about Marie-Madeleine's tone in her letter that promised she wasn't someone to mess with. And that she would do whatever it took to make my great-great-great-great-great... grandmother pay for not holding up her end of the bargain. Whether that meant that she would—or heck, could—cast a curse that would persist for generations was the million-dollar question. And somehow Roseline could shed some light on that.

I was still thinking about what all of this could mean when we finally arrived at Tony Juste's peanut farm. Alternating rows of brown soil and short blades of grass extended for miles, the outskirts of the crop surrounded by overgrown shrubs and large-leafed banana plants, mountains reaching toward the sky in the distance. Jason, Thierry, and Tony were already in place when *Tati* Estelle and I walked up to where the camera equipment was set up.

"You're late," Thierry said gruffly as he pointed to a spot near where Tony stood in front of the camera for *Tati* Estelle to join so that they could begin filming.

"Never," *Tati* Estelle replied with a smile. "I told you an hour earlier because *you're* the one who's always late. Let's get started, shall we?"

Thierry huffed as he got my aunt mic'd up. Jason and I gave each other a little smile but said nothing, standing to the side so as not to become the focus of Thierry's wrath.

"The mission of PATRON PAL is not only to bring aid to the children of Haiti, but also to provide opportunities for the next generation to become self-sustaining. We strive to educate our Patrons on responsible ways to help."

My aunt smiled brightly into the camera as she spoke, Tony standing just outside of the frame, a large grin plastered on his face as he waited for his airtime. I'd pitched a video series idea at our latest meeting to highlight different ways that Patrons could be more informed about Haiti and had been happily surprised when my aunt decided to do it.

"We are at a peanut farm in Novion, a town in northern Haiti," she said. "We are going to show you what happens when we don't hold our government accountable for its actions."

"Okay, that was a good take," Thierry said as he stopped filming. "Let's head over to the rows of peanuts so that we can get the next shot."

"Your aunt is a great speaker," Jason said as we went to where Thierry had instructed.

"It comes with the Dubois territory," I said with a grin. "The very expensive, tutor-filled Dubois territory."

Jason laughed. "There's some natural talent in there too. Do you think that you'd like to have your own show one day like your mom? Or maybe go into public service like Estelle?"

It was my turn to laugh. "I could *never* be a politician. They don't say what they mean, and there's never any mistake as to what I'm thinking. I want to go to Columbia and become a kick-ass journalist like my mom. They're big pumps to fill, but I think I'm up to the task a solid sixty-five percent of the time. I want to have made enough of an impact on the world that people get a phone alert when I die."

"That…is a strange but compelling goal to aspire to," he said. "The phone alert. Not the mom."

I shrugged. "What about you? Have you got any political inclinations?"

"Not right now. I'm a computer engineering major."

"You mean every Haitian mom's dream?"

"Precisely," he said.

I tried to rein in my grin. "What's a freshman engineering major doing here in Haiti during the middle of the school year? That's got to be some kind of breach of protocol."

"When I got the chance to do a semester internship at PA-TRON PAL, I didn't think twice. Coding for a start-up company that not only has cool software but also helps the Haitian people? It's exactly what I want to be doing when I graduate."

"Even if we're not really being put to use?"

"Hey, you're the reason we're here, right?" He motioned around us. "And I'm willing to prove my worth. Besides, my dad's American but my mom's family still lives here, so it's also a reunion. I like to come back and visit as much as I can. It gets pretty lonely when you're away at school. Especially since I'm three hours behind."

"Three hours?"

"Yes," Jason responded. "I'm a student at Stanford."

"That's right! My aunt mentioned that." I groaned and clutched my chest. "Ugh. I don't think that my Haitian woman sensibilities can take any more of this. Engineering major at an Ivy League? What else is there? You've got the solution to end world hunger?"

"We're technically not an Ivy League, but I'll take it. And I'm still working on that—ending world hunger," he chuckled. "In all seriousness though, I know some politicians can be pretty sketchy, but I don't think they're *all* as evasive as we've come to think. Look at your aunt. She's doing great work for this country. We need more people like her who can help get things done."

"We do. But I would rather help tell the stories of people who don't have a voice. Our politicians can't make the changes we need if they don't know there's a problem. My mom does such a great job of bringing issues to light on her show that we never would've known about otherwise. I'd love to be able to do that." I hesitated. "Well…she used to."

"How is she doing?" Jason asked tentatively. It was only a matter of time before someone asked me about my mom's wandering at the last PATRON PAL event. Between my aunt's frantic shouting and my palpable anxiety, anyone could've guessed that something was wrong when we freaked out about an apparently self-reliant, middle-aged woman walking away alone for a few minutes.

I watched for a bit as my aunt chatted with Tony before I responded. I took a breath. "She's not well. She has early onset Alzheimer's."

There it was. Out in the open. An ugly truth that I still didn't know how to deal with.

"Wow. She's so young," Jason said with a shake of his head. He looked at me and held my gaze. "I'm sorry to hear that, Alaine."

I gave a tight shrug.

"All right. Quiet on the set," Thierry said as he adjusted the camera on his left shoulder. He might have been in charge of money, but he was the self-assigned resident videographer too. I sighed away the tension in my neck.

"This is going to be a walking shot, so I need you guys to stay aware of the lens," Thierry barked. "Don't turn your back to me. Got it?"

My aunt nodded and faced Tony when Thierry gave her the signal to begin speaking. "I have here with me Tony Juste. Tony is a farmer in Novion and his only crop is the peanut. Peanuts are a staple food in the Haitian diet because they're loaded with protein and relatively inexpensive to produce.

They grow on a drought-resistant plant that is the saving grace for so many farmers during the harsh, dry harvests that we've been having. Tony, can you show us your crops?"

Tony led us the short distance to the field where three men were bent over, tilling the earth. One of the men had his shirt tied around his head, sweat glistening on his back under the morning sun. Another stood behind two oxen and used a yoke to guide them as they lifted the soil with each dragging step.

"This is Jojo," Tony said in lilting English, pointing out the last man. He wore a tattered baseball cap, his yellow-striped polo shirt filthy with the grime of working in a field. In his hands was a ball of vines, small peanuts dotted throughout. "He is going to show you some of the peanuts that we were able to cultivate."

Thierry stepped forward to get a zoomed-in shot of the plant in the worker's hands. Jojo snapped a peanut from its place on the vine and stuck his hand out toward me to take it.

"M-merci," I said, suddenly aware that I was now on camera. I broke the shell and popped the peanut into my mouth. I gave a thumbs-up. "Tasty."

"My peanuts are the best the city has to offer," Tony said proudly. "We always sell the most when we go to market, but I'm worried that it will not be the same for much longer."

"Why is that?" *Tati* Estelle asked, the ever-attentive interviewer. She might be able to give my mom a run for her money if she kept this up.

"Well, America is trying to give the surplus peanuts that they have to Haiti to feed the children."

"Isn't that a good thing though?" I interrupted. Thierry turned toward me, glaring behind the camera's eyepiece. "Haiti should want to receive assistance, especially if it means helping these kids fight starvation."

"That is what they *want* you to think," Tony said to me with a gentle smile. "When the US brings these peanuts, I will not be able to compete anymore. With so many of the seeds in the market, the price will fall to nothing and I will not make any profit. My livelihood will be finished and the eight people that I employ will no longer have work to support their families. They say that they will distribute the peanuts in tiny bags and give them to the children, only to be eaten at school. But they do not say how this will be regulated. It will be just like the rice situation we had a few years ago."

"Do you mean the subsidized rice imports that came to Haiti from the United States during the 1990s?" *Tati* Estelle asked Tony.

"Yes," Tony affirmed. "All of that extra American rice has made it impossible to grow the grain here in Haiti. They say that they sent the surplus of rice to help feed our people and to remove the burden of making our own food. Have you ever heard such foolishness? What good is a country if it does not produce its own sustenance to feed its people? We all know that the decision to send the extra rice here was a business one. Those farmers in the US were still paid for their product. Without a doubt, they got the better end of the deal. The US government has an entire country dependent on importing its products. Without this system, Haiti will face certain death. The odds are tilted in America's favor. They have a customer for life."

"But Haiti needs the help! There's no way that you can make it seem like this country is self-sufficient," I interjected. Thierry flipped the camera to me again and I'm sure I heard him give a low growl of frustration. Oh well, another thing for him to edit out.

"By no means," Tony responded. "Haiti is very reliant on

other countries for aid. Without it, we would sink into even greater despair. But to act like we are not in this situation partly because of this feedback loop of immense dependency on foreign aid would be naive. And you do not strike me as naive, *ti* Estelle."

"Indeed," said my aunt with a smile. "In fact, this discussion helps to reinforce the importance of PATRON PAL. By donating through our app, you help children all around Haiti meet their basic living needs. You're also helping to educate these children, which is equally important to establishing stability in this country and hopefully will make my app irrelevant in the future. After all, with knowledge comes strength and we all know that *sak vid pa kanpe*. Or, an empty sack can't stand up."

"Cut!" Thierry said. "Okay. We have the scene. Even with the interruptions."

I turned to Tony, ignoring Thierry's pointed look. "Thank you for explaining. I never thought about it the way that you do. You made good points."

"It is a sign of a very mature person to be open to others' ideas. You are definitely Estelle's niece," he said. "She said that it was your idea to make a video highlighting a Haitian worker, so I should be thanking you."

Soon all of us piled into the car to head back to the PATRON PAL office. We passed one of the markets that Tony had told us to keep an eye out for as we wound through the hot and dusty streets. People darted into the road in front of the car, paying no mind to oncoming vehicles and villagers riding by on their donkeys. We saw merchants along the sidelines, each shouting their wares. We drove slowly down a particularly crowded road, cars passing us as they made their way through the streets, ignoring the tentative flow of traffic. Finally, the crowd parted and I saw a stand with a large sign that read *Pistach Tonton Tony*. The two women (wo)manning the stand were hurriedly pouring bushels of peanuts into small sacks for their many customers.

"Tony wasn't kidding about his peanuts being the best in town," I said to Jason beside me in the car.

He nodded in agreement.

Then after some thought he said, "Alaine?"

"Yeah."

"I think you'll fill your mom's shoes just fine."

Wednesday, February 10
From: Tatiana Hippolyte
To: Alaine Beauparlant
Subject: Re: Re: Hey Girl!

Hey there!

Following up on my email since I haven't heard from you. I know you're hanging with your family and all, but I'm starting to worry. Give me an update, girl! There's a *Capitol Post* article that came out today and it's saying that Venegas is heading to Haiti. Did you know this? And there's a mention at the end that your mom might have Alzheimer's. What the heck is going on? Call me or message me or something!

Your best friend that you've clearly forgotten about,
Tatiana

Andres Venegas Heading to Haiti for Beauparlant Showdown

By Colt Rivers, *The Capitol Post*

The plot thickens between besieged cable talk show host Celeste Beauparlant and Florida senator Andres Venegas. The embattled senator is still under fire with constituents for possibly misusing party funds. But with no indictable evidence, Venegas is free to serve his term and run for reelection.

He is expected to announce his candidacy for a second term in the coming months, but his most recent declaration has all but confirmed the inevitable.

"After much prayerful consideration, I have decided to

make a trip to Haiti and return to my roots," Venegas said in a press release.

In the late eighties and early nineties, Venegas's father, Andres Venegas Sr., was the United States ambassador to Haiti, where Venegas spent much of his formative years. The trip is seen as a shrewd move to ingratiate himself with South Florida's Haitian American community, which once loved him for his ties to the poverty-stricken island. His last official visit was in response to the earthquake that claimed the lives of more than an estimated 200,000 people and left almost 1.5 million homeless.

The *Capitol Post* has also uncovered that Venegas and Beauparlant attended sister schools in Cap-Haïtien. The pair presumably remained close before their public falling out. Recently obtained files show that both were early investors in PATRON PAL. The thriving app company is worth a purported $10 million and was created by Estelle Dubois, Beauparlant's twin sister and Haiti's Minister of Tourism.

Two months after her on-air meltdown, Beauparlant remains with her sister. CP is working to verify accounts suggesting she is suffering from a neurological disorder, possibly Alzheimer's disease.

Hi Tatiana,

I guess word has finally gotten out… What you read is right. My mom has Alzheimer's. I've avoided speaking to you these last few weeks because I haven't been able to process exactly how I've been feeling about all of this. If I'm being honest with you (and myself), I was sort of hoping that if I didn't talk about it at all, it would just kind of go away. But it's getting harder and harder to avoid.

The other night, we had a dinner for my grandmother and my whole extended family was there. And, out of nowhere, Mom lost it. She started yelling about something that must've happened decades ago. While everyone else was confused, I was terrified. It scared me senseless to watch her fade away like that. One second we were giving toasts and the next I was shouting my mom's name to bring her back to us.

The worst part was when she came to; she looked so embarrassed. Can you believe it? She has a medical breakdown and isn't even sure what she said, but because of how we were all staring at her, she could immediately tell that something was wrong. The idea of her thinking that we were pitying her…

I can't begin to imagine what it must be like for her. I've been researching the disease to get a better understanding of everything, but there's so much that doctors don't know. Some people deteriorate fast while others can stick around for a while. And there's no telling which side of the coin you'll land on until it stops spinning. What kind of life is that for anyone?

I can't just stand by and watch as everything falls apart

for her, Tatiana. Do you remember when I told you about my family curse? Well, I've learned more about it and I'm going to try and break it. Maybe this is just a wild shot in the dark, but if there's a chance that I might be able to bring my mom back to the light, then I'll take it. Wish me luck.

— A

Saturday, February 13

The Life and Times of Alaine Beauparlant

The next morning, I quickly got dressed to head to Roseline's house. My mom always said, "Never turn down a potential scoop," and if Roseline was the key to potentially breaking this curse, then I was determined to meet with her about it. I wore a short chambray dress with large pockets, the small piece of paper that she had given me with her address tucked safely away. I didn't want my mom to know where I was going, so I left before she even woke up. She'd gone to bed early the night before, quieter ever since she'd read online that Andres had the *cojones* to announce a trip to Haiti. I wouldn't have been able to sneak away without *Tati* Estelle's help.

"I know Celeste wouldn't approve," *Tati* Estelle said when she walked into the kitchen as I finished drinking a glass of orange juice before heading out. "But if I don't let you explore this, I will never forgive myself. And since I won't be here anyway, I know Roseline will show you better than I could ever tell you."

"You won't be here? Where are you going?"

"I have to do some traveling for PATRON PAL, but I'll

be back before you know it. Don't worry about leaving your mother alone. She and Jacques have already scheduled a crepe-making contest that will likely take up the entire afternoon."

Clearly my aunt had planned this all out, so I nodded and gave her what I hoped was a brave smile.

She pulled me into a hug and said, "Whenever the truth is hidden, it always finds a way to come back and bite you. No matter how pure the intentions were. Try to keep that in mind."

She wouldn't elaborate when I asked her what she meant. Instead, she told me that the family chauffeur would be parked in the driveway to take me to Roseline's house at 6:00 a.m. sharp.

I sat silently in the car as Fernand sped through the empty streets. He tried to chat with me at first, asking how I liked Haiti so far. Whether I missed my home in the States. I guess my short answers and distracted tone must've given him the message that I didn't want to talk, because the rest of the ride passed by with no more conversation. I was lost in my thoughts.

I didn't know if Roseline knew that I was aware of what my grandfather had done to her. I didn't know what to say to someone after something so terrible had happened. No matter how long ago it had been. And especially when that some-thing terrible was caused by a person who was related to you. Even though I never knew my mother's father, I still couldn't help but feel guilty about what Roseline went through. Would she look at me and fear that I had the capacity to be just as cruel? I hoped with all my might that she wouldn't.

Soon we arrived in front of Roseline's house, a small shack at the end of a block. I'd followed the names of the roads as we drove past them, but still did a double take to confirm that the tiny house was hers. It dawned on me then that the address she'd given me was for the house she'd grown up in before her mother died, not whatever home she had upgraded to since then. She'd kept it, even after all these years of starting a new life with Pierrot. Each house was crammed beside the next, red, green, blue, and yellow boxes fighting for a place on the side of a steep mountain. I crossed the short yard and hesitated as I lifted my hand to knock on the bare wooden door. It had been a mistake to come. Did I really want to know more about such a terrible time in my mom's and aunt's lives? In hers?

Too late.

The door creaked opened. Roseline stood before me, looking lovely even in a plain, lily-white dress. She was not as dressed up as she had been for my grandmother's birthday celebration, but somehow she looked even more regal. No one would confuse her with a *restavek* ever again.

"Alaine," Roseline said. "You made it. And right on time!"

"I gave up CPT for New Year's," I blurted.

"CPT?"

"Just a dumb joke about black people always being late." This was going well.

"Ah. Do you always keep your promises?"

"I try to."

Roseline pulled me into the house, waving hello to Fernand before shutting the door behind us. The interior was dark, the drawn shutters preventing the morning light from poking through. Two wicker chairs were parked on either edge of a small wooden table. Atop the table sat a bottle of Florida water and another of rum, a box of matches on a clean white plate, and a small mortar and pestle. A thin sleeping mat was off to the right side of the room, with a very flat and lumpy pillow rolled into a ball on top of sheets that were carefully tucked over the makeshift bed. On the wall above the mat hung a brightly colored screen print of a woman with two scars on her face holding a dagger in one hand and a baby in another. A large crown sat perched atop her head, her unsmiling gaze piercing through me. I turned away, a slight shiver racing down my spine. Across the room was a door that led to the back of the house, where food was probably cooked outside.

"How was the ride?" Roseline asked as she looked from the woman in the image to me and ushered us over to the two seats. "Are you hungry? You must be hungry. Let me get you something to eat. Is coffee okay?"

Roseline didn't know where to put her energy. She fluttered around the small house gathering plates and forks and knives, asking me questions without even trying to listen to my answers. The briny smell of smoked herring spaghetti wafted toward my nose when she stepped out of the back door and returned with large plates piled high with food. She placed the pasta before me in one graceful swoop. A second later, a platter of peanut butter and *kassav*, one of my favorite breads made from flattened dried cassava tubers and shredded coconut, followed. She walked in and out, returning each time with more food—sliced mango, diced papaya, a pitcher of soursop juice, a pot of coffee. Finally, Roseline sat down and helped herself to some of the meal. When I finished making my plate, she looked at my portions and clicked her tongue. I didn't bother protesting as she added two more heaping spoonfuls of everything and slathered peanut butter onto my pieces of *kassav*. In true Haitian form, I was going to leave her house three sizes bigger than how I came in.

"Everyone I know seems to eat Tony's peanut butter," I said, motioning toward the glass jar labelled *Tony J. Manba*.

"His business is really booming! Did you know that he's trying to branch out to all of Nord? I hope it works out for him. He seems like a good man."

"Yes," Roseline said. She picked up the jar and inspected it as though for the first time. "He is a gifted farmer."

"I've literally grown up on his peanuts. *Tati* Estelle sends this stuff to me in the States by the boxload."

"How nice of her," Roseline said.

I'm the queen of filling dead air. It was a gift passed down to me by my mother. But believe me when I tell you I was stumped by what to say next. We both knew I hadn't come here to drone on about peanuts. I wasn't just BS-ing a missed assignment (sorry, Sister Wagner). I wanted to say the right thing, not just anything.

Roseline eventually put down her spoon.

"You remind me of your mother when we were girls."

I inhaled sharply.

"I don't get that as often as you would think," I said.

"Oh, she was more serious of course. But just as headstrong. I can sense your independence."

I nodded as I chewed on a mouthful of spaghetti, praying she would continue.

Roseline took a sip of soursop juice and sighed deeply as she placed the glass on the table. "I'm sorry to bring you here," she said, gesturing across the small house with a sweep of her arm. "But it's the only place that I knew where we could sit and talk freely. This is the only home that I grew up in. I closed myself off by the time I was brought to the Dubois family. I didn't grow there."

"Did you ever get to spend time here before you left?"

"I tried. There isn't much to this room, but it belonged to

my mother. Before she died, she told me to return so I could remember all that she ever taught me," she said.

"Can this place help others...remember?"

Roseline smiled sadly. "That isn't quite how it works, Alaine."

"So you know, then?"

"I wish we were not getting to know each other under these circumstances, but *Bondye* does as He pleases. It's why I asked you to come to this sacred place."

"Why *did* you invite me here?"

"We can help each other by helping the ones we love most." The hairs on my neck stood erect. A proposition was coming.

"Roseline, you've gotta tell it to me straight. What are you talking about?"

"Estelle told me you've read Celeste's diaries. You know what happened before. I'm saying we can fix it. For good."

"What has changed from then to now though? Why didn't you do a permanent fix the first time?"

"You have an honest face. I will tell you the truth—I gave up. I may not have grown at the Dubois house, but I did get smaller. Any chance she got, your grandmother would tell me about how Marie-Louise was cursed by Marie-Madeleine for not upholding her end of the bargain. For this, your line was cursed for all eternity. But after my body began to develop and she saw the way her husband looked at me, *I* became the curse.

"Anyone else might think this curse business was just a story passed along to spook children. And yet, my own mother's teachings remained lodged in my brain. 'Never take words lightly, especially *yon madichon*.' Words make us. They destroy us.

"That day Celeste, Estelle, Jules, and Andres made their

way to me... It was the first time I couldn't hear my mother's voice here. I slapped something together. When they stood at my doorstep, I couldn't turn them away, especially when the whole thing was my idea."

"How'd you figure out what went wrong in the ceremony after all this time?"

"I got more in tune with my mother's work and have had years to think about it at a distance. Your mother is suffering today because Estelle did not finish gathering her portion of the required payment. I specifically warned them that no hesitation would be tolerated. Her moment of doubt tainted the whole process, and to make up for this, soil must be collected from four times as many prominent spaces. Ideally, Estelle's direct heir would make this collection. But since Estelle has no children, you are the closest kin. The basic premise is still right—the best way to break a curse is to counter it. But, if my suspicions are correct, then your father, aunt, and, yes, Andres are at risk as well. Money, love, and power will be ripped from each of them without your help."

A shudder raced down my spine as Roseline spoke. But a thought occurred to me that I couldn't overlook. I hated myself for asking but needed to find out. "How did Gregoire die?"

"I can't explain that, because I don't know."

"It just seemed so...sudden."

She didn't break our eye contact. "He was the monster, Alaine. I didn't kill him. I didn't need to when he lived on cigarettes, rum, and fried pork."

Fair enough.

"When Gregoire died, I didn't think. I escaped." Roseline's eyes appeared glazed like marbles, her mind far away from where she sat with me. "I came back to this house with the few possessions I had. I wasn't sure what I wanted to do with my freedom. I had no skills besides cooking and cleaning. I wasn't ready to explore my mother's gifts. But I remembered the Giraud family. I overheard one day that they needed someone to look after the house, so I went. If I brought misfortune upon them the way that I had your mother's family, then I would know that the curse really did lie within me."

"You didn't truly think that, did you?" My heart ached for teenage Roseline.

"You believe a lot of silly things when you're broken. I eventually figured out that I was *not* the curse, that it was something within your family's blood. Meanwhile, your mother sent me money each month from her allowance, but I was too proud to use it."

"You just kept cleaning the Girauds' house instead?"

Roseline nodded. "They were fine enough… But their son, Pierrot… He helped put me back together again. We took to each other like nutmeg in *kremas*. Our love felt right and we wanted to get married quickly."

"How did everyone take that?" I asked, remembering what Félicité had told me at dinner.

"They were all against it. His parents used our age as an excuse, but I knew it was me. Celeste was the only one to send a gift."

My heart glowed knowing my mother had gone against family politics. I knew what *Tati* Estelle's beef was with Roseline, but I was still disappointed in her.

"Have family gatherings since then been…awkward?"

"We don't get invited to many." Roseline chuckled. "An unforgivable amount of what needs to be said among family always remains unspoken. Yet I prefer it that way."

"So it's just been you and Pierrot against the world?"

"Our life is rich with friends and neighbors. This little one," she said as she patted her bulging belly. "We'd given up, but it was the greatest shock. I'm asking you to do this not only to help your mother, but to protect my child, since he or she will also be a descendant of Marie-Louise Coidavid through Pierrot."

Maybe this is what my mom felt like when she agreed to give Roseline's idea a shot the first time. I pled with the universe that something good would come of this and also realized that there was no way that I could look into Roseline's hopeful eyes and say no.

"I'll perform the ritual," I said, my voice stronger than I felt.

With no hesitation, Roseline leaped from her seat and got to work, gathering ingredients and supplies for what looked like a tea and leaving them to boil. She held open the front door so that I could follow her outside, where she pointed for me to scoop my own pile of dirt into a small bucket. When I was done, we went back inside to sit at the table where we had eaten just a moment ago. Roseline positioned her seat across from mine and reached out to squeeze my hand, gratitude written across her face.

"I need your hand. Your blood," she said.

"My blood?!" I asked in alarm, pulling away.

"That was a test, Alaine. I do not need your blood. But if you agree to this, then you *must* be prepared to do whatever it takes. I need us to be in this together. No hesitation. When your mom and the others attempted to lift this curse, they only had one chance and they failed. Your mother was the leader of the group. Her illness proves this as she has been targeted first. You have to try it just as they did. But unlike them, you will be successful. There is no other option."

I nodded in understanding.

Roseline continued with the ritual, repeating some of the same steps that I remembered reading in my mother's diary. She pulled a large red candle from her pocket and used one of the matches to light it, placing the candle in the center of the white plate. Roseline motioned for me to place my hands above the mortar and pestle. She rinsed our hands without a word, splashing the Florida water carefully between our fingers. I watched as Roseline took a handful of leaves from the inside of her pockets and placed them in the mortar and handed it over to me. I took the pestle and mashed up the leaves, focused on grinding them into as fine a powder as I could manage.

"Ancestors, we ask that you protect Alaine as she moves forward on this journey," Roseline said once I was done and placed the container on the table. "She is but a humble servant performing your will."

I watched as Roseline grabbed the large bottle of rum that I'd noticed when I first entered her house. She used her teeth to unscrew it and poured three splashes of the dark liquor into the mortar, then placed the bottle on the ground beside her. She then took a match and with two quick swipes, a bright flame ignited. Roseline tossed the match into the mortar, closed her eyes in what looked like a silent prayer and then, finally, we were done.

Roseline gathered up her skirts and left through the back door. She returned with the now-finished tea. "Drink this, it will open your eyes. But I suspect you've already begun to see," Roseline said cryptically. I squirmed in my seat, thinking about the dream I'd had the night I'd learned of my mom's condition. Her face slowly transforming before my eyes.

The tea burned sliding down my throat. I pressed my lips

together and held my breath, barring any of the salty mixture from making its way back up.

"What should I be—" My head suddenly weighed twice as much. I jerked my head toward Roseline, catching the end of her request. My mind slowly drifted away. I knew that I should feel panicked, but instead a strange calm washed over my body, as if I was settling into a deep sleep after an exhausting day of working in the sun. Roseline's words sounded as though they were being transferred through a tube under water. I could barely lift my arms to wipe my eyes in an effort to shake away the blur from her appearance.

"Send Marie-Louise my best."

The world went black.

PART V

MO NOU GEN ZEL

(OUR WORDS HAVE WINGS)

Sunday, February 14

The Life and Times of Alaine Beauparlant
~~~~~~

RECIPE FOR A TRIPPY DREAM-TRANCE PARTY

- Incurably sick mother

- Snarky youth in need of answers and assistance

- ~180 pounds of an above-average height Haitian woman promising both

- 10 minutes of a freaky ceremony

- A dash of disbelief

- Tightly balled tea bag

- 2 pinches of sugar

- 1 tablespoon of salt

- 3 chopped lemon leaves

- Crushed piece of ginger root

- A mind swirling with letters of desperation

- Approximately 200 years of buildup

Directions: Combine your ingredients in a small kettle before pouring into a chipped yellow teacup. Drink hastily and prepare to have limbs feel like lead. Try not to hit your head when passing out. Remember everything.

Become your ancestor. Experience the strongest wave of loneliness you've ever felt when you stand at your daughters' graves for what you know is the last time. Consider staying put so it won't be. Dry your tears and promise to do better with the next generation. Take a rickety ship back to your homeland. Console your granddaughter when she gets seasick.

Be at peace when reuniting with remaining family. Do not cry when leaving them to fulfill a promise. Dress up. Pretend to be charming. Make a powerful man fall in love with you. Be surprised when you realize one day you've fallen in love too. Feel shame when you can't reconcile the gentle person you've come to know with the man who fought actively against your first love.

Accept the irreconcilable. Cut out the knife you've kept sewed into your pillow for years. Pour out the bottle of poison. Keep his secrets.

Avoid all summons to the palace. Grow old. Watch your child's baby become a woman. Convince yourself that you made the best choice for your descendants. Know deep down that this is not the truth.

Serves one.

Have you read this yet? The writer was thirsty as hell but
your aunt kept right on redirecting to what's important. Estelle is fi-yah.

J

P.S. Please forgive my use of "fi-yah." It was now or never.

P.P.S. How have you not thrown being related to a founding
father in my face yet?

Meet the Woman Who Is Making Millennials "Swipe Right" on Charity

VoxPop | Owen Smith

Estelle Dubois has the easy grace of a member of the Brit-
ish royal family. She's pleasantly aloof when citizens walk up
and thank her for, well, existing. She nods her head as regally
as Meghan Markle but has superseded the Duchess of Sus-
sex in this: Dubois is the descendant of Haitian revolutionary leader and king, Henri Christophe, so she is royal by the
blood coursing through her veins.

"It's absurd to actually *claim* such a thing," Dubois says.
Her laugh tinkles like wind chimes on a breezy day.

Henri I, self-appointed sovereign that he was, tragically

became the first and last monarch of the island nation. He sired four legitimate children, one of whom is a distant ancestor to Dubois. But crown or no crown, it's clear that she is special. The people who engage her in conversation at the crowded Port-au-Prince café where we're dining call her by just one name: Estelle.

"They feel like they *know* me." She shrugs. "And in a way, they do. I love Haiti. It's my biggest passion in life and an integral piece of myself."

When I ask her if she has any other passions in life or any other people to share those passions with, she's coy.

"This has nothing to do with my work," she begins teasingly. "But the people who bring me the greatest joy are my family and friends."

Her most famous relative is without a doubt her twin sister, Celeste Beauparlant, the fired GNN Sunday morning show anchor who is currently battling rumors of dementia. It was recently exposed that Beauparlant and the senator she sparred with, Andres Venegas, both contributed in the creation of Estelle's biggest accomplishment to date. I wondered if there were any suspicions of impropriety between the senator and Beauparlant. Venegas is dodging questions of mismanaging money and he and Beauparlant clearly have history.

But what about the drama between Celeste and Andres? I ask.

"There is no drama. My sister is very dear to me. Andres is a longtime childhood friend. Yes, she and Andres have years of history between them, but we all do. Decades of friendship and support," she says firmly. "Video doesn't always show the complete story."

It's almost as if Estelle's saying that, in a way, Beauparlant's breakdown was like another infamous viral altercation.

But in this case, GNN viewers were watching live TV, not a grainy elevator surveillance camera. This is the perfect segue to ask about Beyoncé's role in the upcoming "Haiti Remembers" music video, so I do.

"I realized that while the world may have forgotten Haiti's plight after 12 *janvier*, the Haitian people have not—and cannot. Beyoncé, Bono, and the other amazing performers on that track were gracious enough to agree," she says. "We've lived in this post-traumatic world for years now. We shouldn't wait until there's another tragedy to uplift this country."

Estelle has enlisted her famous friends to help in another endeavor: tourism, which she has run as minister for more than four years. One of the first items on her to-do list when she was appointed was to shake up the perception that the island is a place of depressing destitution. Paparazzi photos of the rich and famous lounging on the beaches of Chouchou Bay have slowly begun turning that image around.

"Let's say it together," she says. "'Haiti is the poorest country in the western hemisphere.' We know. We *know*. Let's promote a different narrative. That was the crux of my 'Meet Me in the Haitian Sunshine' program."

"Meet Me in Haiti" is a campaign to promote travel to Tortuga, a beautiful enclave on Haiti's northwest coast. Tortuga Island is known primarily as a former hub for piracy and was depicted in the Pirates of the Caribbean films.

"Whenever tourists come to Haiti, there's a good chance they'll spend all their time in Labadie," she says, stirring her scalding cup of coffee before bringing it to her lips and savoring it on her tongue. It being unbearably hot outside does not appear to trouble her. "I love Labadie. It's beautiful. Make my life easier and please keep coming! But."

She pauses.

"It's a very specific sort of experience. I wanted to offer the same comfort and amenities it has but with a more…regional twist," Estelle says. "You have a native tour guide highlighting all the amazing history, architecture, and dignity of this nation. You don't just stay on Tortuga, then get back on your cruise ship and sail away. You engage with Haiti."

And it can use the engagement. As the poorest country in the western hemisphere (sorry), Haiti will take all the boosts to its economy that it can get. The Tortuga plan is a better deal than Labadie, simply by virtue of being headed by the country itself. Haiti earns just $9 per cruise ship visitor to Labadie because it outsources the heavy lifting to an American company.

More Haitian citizens will work on the island, which will also stimulate the economy, I note.

"And that's what PATRON PAL is all about," Estelle says, steering the conversation to the purpose of our meeting. "Our intent is not to be dependent on the kindness of strangers for eternity. We didn't fight for and win our freedom in 1804 to accept handouts. We simply want a fair shot. This little ol' app is connecting our youngest citizens to people who can assist them in gaining the resources to learn what they need in school and in life."

I can speak from experience.

"PATRON PAL is everything," says my fourteen-year-old daughter. I will admit that teaching her the value of generosity has not been my biggest focus over the years. But this burgeoning company, with an estimated worth of $10 million, has succeeded in that aspect of parenting where I and others have failed.

No less an endorser than Oprah Winfrey has lauded the merits of this "little ol' app." Estelle shows me handwritten

notes from some of the Pals, students with hopes of being doctors, lawyers, and maybe even ministers of tourism. They're
like her children, she explains, showing pictures of preco-
cious kids in clean blue uniform vests and white shirts. At
forty-three, she looks at least a decade younger but has none
of her own.

Joseph P., 8: *"I love my new uniform and pencils!"*

Daphne L., 7: *"I'm learning so much."*

Melyssa M., 10: *"I can eat and go to school. Thank you."*

Micheline A., 6: *"Merci beaucoup, Estelle. We love you!"*

My thoughts exactly.

Tuesday, February 16

The Life and Times of Alaine Beauparlant

I came into work this morning with a mission in mind but was temporarily derailed by a certain good-looking intern. Jason was all smiles when he stopped at my desk with a large red box wrapped with an equally large white bow. I could feel the eyes of the others in the office trained on us as they tried unsuccessfully to make it seem like they weren't following our every word.

"I know it was just Valentine's Day, but…um…this is a little abrupt," I said slowly as I reached out for the gift.

"Open it," Jason said with a grin.

I tore the wrapping paper to find a brown baby doll with a small curly 'fro wearing a purple onesie. It was sitting on a new copy of *Alice's Adventures in Wonderland* with an affixed note that read *Figured you could relive your favorite scenes in your downtime at work. Thanks again, Child Whisperer*, scrawled in what I could only presume was Jason's terrible handwriting.

"This is amazing," I said. "I love it! Thank you."

"I was hoping the two-day buffer between Valentine's Day and today would take some of the pressure off, but I guess I was wrong," Jason laughed. "Anyway, it's the least I could do. You saved me from an untimely death at the hands of Thierry. He would've pulled a Red Queen and chopped my head off with that machete he keeps under his desk if he knew that I had mixed up those kids' info."

"You can live another day to buy him a *Cubano*. Maybe for all eternity."

"How long is forever again?" he said, clearly pleased with his allusion.

"Sometimes, just one second."

Jason walked back to his seat and I didn't stop the dopey smile splayed across my face behind his back. I realized that I must've looked like a swooning schoolgirl and quickly fixed my expression into something more dignified for a strong, independent working woman who don't need no man. *Read with neck roll.* My nosy coworkers were probably memorizing every joyful twitch of my face to chat about around the water cooler and snack pantry. Or worse, to tell my aunt.

I arranged the doll so that it leaned against my computer monitor and resisted the urge to reread my favorite chapter (Chapter Five: "Advice from a Caterpillar"). Instead, I pulled up the PATRON PAL database to settle into my first task of the day... Only to be called by Florence into back-to-back morning meetings. Someone needed to take notes to keep our Fearless Leader abreast of everything going on while she was out of the office. I was but a lowly intern after all.

Jason W. 2:15 PM
Finally back at your desk I see!

Alaine B. 2:16 PM
Finally! If I had to sit through one more meeting, I was going to scream.

Jason W. 2:16 PM
Lol what were they about? Thierry has had me teaching him how to scrub his computer clean for the past 3 hours. He can't seem to pick it up.

Alaine B. 2:17 PM
Oh Thierry why can't you just use incognito mode like a normal person... Florence wants to put together some marketing materials to highlight how our Pals are better off after becoming a part of PATRON PAL. We were brainstorming some of the ways to get the info and to present it.

Jason W. 2:18 PM
That sounds like a great idea

Alaine B. 2:19 PM
Yup. I was thinking that I'd look up the kids who were quoted in that article that you sent me and track their progress throughout the program. But first... I'm going to watch some hair tutorial videos on YouTube lol

Jason W. 2:20 PM
Bahaha well you deserve a little break. And honestly, they

can't blame us for being a little unproductive when we have
a chat program called "Slackr"

Alaine B. 2:23 PM
You mean you're not any closer to solving world hunger?
Unimpressed.

Jason W. 2:27 PM
Oh man, I let you down. I think you'll have to sort that all out
once you get to college.

Alaine B. 2:35 PM
Argh first I'd have to figure out if I really want to go right now...

Jason W. 2:38 PM
No clue huh

Alaine B. 2:41 PM
College has always been in The Cards, that's not the problem... And to toot my own horn, I should be getting into pretty
dope schools...but with my mom the way she is right now...I
don't think I want to be away from her.

Jason W. 2:45 PM
Have you thought about taking a gap year? School will always be there...

Alaine B. 2:49 PM
No... I hadn't considered it. Telling my Haitian parents that I'm
not going straight to college would be like one more disappointment I've ladled on them in these past few weeks. PLUS!
Like, am I supposed to be a legit adult in six months? HA.

Jason W. 2:50 PM
If it helps, I don't think I became a real grown-up until...

Jason W. 2:51 PM

...

Jason W. 2:52 PM

...

Jason W. 2:53 PM

...

Jason W. 2:54 PM

...

Jason W. 2:56 PM

...

Jason W. 2:58 PM

You know what, how about I tell you once that happens?

Alaine B. 3:00 PM

Deal! Idk. I feel if I had just ONE more year before I embark on the rest of my life…it'd make all the difference

Jason W. 3:01 PM

To be serious for a moment—you're on the right path. Whatever it ends up being. You wouldn't be interning here if you weren't doing something right.

Alaine B. 3:04 PM

Well… Not quite. Let's say everyone has one pass to do something really dumb and not be penalized too, too much for it…

Jason W. 3:05 PM

Okay?

Alaine B. 3:07 PM
…

Alaine B. 3:08 PM
This is my one pass.

Jason W. 3:09 PM
Welp. At least one good thing came out of that.

Alaine B. 3:10 PM
And that is?

Jason W. 3:12 PM
You got to meet me.

Alaine B. 3:13 PM
Very smooth lol

Jason W. 3:15 PM
Thank you, thank you. Besides whatever you did couldn't have been that bad, right?

Alaine B. 3:16 PM
…

Alaine B. 3:17 PM
…

Alaine B. 3:18 PM
Right

From: Alaine Beauparlant
To: Estelle Dubois
Subject: PATRON PALS in Recent VoxPop Article

Hi *Tati* Estelle!

I'm working on a new marketing initiative with Florence (you have the notes but more on that when you're in the office) and I wanted to surprise her with this idea that I have. In order to put together my brilliant concept, I have to track down the Pals that were quoted in the VoxPop article.

Thing is, none of them come up when I look for them in the database (screenshot attached). Is there some kind of glitch in the system? You'd almost think that none of them existed or something! I would've just emailed Antoine, but he never responds to my messages. I'm sure you'll have better luck!

See you soon,
Alaine

SCREENSHOT OF
PATRON PAL DATABASE SEARCHES

2 results for **Micheline**

» **Micheline** Pierre, Age 10

» **Micheline** Valbrun, Age 9

1 result for **Joseph**

» **Joseph** Timothee, Age 12

3 results for **Daphne**

» **Daphne** Leroy, Age 5

» **Daphne** Jean-Charles, Age 7

» **Daphne** Lubin, Age 10

0 results for **Melyssa**

Hi *chérie*,

Something is wrong with the database. I'll have to discuss this with Antoine and the rest of the nerds. In the meantime, focus on more fruitful efforts. I'm sure that Florence has something specific for you to work on?

On another note. Tell me—how was your meeting with Roseline? I'm sure she opened your eyes in the way only she can do. I know that you must have a lot of questions. We can talk more when I return.

Bisous,
E

——
Estelle Dubois
Haitian Minister of Tourism
CEO of PATRON PAL
L'Union Fait La Force

Wednesday, February 17
From: Jules Beauparlant
To: Alaine Beauparlant
Subject: Guess What?

Surprise, I'm coming for a visit!

I sent a postcard but I couldn't wait for you to receive it so here we are. I was sitting at my desk this week, thinking about how I've missed you and how it's been too long since I've visited what you call "the Homeland." Everyone at work really supported the idea of me being away from the office. I've decided to not let that hurt my feelings and instead will be spending the next few days getting everything ready for my first time out of the office in God only knows how long.

See you in about a week and a half,
Dad

I can only be a second but my stupid little brother Jacobin was using my laptop for homework and went through my email and saw your message about your curse. He told my parents because he's an idiot and now they're freaking out about my soul. That said, I can't email you for a bit. Miss you 🖤

Sunday, February 21

The Life and Times of Alaine Beauparlant

~~~~~~~~~~~~~~~~~~~

Letter Mom Left For Me On The Kitchen Table When She And *Tati* Estelle Went Out For Lunch And A Movie (I Slept In)

Alaine,

I went to the doctor on Friday.

You and I both know I've been avoiding discussing my condition with you. I didn't want to keep you out of the loop so I requested your father tell you when I first found out. But that was it. To be honest, I've been avoiding the truth. I usually feel fine, if not completely myself. I keep up with the news okay. I've been reading books and cooking to fill up my pitifully free schedule. Following a recipe is good for me.

My missing Thanksgiving to go to Germany had nothing to do with work. I went to see a specialist, hoping he would give me a different diagnosis. I've spent the last few months obsessing over my condition. I even flew a renowned neurologist all the way to Au Cap from Massachusetts. Surely this physician's fifth opinion would reveal something the other four doctors hadn't. I was convinced she would see something different. Better. She didn't. I have Alzheimer's.

To borrow your tendency to lean toward the excessive: I am wallowing in a pool of grievous disillusionment at knowing that my life will not work out the way I'd planned. I am drowning. I saw the score of my latest cognitive test and nearly asphyxiated. The doctor told me to keep moving forward, which leads me to this letter. It is important for me to continue to "work out" my brain. Maybe it will help and maybe it won't. In the name of efficiency, I'm killing two birds with one stone and have created my own mental exercise to go along with something I should've revealed to you years ago. Let's bake a cake and I'll tell you a story.

First: grab that white mixing bowl from the pantry and combine two sticks of butter, two cups of sugar, a tiny bit of lemon zest, and three eggs.

Roseline was our *restavek*, which is essentially child slavery. I'm certainly not proud that this is a part of our culture, and at the time, I didn't have the knowledge or resources to fight such a thing. I had that series on my show a couple of years ago because of her.

Preheat the oven to 350 degrees. Throw in a dash of salt.

She was abused by my father. I internalized my feeling of powerlessness into anger. Estelle carefully ignored it. Roseline lost herself in the mythos of her mother's magic to cope, which I can understand.

Pour in a respectable amount of rum. And then a little bit more. Stir gently to keep the batter light and airy.

I don't know what you and Estelle are up to but I'm not so far gone that I haven't noticed the whispers and notes.

Add a tablespoon of almond extract. Two tablespoons of baking powder.

Oh yes, my diary entries. I'm not mad. Those were my real feelings in there and it's time you knew. My father was a terrible man whom I do not miss. I am happy that Roseline didn't allow him to break her. But whatever she or Estelle may have suggested to you, I beg you to use your common sense.

A tablespoon of vanilla extract.

We're all trying to carry on but I don't want you to become obsessed with this curse business. For a long time, my life was spent resenting a family superstition that I decided I didn't even believe in. Part of me didn't want you to come here, to be enveloped in the same insanity.

Final stir.

Unexplainable things happen in this country. I knew that whatever occurred that day in that shack, I'd never tell a soul. I wanted to leave Au Cap and be on my own, someplace far away, because I was convinced I needed more out of life. Not the most noble reason perhaps…but that's where I was at seventeen years old.

Butter the pan thoroughly and pour the batter into the pan. Bake for 35 minutes.

You have your whole life ahead of you. Don't let anything stifle your ability to move on.

COPY OF MOM'S COGNITIVE ASSESSMENT TEST

	EXAMPLE OF QUESTIONS TO USE	SCORE	TOTAL POSSIBLE SCORE
ORIENTATION TO TIME	WHEN IS YOUR BIRTHDAY? WHAT YEAR IS IT? HOW LONG DOES IT TAKE TO GET HOME?	8	10
ORIENTATION TO PLACE	WHERE ARE WE? WHERE DO YOU LIVE? HOW DO YOU GET HOME?	8	10
ORIENTATION TO SELF	HOW OLD ARE YOU? WHAT DO YOU DO? DO YOU HAVE ANY CHILDREN?	9	10

DRAW A CLOCK SHOWING 5 PAST 8

NOTES: *The cognitive assessment sheet was additional qualitative confirmation of MRI and CT results suggesting notable changes in hippocampus and entorhinal cortex volumes. Patient refused to conduct the clock-drawing test, a common marker of inability to do so successfully. Patient scored 25 points on questionnaire, indicating early signs of mild dementia.*

The Life and Times of Alaine Beauparlant

I watched Mom through my sunglasses as she stood at the edge of the pool while I floated on my back in lazy circles.

What? Baking is hard work.

She waited for me to swim over to her.

"Let's check on that cake," she said, then spun on her heels and marched toward the house without waiting for a response. I dried off, slipped on my cover-up, and met her in the kitchen. She inhaled deeply.

"This smells delicious."

"You sound shocked, Mother."

"We both know you're not the best at taking directions."

"That's...fair." The timer went off. I sent a silent prayer to the baking gods, realizing then that I would have never heard the tiny beep from outside and might've burned down the kitchen. (Not that I would ever tell my mom or Jacques that.)

We sat at the table, staring at the now-cooling cake in silence. I was also pleasantly surprised that it had turned out so well.

"So Estelle tells me there's a boy at PATRON PAL who you're getting...close with."

My mouth gaped open as I stared at her. "Are you trying to have the birds and the bees talk with me? Because Dad's already covered that. And he paid special attention to the highly contagious sexually transmitted diseases section."

She chuckled. "If Jules is anything, he's thorough."

"*Too* thorough."

"I know that part is covered," she said. I grabbed her hands. "Mom. Believe me when I say it absolutely pains me to change the subject, but let's not tiptoe around the more pressing issue."

She sighed.

"As the cake demonstrates," I began, "I read your letter. Twice. I've heard your arguments and absorbed them into my psyche and... No."

"No."

"I am not going to just accept Alzheimer's as Celeste canon."

"Wha— Canon?"

"Born in Haiti, Ivy League grad, award-winning hard-hitting journalist, mother of one, sassy divorcée, has Alzheimer's. No."

"I understand that this is hard to take, but it's not healthy to ignore reality. It would be more productive to acknowledge that our remaining time is unknown and extremely limited...and get on with the rest of our lives."

That did it.

"I was barely a part of your life until the rest of your obligations evaporated," I sputtered. "I've spent my entire childhood and adolescence *pining* for you, wishing I'd be good enough, *interesting* enough to hold your attention for more than a five-minute phone call. It's your literal *job* to speak to people for a living, and you couldn't do that with me!"

"Alaine," she said with tears in her eyes. "That's the whole point. I want to get to know you more before I have no choice in forgetting you."

"That's not going to happen. I've already met with Roseline and I'm not going to let her, and especially you, down."

She shook her head.

"I have to lie down, so I won't press this anymore today. But you're going to have to let this go."

"Remind me to bring this conversation up when you're

eighty years old and complaining that I never do anything nice for you," I said, sticking a fork into the slice of cake I'd cut for her.

"Look at the holes." She pointed at the large craters in her piece of cake. "I didn't remember to tell you to use room-temperature butter. And it's naked because I couldn't recall my frosting recipe, or where I wrote it down, no matter how hard I tried. This is happening."

Like a coward, I grabbed my own plate and mumbled that I was going to eat in my room.

The Life and Times of Alaine Beauparlant

〜〜〜〜〜〜〜〜〜〜〜〜〜〜〜〜〜〜〜

For the record: I haven't been ignoring the glow-in-the-dark neon-pink cheetah-print elephant in the room regarding my time with Roseline. I've just needed to process what I went through before putting my thoughts to paper—er, keyboard. It's not every day that someone is given a drink that alters their perception of time and reality (unless *ayahuasca* is your beverage of choice). I would argue that it's a feat that I'm able to even write about it now.

When I awoke, I was lying on the flimsy sleeping mat that was off to the side of the room. I could tell that I had been out for quite some time, not only because it was dark out, but because my body was aching from what I guess had been hours of restless movement.

"You're back," Roseline said as she reached out toward me, a cup in her hand.

I must've looked at that cup like it was the devil himself, because she simply said, "Water." I tentatively took it from her and sniffed it a few times before taking a long gulp to quench my thirst. My throat felt lined with cement, but I welcomed the painful scrape of the cool water.

"What happened?" I asked when I had finished drinking.

Roseline gave what I could only describe as a bitter smile and then it was gone. "You've experienced my gift. It's much easier for you to let it take you, than for me to describe it in advance. It's not exactly pleasant."

"Who are you telling?"

"What did you see?"

"I—I think I saw the world through the eyes of Marie-Louise," I said and explained all that I had witnessed. Experienced.

Roseline gave me another cup of water. "Then it has begun. You wouldn't have been able to tap into her memories without the spirits' permission."

I started lifting myself from the mat and a wave of dizziness swept over me. Even though I wasn't feeling well, I had to get out. This was getting a little too weird for me. Even with all that I had read and now observed with my own eyes, there was still a part of me that didn't want to believe that this was true. How much of my life was from my own free will? How much of it was simply this warped version of fate? Everything that had happened in the last few weeks all seemed to be leading me to this point. And I didn't know how to deal.

Roseline reached out to help me straighten up and I flinched away.

She nodded her head as though she understood exactly what I was feeling, which didn't help to calm my nerves. "The next step is for you to complete the circle and pick up where your mother and aunt left off. You must go to Bois Caïman, Sans-Souci Palace, Labadie, and Citadelle Laferrière and collect the soil from each place, as discussed. The soil is essential and you are the one who is to gather it. I've written each location in a note for you."

"Thank you for your help," I said, trying to hide my uneasiness as I took the small slip of paper from her, careful not to graze my fingers against hers. "Is Fernand still waiting for me?"

"Yes," Roseline said. "He's right outside."

I walked as quickly as I could to the front door. I kept my back to Roseline as she spoke.

"There's no stopping what we've set in motion. If we don't finish what we've started, there's no telling what the consequences will be. For all of us. Your family, yourself, and my unborn baby."

I left without another word.

PART VI

PRESKE LA PA LA

(ALMOST THERE ISN'T THERE)

The Life and Times of Alaine Beauparlant

My father is very in tune with his feelings. He isn't afraid to cry, even if it's just in response to a particularly sappy jewelry store commercial.

"She didn't expect the ring!" he'd say, wiping his eyes as I rolled mine.

But the tears he shed years ago on January 12 and the days following were different, marked by the swollen ring of red around his eyes that refused to fade. We watched a special edition of *Sunday Politicos* on location in Port-au-Prince the day we were set to fly back to Miami from our unintentional DC daddy-daughter vacation. My mother stood solemnly in the midst of cloudy dust and mounds of destroyed concrete. The leader of a high-profile Wisconsin church that had donated thousands of dollars to relief efforts was on the air. I had been only half listening when the sound of my dad sucking his teeth jerked my head to the screen.

"…everything that we can to improve the quality of life in Haiti," the talking head said. "But this catastrophic earthquake was not altogether unforeseen. Some religious scholars pinpoint the start of Haiti's misfortune after the Bois Caïman voodoo ceremony."

My mom tapped her pen on the desk of her makeshift outdoor set.

"Sir, are you aware you're not the first person to make this claim?"

"No, many religious scholars also believe that—"

"And these...scholars, they state this idea as though it were fact?"

"It is fact. Haiti is the *poorest country in the western hemisphere*. Just let that sink in."

"Oh, I don't need to let that sink in. It's been 'sunk in' for years," she said. "So to confirm, you're saying that a 'voodoo' ceremony, with all the bells and whistles of the singing and dancing and blood and chanting, brought Haiti this earthquake—"

"It's quite unfortunate—"

"—that those people planning this insurrection in 1791 made a literal pact with the devil in exchange for their freedom—"

"When you say it like that—"

"—and *that* is what was behind all this?" She gestured toward the pile of rubble that had been the national palace. "It wasn't a slip on a fault that caused a release of energy that produced seismic waves that tremored throughout the earth and resulted in what seismologists consider an earthquake?"

"Perhaps that's the scientific reasoning, but there are things at work that even we don't know about," he said.

"So the countries behind hideous atrocities like colonizing occupied lands and raping and murdering their inhabitants and enslaving millions of people...what has been their retribution?" My mother didn't wait for a response. "Thanks for being here. Let's bring in our next guest."

I kneeled and removed the empty mason jar I'd brought in my large purse.

"Hipster blogger or vodou priestess, you gotta pick one," Jason whispered.

"Why are you whispering?" I said, also whispering.

"I don't know. It just seems like we should…" he said. I'd had Jason come along for his car. *Tati* Estelle's driver, Fernand, was off, but I knew Jason would give me a ride and some company without asking too many questions. And if we're being honest, I didn't want to be alone. Walking late at night in a wide, dusty field would make anyone uneasy.

My knowledge of this place, Bois Caïman, was restricted to the old myth that had informed my ~~epic~~ appalling class presentation and my mom taking down that pastor who came on her show. Yet there I was, taking shaky steps up a hill that was supposedly a contraction in the first labor pains of this country. I was on a continuum that had me oscillating between doubting my mother's warnings and wanting to heed them. If I were reading about a random seventeen-year-old attempting to overthrow an eternal curse to save her mom, I'd say the poor kid's brains were fried.

Except. Except one of the things I've most admired about my mom was her ability to go after the answers she needed. Even she had given Roseline's proposition a shot all those years ago, despite resenting the idea of a family curse her entire life. Meanwhile, I had spent my fair share of energy resenting her for not caring enough to find a solid place for me in her world. Breaking this curse was my way of handing her the world again and hoping I'd have a closer spot in her orbit.

Hitting up a few historic landmarks and scooping up some dirt (which is all Roseline instructed me to do) would help my mom or it wouldn't—it couldn't make things any worse. So I ask again, why not?

I dragged the open jar across the ground, picking up brown clods until the container was a quarter filled. I paused and looked up at Jason, who was leaning against a tree a few feet away from me. He tilted his head as he watched me but said nothing. I waited for a sign—the wind to howl, an alligator to hiss. I'd even take a rustling of leaves. Nothing happened. My mind flickered to the mental picture I'd formed of my aunt writhing in pain on this same land, and I counted my blessings. I patted down the soil on the ground to smooth over the evidence of where I'd dug and twisted the jar's top closed.

"All right. Let's go."

UPDATED TO-DO LIST FROM ROSELINE'S PLACES TO VISIT

~~Bois Caïman~~

Sans-Souci Palace

Labadie

Citadelle Laferrière

Sunday, February 28

The Life and Times of Alaine Beauparlant

My dad's parents died when he was twenty-five. The last time he returned to Haiti was for their funeral.

"There's nothing there for me anymore," he'd say when I'd ask him every so often why we didn't visit. I never mentioned that, when I was much younger, I'd heard him unsuccessfully try to convince my mom to agree to a family trip. The only thing that had changed since then was that I was here now. And Mom too. I suspect she had gone crying to him for backup as soon as I'd taken my slice of cake to my room after our argument.

The morning after he arrived, I was rolling dough to make dumplings with her when he announced that he was going to check out his old "stomping grounds" and told me I'd be coming along.

My mother snorted. It was the most relaxed I'd ever seen her.

"Ha. Your use of 'stomping grounds' suggests you ran things over in Limonade when that's the furthest thing from the truth," she said.

"Ahh, but I am a big man bearing gifts now," he said.

Dad took *Tati* Estelle's car, a temperamental stick shift I personally would've refused to drive *anywhere* near the steep cliffs that formed the path to Limonade. I had mostly adjusted to the bumpy roads and no longer felt the extreme nausea that I had when I first got to the island. But now, the thought of seeing where my father grew up, the environment that made him the obnoxiously nerdy and earnest man who raised me, twisted my stomach in anticipation.

As we continued farther and farther into Cap-Haïtien, the homes got smaller and less vibrant. Many houses were covered in peeling paint, suggesting they were once just as cheerful and bright, albeit more modest, as the ones in my aunt's neighborhood. We pulled up to a wooden fence that was covered in vines and got out of the car. A rickety door that led to the house was propped open with a cinder block, and we could smell the sweet scent of tobacco wafting over to us.

"I don't own the house anymore, since I sold it when my parents died," Dad said. "There are people living here now, so we really shouldn't disturb them, but…"

Dad walked through the doorway and shouted a greeting to the old man who sat on a stool in front of the house. He was smoking a corncob pipe, his mouth opening and closing like a fish washed ashore and gasping for air.

"We're just looking, friend!" Dad said in Creole. "I used to live here when I was younger."

The old man nodded, unbothered, and continued puffing on his pipe.

"This is it," my dad said, turning to me. The land the house stood on was impossibly small compared to my mom's family home. The Dubois estate was ten times as big, the house before us easily the size of the suite that *Tati* Estelle slept in. The exposed concrete bricks were painted a faded salmon color, the ramshackle tin roof a lighter shade of pink. Trees lined the outskirts of the enclosure and served only to make the packed dirt that surrounded the house look even more desolate and barren. I suddenly had a much better sense of why Dad worked so much. Even when you've "made it," you're scared to death about losing it all.

"Home, sweet home," Dad said with a small smile as we turned and left through the gate, waving to the old man as we did.

I followed silently as Dad led the way down a dirt path that acted as a makeshift sidewalk, each house a faded arc in the spectrum of a rainbow. I tried to imagine my dad as a child, growing up and walking down this trail every day for school. Did he always know that he would eventually leave this place and build another life for himself hundreds of miles away?

The farther we walked, the more trailing plants lined our steps. The houses were becoming more scarce until we eventually came upon a large clearing. It was the biggest plot of land that I had seen since coming to Dad's old neighborhood.

"This used to be a farm," he said as we continued to walk. We rounded a bend and I could see a small house a short distance away. "I would spend every afternoon here when school let out."

"Doing what?"

"My father worked for the man that owned this little farm. It's not much land, but the yard was filled with corn, sweet potatoes, and bananas. Whenever there was a surplus, the owner would let my dad take some to sell for himself and he would take it home to my mother. Together, my parents sold enough to get me through school and that was pretty much all they could afford."

"How did you get all the way over to Mom's old neighborhood?"

"I walked. I didn't get these calves 'cause I was blessed with good genes," he joked. "These days, my old neighbors take care of things the best they can, but the owner died years ago."

"It looks like the soil died right along with him," I said.

We finally reached the house and knocked loudly on the dark blue door before us. The rest of the house was painted a bright green, the same exact shade as a chayote. A woman in a paisley muumuu with a baby on her hip answered the door and gasped when she saw my dad.

"Ah-ah! Could this really be Jules?" She hugged him tightly.

"*Oui*, Anne. And this is my daughter, Alaine."

I waved and gave her a peck on the cheek.

"Come in, come in. Daniel, come see!"

Three more children sat on the floor of the small living room.

A middle-aged man in a gray undershirt walked in and made the same exclamation. I guess my dad really was a big man now.

"Well, if it isn't *Ti Blanc*!" he said, referring to my dad as a "white man" the way Haitians routinely did expats or their children.

"Daniel. You have a beautiful family. How are you?" They clapped each other forcefully on the back.

"Not bad. Hungry—but what's new?" I always found it fascinating that Haitians were more likely to tell you the truth about their conditions. No "I'm fine" here, not when the children were so plainly thin. There were no ballooning stomachs poking out from malnutrition, but his children did appear frailer than I looked in pictures at their ages. I tried not to stare at the little girl who greeted us as she adjusted the strap of her dress for the fifth time.

I pressed my cheek against Daniel's and kissed the air beside it. Then I settled onto the floor to get to know the kids.

Nehemie was eight and sucked his thumb as he looked at me warily. Samuel was five and a half and remained curled into a ball asleep on the floor, even through all the welcoming/shouting.

Julmise, ten, was the oldest and only girl. She was named for my father. I'd had no idea anyone admired him enough to do that. I doubt I'd ever been prouder of him than I was at that moment.

"I want to be a doctor like *Tonton* Jules," she said. "I'm good in school."

"That's great!" I said, leafing through the stack of classwork she handed me from their low table. All 100/100. "Keep up the good work and you will be."

"Do you want to be a doctor?" she asked.

"No. But I do want to help people," I said.

"How?"

"There are lots of ways," I said, crossing my arms.

"Like what?"

"The usual ones."

Julmise looked at me dubiously. So much for child whisperer.

"Where's your *maman*?"

"Home." I hesitated. "She's sick."

"I can heal her when I'm a doctor."

My throat suddenly closed up, my eyes prickling with unshed tears as I smiled at Julmise and patted her hand.

There are so many more of these kids we could be helping with

PATRON PAL, I thought to myself. They had ambition and dreams but no outlets to plug them into. My eyes fell on a card.

I cleared my throat a few times before speaking. "What's this?"

"My Patron," Julmise said. She analyzed my face. "Do you have a...Pal?"

"I do, thanks to my allowance. His name is Jeremie... But tell me, what does your Patron do for you?"

"*Eh bien*, are you talking about that PATRON PAL crap?" Daniel called from his seat. "Those people promised us enough money to pay for school. They said that they'd pair each of the children with a sponsor who would then pay for them to complete their studies. At first, we were reluctant to even join. The thought of the children's faces plastered all over the internet was a little alarming. But we went through with it because we want the kids to have a better shot and make it out of here...like you did, Jules. But the payments haven't been consistent at all. These Patrons barely send enough for Julmise, let alone Samuel. And there's always something wrong with the app. We've had to hold Samuel back and use the money towards Julmise. We know that if at least one of the kids is able to finish school, that will help us all."

"Why didn't you tell me?" Dad asked.

"Oh-oh, Jules, this isn't your responsibility," Daniel said.

"Didn't I say I was your family? You can come to me for anything, especially if the kids have been unable to go to school."

"It's just that we know that the Dubois woman was your sister-in-law... We didn't want you to think we were asking you for special treatment," Anne said apologetically.

"I'd never think that," Dad said, frowning.

After about another hour of catching up, my dad cleared his throat.

"We have to get going, but I had to greet you two while I was in town and introduce you to my daughter."

He slipped something into Daniel's hand when he shook it goodbye. Daniel held on for a beat and whispered, "*Merci.*

"God may have taken Davide in that earthquake, but he sent me another brother," Daniel said more loudly, clearing his throat.

"Then please use me as one," my father said. "You know I can help you with anything you need."

"When was the last time you had *bonbon sirop*?" Anne said.

"Too long."

We walked back to the car, arms heavy with bags filled with the sweet-smelling sugarcane cake.

Dad fiddled with the key before sticking it into the ignition. He looked at his hands and then shifted in his seat. Hemmed. Hawed.

"Alaine. I could've been Daniel. Easily. We grew up on the same block, knew the same people. I just had parents who could scrounge up the money to send me to school. And even then I was ashamed of them. I'm not proud to admit it, but I am mature enough to acknowledge that what I was feeling was embarrassment…for something they had no control over. I met your mother near the end of high school, and once I did, I wanted to hide my own life and adopt the lavish one she led just a few miles west. I remember once being too afraid to tell her that I couldn't call home because we didn't have a phone.

"I spent so many afternoons skipping out on my responsibilities to my family, chasing after a life that I would've never even known had I not met your mother. My parents must have been disappointed. They knew they raised me better than that. And I barely came home when I went away to the States for medical school…" He cleared his throat and wiped his eyes with his ubiquitous handkerchief.

"I had some more growing up to do when my parents died. I let this place go and tried not to think of the people I'd left behind. Even after I became a doctor and started sending my money to a few neighbors in the village, I've carried this ghost on my back. But I like to think my parents forgave me, because they were kind people. Modest. They loved what they had and never stopped me from pursuing more than what I could see from the small field they tended.

"I guess what I mean to get at in all my meandering is this—your parents are trying their best. Don't let anything stop you from helping your loved ones if you have the means, even if it feels like you're doing nothing."

I looked him in the eyes and nodded. "I know."

Monday, February 29

SAVED INSTANT MESSAGES ON THE ONLINE WORK
PLATFORM "SLACKR" B/T ME AND *TATI* ESTELLE

Alaine B. 10:16 AM
Howdy!

Estelle D. 10:30 AM
Hi there! Kind of busy, do you need anything?

Alaine B. 10:31 AM
No worries—I checked your calendar and saw you'll be running around all day but I wanted to bring your attention to
something… That family I visited with my dad yesterday actually had 3 kids enrolled in PATRON PAL and they said they're
really struggling…like not-having-enough-to-send-every-one-
of-their-kids-to-school struggling. It sounded like they weren't
getting what they should've been. Shouldn't we be using the
money that some Pals receive above the school tuition towards other students whose Pals might not be as consistent?

Estelle D. 10:32 AM
I can't really get into this right now. I'll take a closer look but
it'll have to wait until after my 10:30. Talk later!

Getting another ride from Jason apparently came with strings.

"Sure," he said over our standing lunch at the best (and ~~worst~~ only) food truck in our plaza on Monday. "But I'm going to need something from you in return."

I lifted an eyebrow. "I can give you gas money."

He laughed. A piece of fried yuca flew from his mouth and he quickly dabbed at his lips. It was gross but slightly endearing? Ugh, forget it, just gross.

"The gas I got," he said. "A date I need... Or in clearer terms, would you like to go to my cousin's wedding with me?"

I smiled, my mind firing off a trillion questions: *What will I do with my hair? What will I wear? What do his shoulders look like in a tux? Equal or better than when he's in a sweatshirt? Can he dance? Can I dance? Am I going on a date with a college boy? Why didn't I ever pay attention when Kaylee Johnson bragged about going out with college guys? Does it even really matter though? Shouldn't I just be myself? Blech. Why do I sound so much like Dad right now?*

What I actually went with was "Can't hold off the *zuzu* girls alone?"

"God, no. I need you to keep me company and stave off any intrusive questions from my relatives. You in?"

"When is it?"

"This Saturday. Sorry." He grimaced. "I would've asked you sooner, but I've been avoiding reality and telling myself I didn't have to go. I couldn't come up with a good enough reason to give my family, so I'm stuck getting a tux."

Images of me in a pretty dress and fluffy, puffy hair vaporized into thin air. My heart sank.

"I'd love to protect you from your family, but I'm being dragged to my own wedding this Saturday. Some friend of my aunt," I said.

"Wait... Is this at Sans-Souci?"

"Yes!"

"Should've known."

"Why?"

"It is a fact universally acknowledged that all bougie black people know each other," he stated matter-of-factly.

The Life and Times of Alaine Beauparlant

Unlike Jason, I wasn't really being forced to attend this wedding. When my aunt mentioned she'd be going to the Sans-Souci Palace with my mom, I jumped at the chance to come with them. It was next on my bucket [of dirt] list.

"It's a UNESCO World Heritage Site," I said. "I'd really like my time here to be fun but also educational. I have so much to learn about my culture."

"Someone's laying it on thick," my aunt observed. "It's so last minute…"

I gave her a skeptical look. "I wouldn't be the first party crasher in the history of weddings. You know there's an uninvited guest provisional budget wrapped into all that planning."

Later on, I texted *Tati* Estelle the real impetus for the visit: some good ol'-fashioned curse-breaking. I still didn't know what the endgame was with these collections, but she was on board once I told her.

So that is how I, my aunt, mother, and father (*Tati* Estelle: What the hell, you might as well come too!) climbed into the SUV in our finest formal wear and embarked on our way to Milot. I told Jason I would meet him there, but the mood in the car had me strongly questioning my choice. The ride was as awkward as you could imagine it would be (squared). Fernand, the driver, must have found it unbearable too and turned on the radio. A popular *konpa* song punctuated the air.

Ma chérie, mi amor, my love.

"So, how's the practice, Jules?" *Tati* Estelle asked.

"Good, good. I've been working in the emergency room in my free time with Alaine being away," he said. "The hospital can always use more consulting physicians for psych evals. Plus, it's more action than the suburban ennui I usually get in my office...but don't tell my patients that!" My dad had gone into group private practice to have more time for me after he and my mom divorced, and he'd cut down his hours moonlighting in the ER for extra cash. The head partner wanted to leave him in charge when she retired and I'd encouraged him to accept the position after he warned he'd be available even less. I could take care of myself by then.

Why can't we just let it gooo?

"Like there aren't emergency rooms in the DMV area," Mom scoffed.

"It wasn't that simple, Celeste," he said.

Somehow be together again.

"You're just jealous!" she spat. "You can be a doctor anywhere. DC is the pinnacle for my career."

I will never, ever forget you.

"No, no, no," Dad muttered to himself. "I'm not doing this."

But it breaks my heart to be near you...

"Doing...what?" I asked.

"Reenacting an argument I had twenty years ago."

We listened to the radio in silence for the rest of the car ride.

Running list of people that my parents have dated
since divorcing (the ones I've known about, anyway)

Mom	Dad

The Life and Times of Alaine Beauparlant

I didn't know where to look first. People in all black held up signs with arrows, pointing to where we were meant to pull up. There were already rows and rows of parked cars in varying levels of shininess and Europeanness.

"Follow here," a man in a stiff vest said, guiding us toward a path we could walk to enter the structure. It was the most beautiful crumbling building. There was an earthquake in 1842, long before 12 *janvier,* that brought down Sans-Souci's walls and the surrounding areas of Cap-Haïtien. The people never rebuilt it. Fitting, considering Henri Christophe forced the by-then freed Haitians into slavery to construct it against their will in the first place.

The fairy lights hanging from the columns and lining the cobblestones cast the palace in an eerie yellow glow. In my research I'd read that the palace had once been considered the Versailles of the Caribbean, and its residents had hosted countless parties and socials. Though it stood in ruins now, I could imagine this place alive with energy, buzzing with the uppity spirit of Haitians who came before us.

My aunt placed us in the third row of the bride's section of the audience, then slipped away to hobnob with the other guests milling around. I scanned the seats for Jason but couldn't find him. I turned to my parents, who had not spoken much since their exchange in the car.

"I'm sorry for upsetting you," my dad said.

"No need to apologize," my mom said. "Or rehash decades-old conversations. It's always a jolt when I realize where I've gone."

"Have these…fugues been coming on more often lately?"

"Are you treating me like a patient or something else?"

"A friend. I swear." My dad lifted two fingers in salute.

"A few nights ago, I was my old self. I felt it in my bones. I've been walking through a fog for what seems like years now…but I was soaking some sweet potatoes to make *pain patate* and my mind felt ten pounds lighter. Right there in that kitchen, I remembered things I hadn't realized I'd forgotten."

"Does that happen? Going in and out?" I asked my dad. My heart thumped as I realized the meaning of my mother's words. Me visiting Bois Caïman had to be behind her improvement, even if it was just for a moment. I know correlation doesn't always mean causation, but…what else could it be? I was doing the right thing. I had to keep going.

"There are better days than others with Alzheimer's," he said, frowning. "I've never heard it described that way, but I suppose anything is possible."

The Life and Times of Alaine Beauparlant

The wedding was on time by Haitian standards—that is to say, the ceremony began at 7:03 p.m., just an hour behind schedule. My parents went on to speak cordially about a range of topics, including me (fine), me and school (on a quick drop-off of garlic and rosemary focaccia at school before his trip, Dad ran into Sister Pollack, who reported being thrilled with how well I was doing volunteering in Haiti, away from her sensitive students), me and college (admission decisions would be coming any day), and me and Jason (just friends, that's all, gosh). My mom was just getting into how she was trying (and failing) to teach me her black mushroom rice recipe when the classical music playing gently in the background increased in volume, leading everyone to take their seats. *Tati* Estelle landed in her chair, looking flushed. She tucked a piece of hair behind her ear.

"What'd I miss?" she asked, plunking down a clam-shaped purse identical to the one I carried on the seat beside her.

Before any of us had a chance to answer, the wedding party began their walk down the aisle. The eight pairs of groomsmen and bridesmaids took a step forward, then backward, then two steps forward, all in rhythm with a young woman singing in the front with the band. She crooned Celine Dion, rejoicing that a new day had, in fact, come. I wondered lazily how long it had taken to get the choreography down. When the final groomsman paused at our row, I gasped. Senator Andres Venegas glanced in my direction before his gaze rested on my mother. He smiled. I grabbed her left hand, just in case she intended to get up, and noticed my father did the same with her right. She shrugged us off, balling her fists before neatly folding them on her lap.

"I'm fine," she whispered.

Tati Estelle stared straight ahead, ignoring us and the nearby guests who noticed our movements. And then he was off with his partner, moving forward, then back, then two steps forward again all the way to where the priest and the rest of the party waited. We stood when the trumpets announced the bride's entrance. She was gorgeous in a strapless dark ivory lace gown with a black veil and black side panels, and just like that, everyone fixed their scandalized ogling on her instead of my mother.

SELECTED ENTRIES FROM THE #CALIXTEDITSOHUMBERTPRISCILLAR-ENECHARLESONIT WEDDING (NOT MY FIRST CHOICE IN HASHTAGS EITHER, BUT NOBODY ASKED ME)

Brandon Larue | 1h
This is already the best wedding I've ever been to and it hasn't started yet **#SansSouci #CalixtedItSoHumbertPriscillA-ReneCharlesOnIt**

Leonette Roquefort | 1h
Do they really expect me to properly spell **#CalixtedItSoHumbertPriscillAReneCharlesOnIt** each time???

Marc Sanon | 1h
Open bar + ridiculous hashtag = ultimate fail **#CalixtedItSo-HumbertPriscillAReneCharlesOnIt**

Nina Jesula | 2h
Are we about to see some #drama ...... **#CalixtedItSoHum-bertPriscillAReneCharlesOnIt**

Félicité Roquefort | 2h
The bride. is. wearing. black. **#SJPregrets #RIPmarriage #CalixtedItSoHumbertPriscillAReneCharlesOnIt**

The Life and Times of Alaine Beauparlant

"Estelle! Look at *you*!" A woman in a midlength rose-print dress shouted from where she stood with three other women. They were drinking champagne from long clear flutes and standing around one of the small cocktail tables placed in front of the palace, looking very Real Housewives of Haitian Hills. There were already a few empty glasses on the table. "Why didn't we see you up there?"

"I'm too old to be a bridesmaid, Ophelia," *Tati* Estelle answered.

"Of course you're not," Ophelia replied. "You have to tell us about that wedding dress."

Tati Estelle turned to my mother.

"I can't deal with them right now. Go ahead," Mom said as she linked arms with Dad. "I've got company."

Dad coughed nervously.

"Come over anytime you'd like!" *Tati* Estelle said, walking toward her friends. I warily observed my father, who was in turn peeking at my mother. I made a cheesy joke to break the tension.

"Is anyone going to explain why this place is called 'Without Eyebrows'?" I said.

Mom sucked her teeth.

"That is *sans sourcils*. *Sans-Souci* means 'carefree,'" Dad said. He didn't smile. He did not pass go. He did not collect two hundred dollars.

In need of your buffering services, stat.

I silently cheered at the text message that popped onto my screen. Jason FTW.

"If you don't need me and aren't going to humor me and my winsome personality, I'm going to look around," I said.

"Don't cause a scene," Dad said.

"Don't touch anything," Mom said.

"My ten-year-old self thanks you for the life skills and manners, *monsieur* and *madame*," I said and headed toward the large appetizer table, which was covered in glorious meat patties, conch fritters, and deviled eggs. I tapped on Jason's back to get his attention and he nearly choked on his toothpick of prosciutto-wrapped melon.

"Alaine," he said and let out a low whistle.

"My sentiments exactly," I joked, half twirling in my structured gold evening gown. Mom's closet didn't quit. I looked like an Oscars statue.

"I wanted you to deflect any personal questions, not make everyone jealous," he said.

"One and the same, my friend. And I don't see anyone here that I need to protect you from."

"I just snuck away...but I still wanted to see you," he said sheepishly. I had never been more grateful to have melanin to conceal my blushing.

"So was the bride's side of the family as outraged by the black fabric as the groom's?" he asked.

"I think they were happier she was finally getting remarried and would stop 'living in sin,'" I said. "Plus, my aunt said she had to talk Priscilla out of dressing *completely* in black for 'giving in to the patriarchy again.' The side panels were a compromise."

"Estelle Dubois—ministry official, app developer, crisis manager," he said. "How do they know each other?"

"College roomies," I said. "This is Priscilla's second marriage and she didn't want to deal with all the pomp and circumstance, but my aunt talked her into that too. Can't say no to a party."

"Humbert's my mom's older cousin's son," he said. "They were freaking out in the back because they couldn't find Andres Venegas, who I'm sure you noticed is one of the groomsmen. I was almost forced to walk in his place."

"Yeah, that was unexpected... I hadn't realized he was going to be here," I said. "I'm pretty sure my mom wouldn't have shown up if she'd known."

"They were all old friends back in the day, weren't they? Maybe they wanted a reunion," Jason said.

"Or Venegas wanted lots of pictures of him at a high-society Haitian wedding to get around so his poll numbers go up in North Miami and Little Haiti."

"That too."

By then, we had claimed one of the tables for ourselves and were grinning goofily at each other while grazing through our pile of food and waiting for the cocktail hour to be over to head for the reception tent. I angled my head to where my parents stood at their own table, sharing a plate of guava pastries and cheese. Jason turned to see what had caught my attention.

"Don't mind me," I said. "I'm just doing the child-of-divorced-parents thing where I observe their every interaction to jot down and analyze in my journal later."

"I used to do that," he said. "Then I realized my folks were better apart and I stopped sweating them."

"I'm not trying to *Parent Trap* them or anything. Their relationship has always erred on the side of cordially irritated, which is fine by me," I said. "But ever since my mom got sick and my dad arrived in Haiti a few days ago, they've been either really into each other or super annoyed."

"My parents never went through that," he said. "My mom's been consistently aggravated with my dad since I was eight."

"What happened when you were eight?"

"She caught him cheating with his assistant," he said.

My jaw dropped.

"It's fine." He shrugged. "He's now married to said assistant and my mom's married to my stepfather, who's a great guy."

Before I could ask more about his family (a group of people with more drama than mine perchance?), a man in a purple velvet jacket clinked a glass.

"The reception area is now ready. Please follow me."

I dabbed my mouth with a napkin and quickly opened my clamshell purse to apply my lip balm. Then the stupid tube wouldn't fit back in the purse. And because I live in a romantic comedy, all of the contents bounced out and onto the ground. I crouched down, hoping to keep my dress clean. Jason scrounged around with me, picking up a hair tie here, a package of blotting paper there.

"Here you go," Jason said, handing me a tampon. I took it from him quickly. He kept staring as he helped me up.

"What?" I asked him nervously. I snapped my bag shut.

"Did I mention how beautiful you look tonight?"

My neck grew hot. *Melanin to the rescue!*

"You look pretty great yourself," I said. He just smiled.

Jason placed his hand on my lower back and steered us toward the "youth table." I concentrated on not tripping in my strappy gold heeled sandals. We slid into our seats and introduced ourselves to the people nearest us. There was my dearest cousin Félicité, her younger sister and doppelgänger, Leonette, and Jason's cousin Marc, a handsome guy around my age with closely cropped hair and blindingly white teeth, who gave Jason a nod and wink when we sat down. Before we could dig into any more conversation, the music started.

"Introducing our favorite newlyweds of the night, Mr. Humbert Calixte and Mrs. Priscilla Rene-Charles!" We were all on our feet again, shouting and clapping to welcome the brand-new couple. They sashayed around the tables, to the tune of Starship's "Nothing's Gonna Stop Us Now," pausing and pointing occasionally at each other from across the tables. They reunited at the front on the elevated stage and kissed. "Single Ladies" blasted. The crowd roared. Someone complained loudly about the hashtag. Priscilla squeezed Humbert's hand and lifted it up like a prizefighter in victory and I laughed along with everyone else. I'd never met her, or Humbert for that matter, but it wasn't hard to feel the love in their glances at one another and wish them well.

They weren't exactly a typical *zuzu* couple. *Tati* Estelle had given me the highlights when I said I was coming to her friend's (and lawyer on retainer's) wedding. After graduating from L'Université d'État d'Haïti with my aunt, Priscilla went on to Harvard Law before coming home to represent poor rural women in pro bono cases. Her latest project was representing dozens of mothers in a class-action lawsuit against UN peacekeepers who impregnated them when visiting their villages and provided no support. Humbert, according to Jason, was the son of Cap-Haïtien's mayor and ran a medical clinic in Cité Soleil, the poorest slum in Port-au-Prince. They chose to get married in Sans-Souci because of their family ties but already owned a home together in Pétion-Ville.

"Can you believe Priscilla got married here the first time?" Leonette said as she sucked up the final dregs from her wine. She tipped back the glass and chomped on an ice cube.

"I'd get married here for a second, third, *and* fourth time if I could get the reservation," Félicité said, frowning disapprovingly at her younger sister. "You're diluting the flavor."

"I'm anemic. You know I have pica," Leonette whined. She bit into another ice cube. "Besides, you'd need a boyfriend to even think about having a first wedding."

Jason gagged on his rum and coke. I stifled a laugh.

"I didn't know ice was a no-no with wine," I said.

"It's a huge faux pas," Félicité said. "Right, Jason?"

"To people who care about that stuff, sure," he said. "I say drink what you want."

I suppressed the impulse to grin.

"Here, here," Jason's cousin Marc said, lifting his own cup in the air.

"I'm not a huge drinker," I said. "The legal age is twenty-one in the States and I'm seventeen."

"It's sixteen in Haiti," Félicité said. "We're much more mature here."

In reality, she didn't seem all that mature. My cousin struck me as an adolescent mean girl you'd find in any country, not just Haiti. Good to know some things are universal.

"I wouldn't say all that now," Jason said.

"And Jason would know, Mr. Go-to-College-Early Man," Marc said. "This guy right here? Makes me so proud. Don't break his heart."

"I would *never*," I said. "Jason, breathe."

"Marc promised he wouldn't act like this," he grumbled. His complexion was light enough that I could actually see the creeping of blush on his neck.

"Do you live here, Marc?" I asked.

"God no, this place is much too provincial for me," he said. "You see these groups of tables right here in the not-kiddie-not-yet-adult section? We're all pretty much classmates at school in Pétion-Ville or abroad. Our parents came up for the wedding."

"Nice." Suddenly, a light bulb of an idea sparked in my mind. "Casual question, when do you head back to Pétion-Ville, Félicité?"

"I'm here for the weekend, but I visit all the time. Port-au-Prince is so stuck-up," she said without a milligram of irony. "Why?"

"Well, I'm dying to go to Labadie before my internship ends and tomorrow might be the best day. Of course, you all are invited too!"

There was no way my dad was letting me near any ~~sensual, seductive~~ beaches with two guys alone. And I noticed the furtive glances Marc kept throwing Félicité's way. If I could visit the third place on my dirt list and hang out with Jason, that's what I would call a win.

"Leonette's too young, but I'm in," Félicité said, lifting her hand to halt her sister's protests. "Sounds fun."

"Me too!" Marc beamed.

Jason extracted the drink from my hand and placed it on our table. "Oh no, we're gonna have to get up for this one," he said.

"What are you—" I stopped midsentence, recognizing the first bars of that popular love song on the radio from the car ride. I hung my head and laughed.

"What's so funny? You haven't even seen my moves yet," Jason said. He bent over at the waist and let his stiffly angled right arm swing from his elbow.

"My parents—" I stopped and got out of my seat. "You know what, forget it."

DEAR HAITI, LOVE ALAINE   331

I shuffled my feet in place, miming the running man. "You haven't seen my moves yet either."

"Impressive," Jason said. He took a step closer and reached out his hand. I hesitated, then took it and walked to the dance floor.

"I don't know how to *konpa*," I said.

"Then you haven't *lived*." He smirked. "What's that line? 'The best way to explain it is to do it...' Follow my feet. Left, sway, right, sway."

"You're cheating," I said. "I wouldn't even be able to tell if you're doing it wrong."

"You're in good hands. The best probably. My mom made sure I could do this," he said, spinning me. He motioned to where a tall woman danced with an even taller white man a few feet away. He knew the moves perfectly, albeit executed ungracefully.

"My stepdad. My mom has a type," Jason joked, tugging at his wavy hair from presumably his own father. "She wouldn't marry him until he took lessons."

I loosened up with each beat, even adding an extra twist in my steps when I felt it. But something distracted me from fully focusing on my moves. My mom's laugh. I spied her at a table with my father, their heads close, in deep conversation. The dancing was fun, but seeing my mother so engaged reminded me why it was important for me to come to Sans-Souci at all. I had lost track of Andres after the "I dos," but it didn't seem like Mom was wasting any time stewing about him anyway. I spun around, taking in the entire reception tent. My aunt was nowhere to be found. I suspected it wasn't a coincidence that Andres wasn't around either.

"I—I have to go to the bathroom," I said absentmindedly.

Jason's face fell. "I'll be back before you're even done dancing with all your fans."

A few of the *zuzu* girls gawked at Jason unabashedly from our surrounding tables. I stepped away from him and headed out of the tent. I tiptoed through the path leading to the cars, hoping to avoid *Tati* Estelle and any of her questions in order to grab my mason jar from the back seat. I cursed silently when I reached it, realizing I didn't have the key to unlock the door or any idea where the driver was.

"Someone's up to no good."

My hand froze on the door handle. Thierry stood behind me in the tightest, most crimson cummerbund I'd ever seen, holding a glass of what looked like rum and coke. I hadn't known he was going to the wedding too. His hand caressed the trademark ring that dangled from his neck.

"Weddings always make me so sentimental," he said as he moved forward to lean against the car. "It's not gonna last, you know."

"Now, that's not a nice thing to say tonight of all nights."

"You ever been in love, kid?"

"No?" This was moving into weird territory.

"Trust me. It's not worth it."

"Thanks for the advice, I guess."

He took a sip. "What did you say you were doing here again?"

"I was looking to see if my powder was in the car. I wanted to freshen up," I said, thinking fast. In reality, I'd forgotten my compact on the vanity in my room.

"I saw you with the other intern earlier. He's a good guy. Smart guy. Trustworthy. You can't trust most people these days, even after you stick your neck out for them." Okay, we were officially in the land of weird *and* unseemly.

"Did he pay you to say that?" I joked without feeling any sort of amusement.

He swallowed the final drops and placed the glass on the hood of the car and leered at me. "What's this, a shakedown? That's my job."

I didn't know how my aunt could work with a man like this. He was a walking, talking dirtbag cliché. Weddings didn't just make him sentimental; they made him moody and inappropriately talkative too.

I saw my opening. A valet who was zigzagging around the maze of cars made eye contact and I waved him over.

"Where's your car?" I asked Thierry, who looked about ready to doze off. He nodded his head toward a platinum-plated Hummer a few paces away. Ew. A jerk of a car for a jerk of a driver.

"Can you please find his keys and take him home? Let your boss know that Estelle Dubois sent you."

"You're okay too," Thierry said, dragging his feet behind the nervous valet.

I smiled tightly and went back to my original focus. Crap. I looked down at the vintage metal-chain clamshell purse I'd borrowed from my mother's wardrobe and sighed. This would have to do.

I gathered my long skirt and wrapped it around my hand to run quickly down the stone steps that led to the shallow valley I'd noticed coming in. I looked for a stick to dig with, but the ground was bare. Instead, I dropped to my knees and scratched at the flattened earth with my fingers. My index finger hit a sharp rock and I pried it out. I stabbed at the little hole until the mound of dry powder was substantial enough for me to pile into my purse.

I shook as much dust from my skirt as possible, but it didn't help. Overhead the sky cackled and thundered before unleashing a torrent of rain from the clouds. I could already predict the inches of my curly hair that would shrink into itself, seeking refuge from the moisture. The ground was suddenly saturated, and my foot made a squishy sound as I pulled the heel of my shoe out of the muck. There was nothing I could do to keep my already soiled dress from clinging to my body.

A cheer erupted from the tent as I walked toward it. My mother looked rapturous midspin on the dance floor with my father. Even though I suspected I looked the hottest of messes, I was pleased. Rain at a wedding was supposed to be good luck.

As I got closer to the party, I noticed a couple loitering beside another car.

"This will be over soon," I heard a muffled male voice say. "We didn't even talk tonight."

"You can tell me anything," a breathless female voice replied.

They were clearly taking advantage of the low light to get closer than they could on the dance floor (and still look decent, that is). I quickly averted my gaze, then did a double take when I saw my aunt's clam-shaped purse on the ground beside their feet.

"This has to be a joke." I blinked to make sure the champagne I'd drunk wasn't deceiving me. I tiptoed closer to them.

My aunt jerked her head from where she'd tucked it into Andres Venegas's collar.

"Alaine! I—"

"Could not possibly have any reasonable explanation for this, so just stop there," I said.

"She has a temper just like her mother," Andres said, leaning on the car.

"How dare you speak to me!" I hissed.

Andres lifted his arms in surrender. "I'm not going to fight you."

"You are scum," I said. I looked pointedly at my aunt so she wouldn't miss that I meant her too. My hands were shaking. Was I more upset at *Tati* Estelle for being with him? Andres Venegas was a monster, worse than those translucent bottom-dweller anglerfish. My mother's diaries attested to that. After his betrayal, how could *Tati* Estelle let him anywhere near her now?

"What are you doing here?" I demanded. I was within striking distance, and *Tati* Estelle's gaze fluttered anxiously between my hand and his face.

"I'm a groomsman," he sniffed.

"Yeah, sure. So am I," I said.

"Don't you have to be digging up dirt somewhere? Isn't that what you said, Estelle?"

"Alaine—" *Tati* Estelle interjected sharply.

I shook my head in disappointment. *She told him.* "I'm not an idiot. Is this some sort of sick joke?"

"This is out of your high-school-paper league," Andres said. "Even if you're the kid of the once-great Celeste Beauparlant."

I don't have to tell you what I did to him, because I didn't have the chance to unleash my full rage. We were interrupted by two men in white shirts bearing the insignia of the *Police Nationale d'Haïti* on their sleeves.

"Estelle Dubois, you are under arrest."

PART VII

MEM GWO WOCH PA KA KANPE DEVAN DLO LANME

(EVEN A BOULDER CANNOT WITHSTAND THE SEA)

Saturday, March 5

UPDATED TO-DO LIST FROM ROSELINE'S PLACES TO VISIT

~~Bois Caïman~~

~~Sans-Souci Palace~~

Labadie

Citadelle Laferrière

Sunday, March 6

SPOTTED: Andres Venegas returning home from a soul-searching trip to Haiti, welcomed by his wife and two kids at Ronald Reagan Washington National Airport carrying a homemade Welcome Back! sign. The senator and his wife are expecting their third child in May.

CAP-HAÏTIEN POLICE DEPARTMENT
CAP-HAÏTIEN, HAITI

INCIDENT REPORT:	#5068531
REPORT ENTERED:	03/05
LOCATION:	Palais Sans-Souci, Milot, Haiti
INCIDENT DATE:	Started approximately July of previous year, ongoing
INCIDENT TYPE/ OFFENSE:	Embezzlement
REPORTING OFFICER:	Josue Antenor
APPROVING OFFICER:	Evens Cazimir
OFFENDERS	
STATUS:	Defendant
NAME:	Estelle Dubois
SEX:	Female
AGE:	43
PHONE:	+509 55 55 1243
ADDRESS:	Le Cap-Haïtien Arrondissement, Nord Department, Haiti
WITNESSES TO INCIDENT/OFFENSE	
NAME:	N/A
SEX:	
RACE:	
AGE:	
DATE OF BIRTH:	
PHONE:	
ADDRESS:	
WITNESS:	

NARRATIVE:

After months of investigation, it was discovered that Estelle Dubois was allegedly complicit in an active embezzlement of her charity, PATRON PAL. Dubois, along with multiple unidentified parties, allegedly siphoned donor funds in numerous small quantities from the organization into multiple accounts in banks mostly located in Belize. It is estimated that as much as 3,000,000 USD was misappropriated.

On Saturday, March 5, Dubois was placed under arrest at Sans-Souci Palace. As we approached Dubois to perform the arrest, we observed that Dubois was accompanied by a Latin man who appeared to be in his early 40s. The pair was speaking heatedly with a young woman, approximately age 18. The young woman was covered in dirt and drenched in rain. As we approached, we could hear the young woman raising her voice while waving a clam-shaped item. It appeared that she was lifting her hand to strike the gentleman, who then covered his head to protect his face. As we moved to place Dubois under arrest, the gentleman quickly excused himself and left the scene.

The young woman said that we must have been mistaken, but after presenting the arrest warrant, Dubois told her to remain calm and that it would be all right. Dubois then instructed the young woman to alert her mother to the situation. The young woman's mother reached the scene quickly. Upon recognizing her as Celeste Beauparlant, Officer Antenor requested a picture and autograph but was met with a stream of swear words by both Beauparlant and her daughter. After this, Dubois did not resist arrest and was cooperative as we led her away.

The Life and Times of Alaine Beauparlant

"Should I change my moisturizer? I can't believe the police officer thought that I was eighteen," I said as I handed the police report back to my mother.

"Alaine," *Tati* Estelle said with a small laugh. "You have an amazing knack for pointing out the humor in any situation."

I ignored her.

My mom, aunt, and I were sitting around a small table in the Au Cap Police Department. The room was lit with a—get this—single bulb swinging from the center of the room, its yellow light flickering every so often. I'm sure there was a grimy pot of coffee in the kitchen as well. Technically, we weren't supposed to be sitting here with *Tati* Estelle. But two crisp American fifty-dollar bills went pretty far in helping watchful eyes turn the other way. And arrested or not, *Tati* Estelle was still one of the most powerful and well-liked people in Haiti.

"You guys really didn't need to spend the entire night here," *Tati* Estelle said. "I don't want you to see me like this."

"We're family. This is what we do," Mom said firmly. I swallowed the words I wanted to say about family loyalty.

"Yep, bribing public officials, that's what we do," I said instead. "What did you do to get here in the first place? I thought you said you loved those kids as if they were your own."

How could you be so stupid?

"Watch that tone," my mom said with a warning look.

"It's a fair question," *Tati* Estelle said. She rubbed her eyes and blinked rapidly as if to confirm she was in fact where they showed her to be. "My lawyer said that I don't have to worry about anything. They'll be here any moment to let me out."

"But that still doesn't answer the question—"

"I demand you release my client, immediately!" Right on cue, we turned toward the voice making the commotion and saw none other than Priscilla. She had changed into black jeans but was still rocking her veil and intricate updo.

"Madame Calixte—"

"Rene-Charles. I left my own wedding early. I wouldn't do that for just anyone. These absurd charges you intend to bring on Ms. Dubois can wait until a respectable hour. She has no record, she's an upstanding member of this community. Frankly, this is a total insult, Chief Durand."

"This case is very sensitive and we reacted in the manner we felt most appropriate, Madame Rene-Charles," Chief Durand said. "If you would follow me to my office, I can further explain."

Priscilla strode through the station, clearly comfortable with all the officers. When the police chief opened the door, I peeked inside the office and saw a man rising from his seat. He wore a navy blue jacket embossed with gold letters: FBI. *Oof.*

After about an hour, Priscilla walked out of the office looking much more subdued.

"We will be releasing you but expect you at the tribunal in one week's time," Chief Durand said.

No one stopped my aunt as she jumped out of her seat.

"What was that all about?" I asked once we were packed in Priscilla's car. "And you're amazing."

"Durand is a friend of my father-in-law's. I knew things would move faster if I came myself."

"What about your honeymoon?"

"I'm heading to the airport tomorrow." Priscilla shrugged as she scrolled through her phone. "We eloped three months ago. The wedding was just so everyone would leave us alone."

The Life and Times of Alaine Beauparlant

You know what's the worst? Spending hours in a police station after watching your aunt betray your mom and get arrested at a wedding the night before, and then having to pretend everything is hunky-dory with a bunch of fancy-pants Haitians. I wanted to cancel my Labadie plans, but then I remembered Félicité was leaving soon and I had to work at PATRON PAL during the week. I hadn't told my father what I'd been up to, because I still wasn't sure if he would support my decision to pursue curse-breaking out of love for my mother or recall his own haunting experience dabbling in the spirit world and double down on forbidding me to take these steps...out of *his* love for my mother. So when I explained why I was going to Labadie to my parents and aunt early that morning at breakfast, I simply said we were going "for fun."

The only way to get to Labadie from where we stayed in Au Cap is by driving forty minutes to Cormier Beach and taking a boat. It's not a neighborhood beach anyone can readily drive to and enjoy "just because." It's cut off from the rest of the country, reserved for the foreign tourists who grace the sand with their toes and are willing to pay a few dollars for a local to braid their hair or chop open a coconut for them to drink.

My parents were still on each other's good sides and my mom's positive mood was holding up. I needed to get to Labadie and their sand to make sure she kept feeling that way. *Tati* Estelle offered a way to the beach.

"It's not the easiest place to reach from the mainland. The locals are isolated from most residents in Nord, but Tony heads into the market there and I'm sure he wouldn't mind taking you and your friends," she said. Her eyes bored into me: *don't say anything.*

"It's fine. We can get there the normal way," I said, not entirely sure what the "normal" way entailed.

"Alaine, take the free ride," my mom said.

"I'd be much more comfortable with you going on this trip through your aunt's assistance," my father said. (*Dad Translation*: I have no clue why you're insisting on going today of all days. Unless you take Estelle's escort, I won't let you go and will talk your mother into agreeing with me.)

I didn't want anything from *Tati* Estelle, regardless of the convenience it offered—even if it was from Tony.

"Okay," I said stiffly. "Whatever you want."

I knew that Andres and my aunt were a couple once upon a time, and I suppose it wasn't a stretch that they'd rekindled their affections in the years since high school...but I'd assumed such things would cease when one of the involved parties *got married and had 2.77 children*. I mean, I get it. I've watched *Scandal*. I could even begrudgingly admit that Andres had the smarmy coiffed handsomeness customary for politicians. But I'd never thought my aunt would be the Other Woman. Not when she'd worked so hard for everything in her life and was such a champion of women and one of the two most confident people I knew.

And let's not forget that Andres *had unsettled my mother to the point of her attacking him on live television*. I was obviously #TeamCeleste #allday, and it was disturbing to discover that this distinction wasn't black-and-white for *Tati* Estelle. *Thou shalt not indulge in carnal pleasures with your sister's mortal enemy* was hardly something that needed to be carved on a stone tablet to be understood. But whatever my mother knew or hadn't known about their current relationship status, I refused to be the person to break that news to her. *Tati* Estelle had gotten a night in the slammer, and Andres had gotten a ticket straight home without anyone realizing he was even there at the time of the arrest. Mom had enough on her plate. A disloyal twin would add to the stress.

I used to love that my aunt knew me so well. Now it made me feel exposed. When she stopped me on the way to my room to grab a few items for my trip, she took one look at my face and was pleading for me to follow through.

"Go," she said, correctly assuming the true nature of the Labadie visit. "Your mother's depending on you. This can't wait."

But now I resented her. She had told Andres about my moves. Was this benefiting him in some way? Was it part of their pillow talk? Seeing them together, learning about my mother and Andres's disagreements in Mom's diary, reading articles claiming that both were early investors in PATRON PAL showed me that *Tati* Estelle held two allegiances. I didn't know what to think anymore. But my mom's offhand comment at the wedding about feeling like herself, and seeing how content she was at breakfast, was enough to keep me going, even if I was wary of believing a word *Tati* Estelle said. I paused.

"I'm not doing this for you," I said, slowly closing the door.

**Engraved wood carving on the
SS *Bateau d'Amour*'s king-size headboard**

Welcome to the Love Nest
Rest your head on the pillows of your lover
Soak your feet in the hot tub of desire
Blush the deep, deep red of lust
Embrace the heat of passion's fire

The Life and Times of Alaine Beauparlant

Turns out Tony Juste's brother-in-law was quite the poet. Tony had been feeling especially grateful to *Tati* Estelle since the YouTube interview and had practically begged her to reach out if she needed "anything, anything at all." So it was no surprise when he agreed to give me and the others a ride on the SS *Bateau d'Amour* when she called on short notice to cash in her favor. He spent weekends selling peanut butter to the tourists at Labadie using his sister and brother-in-law's boat, so it really was "no trouble at all."

Fernand had first picked up me, then Félicité, followed by Jason and his cousin Marc.

"It's the tall, skinny one, isn't it?" Fernand whispered, leaning over to me in the passenger seat. "Your *chouchou*? You smiled the biggest when he came into the car."

I rolled my eyes and mimed zipping my lips.

Part of the deal with my dad to let me go to Labadie was having Fernand drive us to the marina where we would meet up with Tony. We rolled the windows down the whole way and sang along to the radio. As we came to a stop at the dock, I felt a nudge in my back. I turned in my seat and met Jason's laughing eyes. He raised an eyebrow as he trained his gaze toward our cousins, who were very seriously alternating the singing and rapping parts of a song.

"Okay, Beyoncé and Jay-Z, we're here," Fernand said. "The concert is over."

"Tell me. Do you charge extra for the jokes or does that come with the service?" Félicité huffed over his chuckling.

As we piled out of the car, the briny scent of salt and sea deluged our nostrils. A few women in wooden canoes were gliding along gently in the water, heading toward the tiny mint-green and lemon-yellow shanty houses embedded precariously into the rocks of a jagged mountain. It was a miracle that they stayed up when the wind blew.

"Allo!" Tony Juste called out from where he stood at the dock, ready to escort us onto the boat.

It was a fairly large yacht, painted a stark white that reflected the sun directly into our eyes. Tony was apologetic when we took in the decor. I brought my hand up to shield myself from the glare. There was a flashy red stripe painted around the perimeter of the vessel, hinting at the gaudiness that awaited us on board.

"My sister and her husband are very…affectionate," he said. "He bought this for their anniversary but is kind enough to let me borrow it when I sell my food."

"Yo, your aunt hooked it *up*," Marc said from the chair he "nonchalantly" reclined in beside Félicité. "Did she use her connects from prison?"

The police showing up had livened an already eventful party and hijacked all conversations.

"Ha ha. She's already out," I said. "It was all a misunderstanding."

At least I hope it was.

"Seeing her get led away in handcuffs was the biggest moment of the night," Félicité said. "Even bigger than the black dress."

"Let's take a tour," Jason said, changing the subject.

"Smart man," Tony said as he walked to the cockpit of the yacht at the center of the boat.

The bow of the ship had been converted into a makeshift bed with four patio lounge chairs pushed side by side and crimson throw pillows strewn about. The seats along the border of the bow were lined with the same red cushions. Below deck was a long table with enough space for six people to sit comfortably. A large platter topped with all sorts of meats and cheeses was positioned in the center of the table, four bottles of *Prestige* beer arranged side by side. I grabbed a drink and stopped short when I saw the long silver pole that was planted in the center of the room. I glanced at Jason and he blushed.

"Very classy," Félicité sniffed.

I spread a bit of smoked goat cheese and lentils onto a cracker and headed to the other side of the boat. I carefully climbed down a small staircase that led to an unlit room, making sure to not spill my drink. The sound of the others' steps told me they weren't far behind, taking their time as they descended into the dark space. I walked with one hand outstretched to the side, feeling around for a switch. With a flick of my wrist, light flooded the room and I cackled.

There was a trail of rose petals leading to the bed in front of us, with the flowers carefully organized in the shape of a heart. At the center was a small collection of gadgets that I didn't want to know if they were new or used. There were champagne glasses on the bedside table, and when we went into the bathroom, we saw an almost empty box of bubble bath soap beside a huge roman tub. A row of jars filled with vanilla-scented candles were set on the counter with a safety gas lighter settled gingerly across the top.

"I'm personally always ready to soak my feet in the hot tub of desire," Marc said.

"Who isn't?" Jason said.

When we got back to Tony, I sat down on one of the seats toward the front of the ship and observed as the prow sliced through the water with a low rumble. The blue water splashed on either side of the boat, frothing into white as it made contact. I watched, hypnotized, not hearing when Félicité sauntered over. She lowered herself beside me, her movements as graceful as Misty Copeland even when the yacht bounced over a particularly choppy wave.

"It's awful what happened to *Tati* Estelle," she said in a low voice.

"Yes..." This was foreign territory.

"To be imprisoned for something she didn't do," Félicité said. "That curse is trying to ruin all our lives, but we won't let it."

She squeezed my hand.

"Wait. You believe in that?"

"Of course I do. Don't you?"

"I just didn't expect you to, is all." I considered my cousin, a girl my age who was living the life I might have lived if I'd been raised in Haiti. "*Tati* Estelle talks about it sometimes, but my parents make a point of ignoring it."

"That's exactly what the curse would want—for us to pretend it doesn't exist. It'll wreak havoc either way," Félicité said.

"I've started taking it more seriously since I've gotten to Haiti. I dunno, it just seems easier to do that here." I hesitated before continuing. "And you know what, Félicité, I have a feeling our luck is going to change soon."

"How is that exactly?"

"Let's just say Roseline and I are working on it."

"Hmm... I'd be careful about her, Alaine. She's not very... nice."

I scoffed. "No shade, but you didn't even acknowledge her at my grandmother's birthday dinner." I'd held it against Félicité ever since, frankly.

She sucked her teeth impatiently. "All I'm saying is that some people in the family find it very suspicious that Pierrot fell in love with her so fast and so hard and hasn't come up for air since."

Roseline's somber disposition was off-putting, yeah. And she could probably blink more. But Félicité and the rest of my *zuzu* family didn't know or chose to ignore the truth about her childhood. Roseline didn't owe them anything and, after all she had endured, she didn't need to ingratiate herself with in-laws who made it diamond clear that she wasn't good enough to share their name or wealth anyway. But I kept my lips shut. Maybe there were things I just didn't understand from my perspective. I doubted it though.

"So what's your thing?" I asked politely.

She paused. "I'm not sure. But it's coming."

The Life and Times of Alaine Beauparlant

Across the sea, an enormous ship no doubt holding tourists within its metal confines was also proceeding slowly to the shore. Since we'd met Tony at a private marina closer to Labadie, we had a much, much shorter trip than the almost five hundred miles the luxury cruise ships coming from Nassau, Bahamas, did. We would dock before them and have the island all to ourselves for about an hour, Tony explained.

I grunted. "This place can't be that hard to get to on your own."

"You would've had to take a tap tap to a water taxi stand farther away from your aunt's home and then another boat if you wanted to go deeper into the village," Tony said. "Very unreliable."

"Yeah. That's usually how we get to Labadie when we go," Jason said.

"It's nice to commune with the people," Félicité said magnanimously. She poured herself another glass of wine (iceless in her sister Leonette's absence).

"Is that what you call traveling a few minutes on public transportation to get to a private island that said people aren't allowed on?" I asked.

"Labadie isn't a real island," she said. "It's a peninsula. And this sympathy for the masses is rich coming from the girl who got us the private boat."

So much for our moment.

"My parents insisted I take it," I said between gritted teeth, completely aware of how silly I sounded. I tried not to think of my dad's old neighbors who surely had never stepped foot on Labadie.

Tony jumped in.

"Estelle is a great woman," he said. "She cares. And go to Labadie, don't go to Labadie, there will still be poor people in Haiti."

Jason shrugged in agreement.

"I don't see any trouble with enjoying the isl—peninsula," Marc said, meeting Félicité's eyes. "Just because we're touristing it up here doesn't mean we can't still help the rest of the island. PATRON PAL hasn't gone anywhere."

"This is true." Tony slowed down the boat and observed the water for a moment before turning the wheel to move the yacht against the direction of the gentle currents and wind. He sped up slightly to get as close to the dock as he could before shifting to reverse the boat to stop its movement. I watched nervously as Tony then moved from behind the steering wheel to pick up the ropes sitting on the side of the craft near the dock. He handed one to me expectantly.

"Will you help me do the honors?" He smiled.

I put my four middle-school sailing lessons to use and looped the line through the metal cleat attached to the dock to tie off the rope and secure the boat. I landed gracefully-(-ish) on my feet as I got off the yacht. When we were all on land, we walked over to the entrance of the tourist area, where soldiers carrying menacing guns stood looking bored.

"*Bonjou,*" Tony said pleasantly. "I sell in the market and this is Estelle Dubois's niece and her fine friends."

The soldiers straightened up slightly. Tony flashed his ID card and motioned us to follow him through the now-opening gate.

We were officially in Labadie.

I will admit that sometimes it takes more effort to see the beauty in the darkest corners of Haiti. But this place was stunning. The sand was as glittery white as crushed-up vampire bones and the sky and sea were the same shade of startling aquamarine. The vendors peppered across the beach in between giant umbrellas and long reclining chairs advertised their treats with scintillating scents of barbecue and fried pork. Salty air filled our nostrils as we walked to the edge of the shore and looked up when a flock of laughing gulls flew overhead and then touched down on the water. It took us no time at all to get the lay of the land from the employees waiting for the cruise guests and to find the neon yellow and orange signs that pointed out places like Pirates' Port and Adventurous Alcove.

I felt guilty, banishing the images of Julmise and her brothers from my mind so soon, but the conch was so tasty, even more so when we licked the lemon juice dripping from our fingers. We soaked up the sun that blinded us warm.

We broke off in pairs for the roller coaster that had no lines yet. When I heard Jason's piercing scream beside me, I jumped in my seat, then laughed. Instead of looking embarrassed, he grabbed my hand and didn't let go until we got off the ride. I could feel the sweat beading in my palms, but I didn't care. In that moment, I would've been happy for the roller coaster to go on forever.

Our personal deserted island bubble burst when we spotted the cruisers, who had officially docked and were sauntering across the beach in various levels of undress.

"Wow, I still cannot believe this place is *Haiti*!" said a woman who had missed a spot in her sunscreen application. The top of her nose was peeling from exposure.

Her companion lazily tugged up his drooping shorts.

"It's absolutely amazing what they've done here. I read online that the cruise line didn't even use to label this place in their marketing pamphlets. Just called it Hispaniola."

We took turns zip-lining across the water, shrieking at the top of our lungs. As I surveyed Labadie from above, I sensed in my gut that the sand from this beach wasn't what I needed. If I squinted, I could make out a fence far away, separating the tourist area from the rest of the village. The developers had done a good job of tucking this section of Labadie away from their guests, effectively segregating them.

Later we moved on to taking turns sharing details about ourselves as we sat on the edge of the shore, close enough to have the waves crawl up our legs and lick our calves.

"I'm definitely getting out of here," Marc said when Félicité "casually" asked about our hopes, dreams, and life goals. His father was an executive at Haiti's top cell phone company.

"Don't you feel the need to stay and help?" I asked.

"No amount of help I could offer will save this country," he said matter-of-factly. I couldn't reconcile the good-natured guy I'd met with this person with no hope.

"Well, sure, if you have that attitude," Jason said.

"No, I get it," Félicité said. "Look at it this way. You and Alaine *chose* to come here. Your place is in the United States. The land of the free. Home of the brave. Whatever. When your internships are over, you're going to hop on a plane and go back to all that."

"Sometimes you don't want to be responsible for everyone else's problems," Marc said.

"Or feel guilty for what you have," Félicité interjected.

"Yeah! It's hard to look down the hills of Massif de la Selle and know there are people looking up at you, wishing they could take your place."

"And when you go abroad, everyone thinks all Haitians live in poverty," she said.

"That's a huge pet peeve of mine," Marc said.

Jason and I exchanged a look. Our cousins were entitled to their opinions, but it was disconcerting nonetheless. I'm sure this was part of the angst that had pushed my mother to New York for school and eventually to DC—the irony of a privileged life in a bereft nation. Until this trip, I'd spent my entire existence away from either side of Haiti, and I couldn't see myself ever living here full-time. Félicité was right. I couldn't fully understand their disdain when they'd spent their lives on the periphery of such pain.

"Doesn't the poverty affect you at all?" Jason asked. Deep down, I knew how easy it was to be wrapped in your own world, no matter where it was located. A few rides on a roller coaster had me forgetting my dad's lecture and Daniel, Anne, and their kids.

"Of course it does, man," Marc said. "I just need to get away for a bit. Maybe go to Stanford for four years." He grinned.

"I wouldn't stay away *forever*," Félicité said. Her parents ran a popular hotel near the US embassy that was always featured on travel documentary shows. Someone would need to take over when they retired.

"It's still home," Marc agreed.

I looked at the grains of sand around us. The cruise company had shuttered its passengers away from what—and who—resided beyond Labadie's barbed gates.

"Has anyone ever gone past the tourist spots here?" I asked.

"No," Jason said. "But I'm down if you are."

"Sure. Why not?" Marc said. We turned and waited for Félicité to weigh in.

She sighed. "Let's go."

We picked up our towels and walked back to where Tony's boat was docked. While Jason, Marc, and Félicité left their things on the long table below deck, I walked around the yacht searching for Tony. I wanted to let him know that we would be right back, but he was nowhere to be found.

"I can't find Tony, but we won't be long anyway," I said when I got back to the others. "Let's head over to the locals' section before he returns." From the boat I could see the concrete wall that surrounded the entire tourist beach. And even though it was shrouded in trees, there was no denying that it was there to keep the tourists in...or the locals out.

We left the yacht and headed to where the concrete wall transitioned into a chain-link fence. It towered five feet above us, barbed wire perched at the top like an unraveled slinky.

"Let's go through there," I pointed.

We neared the opening in the gate and were immediately stopped by a man in green wearing a black hard hat.

"Where do you think you're going?"

"We live right through there, boss man," Marc said, pointing past the guard to nowhere in particular. He flashed his affable smile, clearly hoping that he could charm his way through to the other side of the barricade. The guard blinked.

Félicité sucked her teeth as she looked through her purse and handed him a few bills. "We expect to be let back in, *san pwoblem*."

The man smiled widely and gave a mocking bow as he let us pass. "Of course, *mademoiselle*."

"Nice," I said.

"Money talks," she replied.

"Sure does," I said, thinking of *Tati* Estelle's night in jail.

"I don't know what she has you doing, but hurry it up," she said more quietly beside me.

As we walked away from the tourist-designated area, it was clear to see that the rest of Labadie was not developed. Wooden walkways quickly turned into rocky roads, the island music that played nonstop once passengers got off the cruise ships fading into a dull din of steel drums. After a short while, we reached the edge of a sizable cluster of trees, ducking as we stepped through a patch of low-hanging leaves. I led the way, the sound of dry twigs snapping beneath our feet now the only noise as we wound deeper into the small forest. A group of beetles swarmed around a dark mass that I didn't care to get a better look at and I quickened my steps to put some distance between us and what I could only guess was a dead animal. Jason and Marc followed closely behind Félicité and me, our surroundings growing darker with each step.

Here.

I couldn't explain why, but *this* was where I needed to stop. Where we stood looked just as similar as the rest of the forest, except for a small cluster of hibiscuses. Félicité gasped in delight as she bent down to inspect the beautiful ruby flowers, Jason and Marc following her lead. While they were distracted, I pulled out the small jar from my bag and unscrewed the top. I sent up a small prayer of thanks that the others paid me no mind, because I knew that there was no way to logically explain what I was doing.

I used the lid of the jar to quickly fill the container with soil and silently screwed on the top once I was done. I took one more look at my collection before placing it into my bag and noticed a small spider hanging on to the outside of the jar for dear life. I stifled a scream and silently shook the creature off, resisting the urge to throw the entire jar away. I slipped the spider-free container into my bag just as Jason called for me to join them.

I skipped over and noticed the bright red hibiscus he extended toward me. I looked up at him to comment on it, and as I did, he took the flower and tucked it behind my ear.

"Pretty," he said quietly.

My heart fluttered and I looked away, suddenly forgetting what I was about to say. Thankfully (or not so thankfully), Félicité and Marc joined us and soon we were headed back to the tourist section of the peninsula.

The guard let us back in *san pwoblem*, as promised. We all agreed that we needed a bite to eat before heading back to Tony, so we made our way to the buffet station that the cruise line had ready in a teal, open-air building. An easy rhythm fell over us as we grabbed some food, teasing and laughing the entire time. Once our plates were piled with slices of melon, pieces of fried plantain and yuca bathed in *pikliz*, and tender chunks of *griot*, we headed back to the beach and hung out on a large blanket in the sand.

Somewhere between stuffing my face and giggling at Jason and Marc poking fun at Félicité, I must've fallen asleep, because I awoke to a cold *splat* on my stomach. My eyes flew open and I saw Jason standing above me with his hands dripping wet sand. I jumped up and chased him into the water, splashing, laughing, and shouting like a child in an amusement park. Félicité and Marc joined us and we played around until we were lying on the shore again, catching our breath.

"We should find Tony," I said. I'd had a better time than I'd expected, but I wanted to go home and check on my mom. Confirm my parents hadn't killed each other. Glare at *Tati* Estelle.

We grabbed our belongings and left for the makeshift harbor.

"I think that's him," Félicité said, squinting toward the man showing his ID card to enter the tourist-designated area of the peninsula.

Tony flashed a wide smile as we walked toward him, his empty peanut butter crates in tow.

"Ah. Just the young people I wanted to see. There's a storm coming," Tony said. "Maybe we should wait it out."

"Storm? What storm?" I said, looking up at the nearly cloudless sky. The sun would be setting in about an hour and a half and I wanted to be back on the mainland before then.

"I have a bad leg," Tony said, tapping on his right knee. "And I can taste it in the air. Can't you?"

"Not really," Félicité said flatly.

"We'll be fine!" I said, waving my hand at my cousin to keep her from saying anything else. I pointed at the empty crates that Tony held in his hands. "And you can tell us all about the sales you made today on the way back."

Tony looked up at the sky and shielded his eyes from the sun. Finally, he said, "*Eh bien*. Let's pray that I'm wrong and that we have an easy trip."

We boarded the yacht and went down to the lower deck to leave our bags for safekeeping. As we joined Tony in the cockpit, we watched the sun set, burnt orange bleeding slowly into the horizon. The four of us stood behind Tony as he steered us to Cormier, recapping our day among ourselves while he hummed along to the music that played throughout the boat.

I will never, ever forget you.

But it breaks my heart to be near you…

"Can you turn it up, please?" I asked, tapping Tony on the shoulder. It was that same song from the ride to Priscilla's wedding and the reception. I grabbed Jason's hand and led him out to the prow of the boat, the music leading the way. I pulled him close, wrapping his arms around my waist. I could blame my boldness on the beers we had earlier in the day, but I knew that wasn't it. Marc whistled over the speakers from the cockpit.

Jason and I swayed to the music, my head resting on his chest. No one would ever call me a smooth operator, and normally I would've talked myself out of even suggesting that I wanted to dance. But for once, I didn't overthink. Jason made me forget how self-conscious I usually was with guys I found even marginally attractive, and I let out a contented sigh as we continued to glide around the yacht. There must've been something to this song because soon Félicité and Marc joined us at the front of the boat. I watched as the two of them moved closer together, staring out at the water, whispering with their heads bowed.

"Eps!" Tony tutted over the speakers that Marc had used earlier, glancing exaggeratedly between where Jason and I danced and Félicité and Marc stood. "Hands where I can see them, lovebirds." He chuckled to himself as if he had just told the funniest joke.

I was twirling when the first drop of rain landed on my forehead. Then my nose. My lips. The once-orange sky was now a dark sheet of clouds, heavy with water.

"Uh…what's your knee telling you now?" Félicité shouted to Tony, her voice trembling slightly. The sky crackled with electricity, with thunder booming seconds after.

"We're almost to Cormier," Tony said over the speakers. Even from where we stood I could see him frowning. "We have no choice but to keep moving forward. Head below deck, you guys."

We listened to Tony and went into the interior section of the ship. Félicité and I sat on a low bench along the wall of the cabin while Marc and Jason paced restlessly nearby. Soon the waves that had been gently lapping against the sides of the boat turned vicious, each surge of water slamming harder against the hull, the boat rocking back and forth like a rogue bassinet. The heavens ripped open and released bullets of water, washing away our high spirits. The wind picked up with a low howl and I scooted closer to Félicité. Another shriek tore through the boat, and this time the force of it knocked Jason over to where we sat. He tripped over me and landed on my lap in a clumsy heap that I didn't have time to brace myself for.

"I'm sorry," he yelled over the ocean roar as he tried to straighten himself. "Are you all right?"

"I'm fine!" I said although I feared I would not be for long.

In the distance, we could see that we were nearing Cormier Beach's shoreline. A collective sense of relief washed over us as we all relaxed, if only for a moment. As Tony pushed forward, the wind reemerged, singing a dangerous medley, seducing us to give up the fight for safety. The boat swung forcefully to the left and a flash of lightning illuminated a wall of rocks that seemed to appear out of nowhere. There was a sickening crunch as the left side of the boat scraped along the small boulders.

"Brace yourselves!" Tony grunted over the speakers as he tried with all his might to steer the boat away from danger. But there was nothing he could do as the wind picked up a second time. We slammed against the stones again and again, a rag doll being yanked back and forth in the teeth of an angry dog. Tony must have lost his grip on the wheel, because without warning, we were all tossed to one side of the boat.

The cabin glowed brightly as a thick bolt of lightning streaked through the sky. The deafening sound of wood splitting crashed through the air and we could see a cloud of black smoke follow in its lethal wake. It felt as if Zeus himself was hurtling lightning bolts toward us with each flash of electricity. I racked my brain, searching for anything I might have learned at school that could've prepared me for this, and came up with nothing. My voice was trapped in my throat. I couldn't scream. My mind was inundated with a flurry of thoughts. *This is all my fault. How could this happen? We could very well die here. I might actually die before my mother.*

Tony burst through the doors to where we were below deck. "She's taking on water! We have to get off!"

Tony motioned for us to follow him. We scaled the perimeter of the yacht as fast as we dared back up to the cockpit, where the life jackets were kept. Suddenly, I remembered my collection from Labadie. Without hesitating, I raced past the others to head to the lower deck, where our bags were stored. Tony's eyes bulged, the wind ripping his words away as he shouted for me to come back.

If there's a chance that we might live through this, I can't mess this up!

I could feel the water sloshing beneath my feet as I ran over to our things. I quickly grabbed my satchel and put my arms through the straps to secure it onto my back.

"Alaine! What are you doing?" Tony bellowed as he burst through the doors to the lower deck. "Put on your life jacket and let's go!" Tony shoved the life jacket onto me and over my bag, quickly snapping it into place. He took my hand and dragged me back up to the cockpit to join Félicité, Marc, and Jason.

We stood at the front of the bow waiting for Tony to let us know when it was time to jump, and another wave of guilt hit me. *Why did I insist on leaving? Would it really have been the worst thing for us to stay a little while longer in Labadie?* And then I thought of the dirt that sat in the mason jar in my bag. If I lost it because of this terrible storm, I *knew* my parents wouldn't let me return to collect more. I couldn't have come this far for it to all fall apart.

I glanced at Tony and saw the anxiety that painted his face. I was worrying about losing this dirt for something that I wasn't completely sure I believed in, while a part of his livelihood was being ripped right away from him. And it was because of me. Still, I sent up a prayer that nothing would happen to my collection. Or us.

Tony signaled that it was time and we jumped on the count of *trois*. The ink-black water was freezing, and my teeth immediately began to chatter. When my head broke the surface, I was relieved to see that Tony was right; land wasn't too far out. I looked left, then right, and saw a bouncing orange life vest. It was Jason, yelling what I could safely guess was *Swim!* I sent up another prayer that we would make it safely to shore and propelled my arms with every ounce of force I had left in my body. Each stroke left me weaker than the last as the water battered us in relentless waves, slamming down on our heads in painful sprays. The wind gave another howl, an unforgettable tune that I wondered if the others heard too.

My head dunked below the surface and water flooded through my mouth into my chest. I flailed my arms as salt stung my eyes. Strong arms took hold of me and pulled my head above water. My lungs were on fire. Each cough that racked my body stoked the flames. I looked dazedly into Jason's eyes.

"We need to get to land!" he yelled over the laughing wind.

"Félicité," I croaked, and Jason gestured toward my cousin and Marc, kicking furiously up ahead.

"Can you make the swim?"

I glanced to the shore and saw a bright orange jacket drifting up and down like a lazy yo-yo ahead of Félicité and Marc. It was Tony. Farther and farther, he drifted toward shore.

I took a deep breath and nodded. Jason loosened his grip on my arm and we pushed through the water. The waves slapped nonchalantly against us, as if we were no longer worth the effort of a true battle. After what felt like hours, our feet touched sand. I could see three bright orange life jackets already ashore, two huddled near one another, the other a short ways off. Alone. Jason and I crawled over to the first pair of jackets and only when we were right near them did I see that it was Félicité and Marc. We all lay back together, a tangle of limbs not unlike how we had been earlier in the day. The wind gave a final, deafening cry of defeat, and then the world was calm again, all traces of the storm erased.

"Is everyone okay?" I asked when I finally caught my breath.

Three voices confirmed that they were fine.

"Tony?" I asked.

I looked over to where Tony was lying facedown in the wet sand.

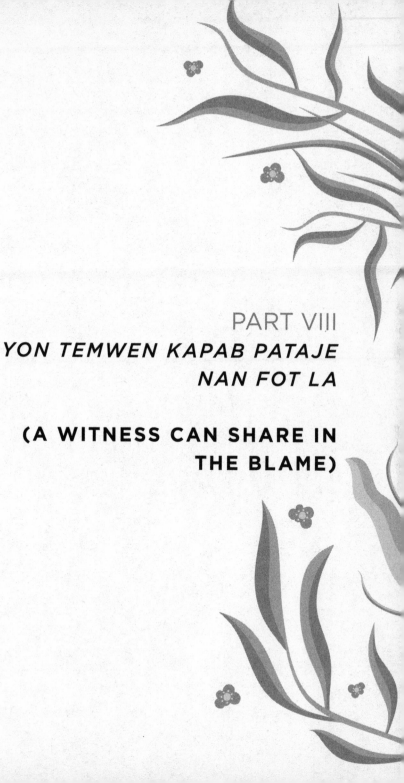

PART VIII
YON TEMWEN KAPAB PATAJE NAN FOT LA

(A WITNESS CAN SHARE IN THE BLAME)

Sunday, March 6

The Life and Times of Alaine Beauparlant

Everything moved in a blur: me dragging myself to where a bloody Tony with a gash on his forehead and blue lips lay not breathing, Marc screaming for help, Jason pulling me away while Félicité ran as fast as she could to find someone, anyone who would know what to do. I couldn't believe this had happened.

I couldn't believe Tony was dead.

I couldn't believe that it was my fault.

It was *my* fault.

I kept saying this over and over as Jason tried to console me. I hardly noticed when help finally arrived with Félicité, three men yelling that it was *Monsieur* Tony and how they had to get to the hospital *now*. Someone lifted me into the bed of a white truck and we bounced around as the driver crashed through traffic at breakneck speed. I don't know when I passed out, but I awoke for a moment when Tony's cold, lifeless hand grazed my arm. There was nothing I could do as bile rushed to the top of my throat and I leaned over the side of the truck to vomit and cry.

At the hospital the emergency workers were organized chaos as they pulled us out of the truck bed. I was quickly placed in a wheelchair and rolled away.

"…hysterical," I heard someone say as we neared the front door of the hospital.

I looked back at the truck to see that the nurses had moved Tony onto a stretcher. A tall man worked diligently to bring him back, pumping his arms up and down over Tony's chest. And then a short doctor who was standing to the side came up and placed a hand on the shoulder of the man performing CPR. She shook her head and looked down at her watch.

"18:32," I heard her say as the doors to the hospital closed behind me.

The Life and Times of Alaine Beauparlant

My mother was livid. The details of what happened came trickling out as Jason, Marc, and Félicité were cleared by the doctor and discharged. The doctor wanted to hold me for observation because of all the water I had taken in, so my dad insisted on driving the others home to speak with their parents himself. I wasn't ready to face my mom and kept my eyes tightly shut as she walked from one end of my hospital room to the other. The shuffling sound of her pacing near my bed stopped for a moment and was replaced with the unzipping of a bag and the clacking of a bottle of pills. I heard the door open slowly, then close. She spun on her heels.

"What is she doing with this, Estelle?" Mom whispered. I squeezed my eyes shut even tighter.

"Saving your life, if we're lucky."

"She almost lost hers," my mom said, her voice rising in anger. "That man hit his head so hard he drowned and *did* lose his. I told you to leave her alone. I don't want my daughter traipsing all over Haiti to collect dirt. It's giving her false hope."

My mason jar.

"You know that Roseline can help you."

"Help me? I'm not in the business of wasting my time, or my life."

"Is that right? All you've done for the past three months has been feel sorry for yourself."

"At least I have something to mourn," Mom spat. "I didn't spend three-quarters of my existence entangling myself with a man who has no intention of ever moving forward with me. It's wishful thinking to believe otherwise."

"It's wishful thinking to believe that you've *just* gotten

something to mourn, Celeste. You lost your daughter and your husband a long time ago."

"I made a choice," my mom snapped. "I refused to let this foolishness overrun my daughter's life."

"And your solution was to neglect her? Is that not a curse of its own? The thing that you tried so hard to keep from her has been impacting her from the very beginning! I understand that it was your decision to make, sister, and I have not questioned you for it once. Do me the courtesy of not questioning *my* decisions either. We need Alaine and Roseline's help. So does Jules and the rest of this family."

"And Andres? Like he helped you with PATRON PAL?"

"Yes. Him too. You despised anyone who chose to spend time with me over you," my aunt hissed. "Ironic, isn't it? Since you were the one to turn your back on me for Rose—"

"Enough!" my mom said, all pretense of keeping her voice down gone. "Maybe you're the one who needs your head checked. Because this? This has not solved one problem for us."

I opened my eyes just as the crash of broken glass filled the room.

UPDATED TO-DO LIST FROM ROSELINE'S PLACES TO VISIT

~~Bois Caïman~~

~~Sans-Souci Palace~~

~~Labadie~~ (?)

Citadelle Laferrière

PAGE FROM
TONY JUSTE'S FUNERAL PROGRAM

In Loving Memory

Tony Juste

Obituary

Antonie Rivière Hérard Juste, 37, was born on Valentine's Day in Kingston, Jamaica, to Preston and Claudette Juste. His parents were university professors who instilled in him the importance of hard work.

Above anything, Tony was curious. He grew up learning of his cultural heritage in Haiti from his parents, particularly his mother, who descended from one of the early leaders in the country's history. When he turned 18, he decided to move to Cap-Haïtien to explore his history and try his luck as a peanut farmer.

He lit up any room he entered with his easygoing charm and was beloved by his growing number of customers. Tony was a permanent deacon at Cathédrale Notre-Dame for many years. In his spare time, he often conducted planting and grinding workshops for hopeful entrepreneurs. It was while he was on a boat returning from one of these volunteer sessions that he met his untimely end during a storm.

Tony is survived by Suzette, his wife of 16 years; Brille and Claude, his daughter and son; and his older sister, Neddie.

ACKNOWLEDGMENTS

The Juste family would like to offer their sincerest gratitude to every single person who has called, prayed, visited, and supported us during this extremely trying time. Thank you.

Special thanks to Estelle Dubois and family for your consideration and compassion.

MEMORIAL SERVICE

Cathédrale Notre-Dame du Cap-Haïtien
Rue 18, Cap-Haïtien, Haiti

The Life and Times of Alaine Beauparlant

It had been a week since Tony's death and sleep still did not come easily. Something nagged in the back of my mind, but I couldn't quite place my finger on it. I spent all night after the funeral thinking of Tony and his family. They were undoubtedly lying confused in their beds, grieving and unable to understand why he was taken from them. The next morning, I got up with only one goal. Today would be the day that I put this whole ordeal to rest. I'd spoken with Roseline on the phone the night before, and we'd agreed to meet at Citadelle Laferrière at 7:00 a.m. My mom and dad were still asleep, and I didn't even let myself worry about whether my aunt would get in the way. She had made herself scarce of late, probably feeling unwelcome in her own home. I still couldn't bring myself to look at her, let alone speak about whatever was going on with PATRON PAL and Andres or, more important, her conversation with my mom at the hospital.

The house was silent as I finished gathering up my jars and prepared to head to the Citadelle. I couldn't help but think about the Labadie collection. I had gotten on my hands and knees in the middle of that hospital room to collect as much of the dirt as I could. My mom hadn't tried to fight me when I'd leaped out of my bed after she'd slammed the jar to the floor. She'd only looked on as I'd tried my hardest to move as much of the dirt as I could to an empty box of gloves. Even now, the glass shards glimmered through the new jar that I had transferred the dirt into when I got home. I prayed that the glass wouldn't interfere. I had debated finding a way back to Labadie, but after what happened to Tony, I knew that my parents would never let me go…and I couldn't stomach the idea of returning there either. In the last few days, they had become closer than I ever remembered seeing them. A true unit. They were all smiles and lingering touches, even with all the craziness that had been happening. Just as I made my way to go out the back door, wondering what it would be like to have them together again once this was all said and done, I heard someone clear their throat. I turned to find my mom standing behind me, her arms crossed.

"Going somewhere without me?" she said.

"Uh…what are you doing up?" I answered with a question of my own.

"No need for the charade, Alaine. I could practically see the wheels spinning in your head all week. That…and Estelle told me you were meeting with Roseline this morning."

"Trying to earn back your loyalty," I said, crossing my own arms.

We stood that way for a while, staring at one another. Finally, my mother sighed, "Well, if you're going to go through with this, I'm coming."

And so we went out the back door together. Fernand was there, waiting with the car just as I had asked him. When he noticed my mom coming with me, the smile dropped from his face. He knew that my visit to Roseline was supposed to be a secret.

"Uh...Ms. Beauparlant...I'm here to...uh..."

"It's okay," I said. "She knows."

Fernand gave a sigh of relief and opened the car door with an exaggerated bow. The drive to the Citadelle was uneventful, the world a silent fog as we twisted and turned through the streets. When we arrived, I thanked Fernand and told him that he didn't have to stick around, since my mom was with me.

"We have a ride back home with Roseline. We'll be fine, I promise," I told him.

He seemed reluctant to leave, even mumbling something about *safety*, but finally agreed after I glared at him in what was my best seriously-just-take-the-day-already face.

We watched as he drove away, then began the walk up the mountain, quietly taking in the sprawling views of the countryside. Green hills rolled as far as the eye could see, white clouds kissing their peaks. There were very few people milling about the Citadelle when we arrived at the fortress. One man caressed a jagged stone wall in admiration, while a girl about thirteen took selfies in front of a wide pyramid of stockpiled cannonballs. The sole tour guide at this hour watched her grimly, shouting, "Get off the pyramid!" when the girl handed her phone to a friend and made moves to climb the arrangement.

The fortress was breathtaking. Seeing it in person was nothing like reading about it in Mom's journals or searching online. There was no giant flashing sign anywhere that would lead us to the exact spot my mom, aunt, dad, and Andres had met all those years ago. And I didn't want to ask my mom for fear that she wouldn't remember and would spiral into another outburst. We walked around silently, moving farther and farther away from the most populated areas of the Citadelle. I was just about to tell my mom that we could check out another part of the site when I tripped over a gnarled tree trunk and my eyes fell on (eye-roll-inducing) gold.

$$ED + AV = \heartsuit$$

Tati Estelle's trunk engraving. If that wasn't a sign, I didn't know what was. I bent down and quickly filled my final jar. My mom still didn't speak, but as she watched me, I knew that all she wanted to tell me was to not get my hopes up. We continued on to find Roseline and before long we saw her already at work. Her back was to us, and she was staring intently at the Citadelle. She stood as still as a statue cursed to gaze upon the culmination of the paranoid thoughts of a self-proclaimed king. I cleared my throat, and Roseline turned around. One hand rested over her stomach, a slight breeze pushing back the flowy folds of her polka-dot maxi dress like the wings of an enormous butterfly.

"Celeste?" Roseline asked apprehensively. I could tell that she was worried my mom had come to put a stop to the final ceremony.

"Hi, Roseline," Mom answered. "I'm here to help see this through. No matter the outcome."

Roseline simply nodded and asked, "Do you have the collections?"

As she stepped toward us, I noticed the items placed in a circle that she had dug into the ground behind her. A pile of small logs sat in the middle, and a bottle of rum rested outside the circle with a small jar and box of matches.

"Yes," I said and pulled out the four small jars that were each filled with earth from Bois Caïman, Sans-Souci Palace, Labadie, and now Citadelle Laferrière. The jar from Labadie held markedly less than the others. Even now, my mom's gaze lingered on that partly filled jar, the shards of glass that I couldn't get rid of from the old container twinkling in the sunlight. She didn't apologize for what she had done.

Roseline took the jars from me carefully and placed them beside the small box. "It is time."

My stomach did a little flip as I looked at my mom. As resistant as she had been throughout this entire process, I couldn't ignore the hopefulness in her gaze as she watched Roseline. If my mom (ever the pragmatic journalist and refuter of the supernatural) could allow herself the moment to *believe*, then who was I to think that all of this couldn't work?

Roseline crouched before the circle she had arranged, more nimble than should be possible with a belly that size. She picked one of the matches from the box and scratched the head along the container's gritty side, then dropped the new flame onto the pile of wood. The fire crackled softly as she poked it from different angles to coax the heat and smoke to grow. She took the bottle of rum and poured an ample splash on the fire, followed by two more for good measure. The flames rocketed up with a roar, and I took another step back. Roseline was unafraid.

She unscrewed the first jar and looked at me and my mom. "The relationship between a mother and child is like none other. As a mother, you are a vessel to the spirit world, guiding a new life into the physical realm. It is no coincidence that you both are here. We are asking the ancestors to end this curse that has plagued your family for generations, and your connection will help us with our offering. You must complete this final step together."

Mom stepped forward and I followed, praying my eyebrows wouldn't be singed off from the licks of the fire.

"Repeat after me and scatter the contents of each jar as you do so," Roseline said, handing the first jar over to us after she had unscrewed it.

Mom and I crouched beside Roseline, holding the jar between us. As I inspected the dirt from Bois Caïman, the same something that had been haunting my thoughts all last night and this morning tugged at me. My apprehension must have shown.

"We've come this far," Roseline said, placing a hand on her bulging middle.

Mom smiled encouragingly at me and I nodded for Roseline to continue.

"Ancestors and spirits, we are here before you with our plea to lift the curse that has plagued our family for so long," Roseline began.

My mom poured a handful of dirt into her palm from the opened container. I scooped out the rest. We repeated after Roseline and each threw the contents into the flames. The fire hissed.

"We've come to uphold the agreement that Marie-Louise Coidavid made all those years ago," we continued, adding the dried mud from Sans-Souci Palace.

"We know that there is always a price to pay when seeking your aid. We accept the consequences of our inaction." My mom gingerly scooped out a handful of the Labadie mixture of dirt and sand and glass. I poured in the rest of the contents after her.

"And we come to you again, in the very place where the course of our family history was forever altered after the death of Henri Christophe." I tried not to cough from the dust of Citadelle Laferrière.

"But now we have the chance to amend our sins. We beg for your mercy and agreement in ending this curse once and for all."

Together, my mother and I each held one side of the small jar that Roseline had placed on the outside of the circle. We tossed the soil inside over the fire, the dirt rushing to meet the flames like iron filings to a magnet. An acrid smell rose up from the blaze and black smoke hovered in the air. Roseline said nothing as she splashed some Florida water into the fire, followed by a handful of dried leaves that she removed from her pockets.

"One last thing." Roseline reached into the neckline of her dress and handed me a folded piece of paper. "And we understand the sacrifice that was made for this chapter to come to a close."

"And we understand the sacrifice that was made for this chapter to come to a close…" I don't know why I looked down at the paper in my hands. Maybe because I'm nosy and like knowing what I'm setting on fire. But when I did, I saw the smiling, twinkling eyes of Tony Juste boring into mine.

I shrieked and rushed to my feet, throwing the obituary from my hands as if it were poison. A gust of wind swept through the heavy curtain of smoke, guiding the pamphlet into the pit. I reached for it in vain, trying to prevent it from landing in the fire. The flames surged forward in a grand show of light and sparks, and swallowed the paper in one burning gulp. Just as suddenly, the fire died.

"What have you done?" I roared at Roseline. "How could you do this? Why didn't you tell me this would happen?"

Roseline stood from her spot beside the circle. "What did you think would happen? You're a smart girl, Alaine. You read those letters. You saw for yourself that Marie-Louise didn't keep her promise. She was weak."

The creeping dread I'd sensed since we'd begun flooded my body. I remembered. Marie-Madeleine Lachenais's words had made me shudder even then, but I'd written her admonishment off, distracted by everything else that had happened since my arrival in Haiti. I had barely considered what all this collecting was leading to. That was Roseline's job.

I want Rivière-Hérard to be dust in my hands. In every sense of the word.

"You knew this was how it was meant to be," Roseline said. "Did you not notice Tony's full name listed in the funeral program?"

My mom stood up silently, her arms wrapped around herself as if to keep her emotions from spilling out of her body.

"What was in that last jar?" I wouldn't put anything past her anymore.

She cocked her head. "Don't worry. Just dirt from his burial site. *He's* not in there, if that's what you're thinking. It is finished."

Roseline handed the jar back to me, the hastily torn label of *Tony J. Manma* still partially attached by gummy adhesive now unmistakable.

"H-how could you be so heartless?" I said through tears as I wiped my face.

"Heartless? Heartless is for men like your grandfather. I did this because I love my child. One day when you have children, you'll understand."

"This is what it means for you to love a child?!" I asked incredulously, my voice rising an octave.

The look on Roseline's face should've made me stop, but I was so repulsed that I continued, "Tell me, Roseline, what did you wish for that day my mom and the others joined you for the original ceremony?"

Roseline's eyes filled with tears. "Freedom."

She opened her mouth to speak again, but instead of words, a low moan escaped her as she doubled over in pain. "I think I'm going into labor."

Instinctively I stepped toward Roseline. "Something's not right," she gasped.

My mom, who had been standing silently the whole time, finally seemed to shake the cobwebs from her mind. "Estelle?" she said, tears streaming down her face. "Are you going to be okay?"

My vision blurred with tears of my own as realization hit. *It didn't work.*

Amount of time it takes to get from Citadelle Laferrière to Hôpital Sacré Coeur in Milot:
23 minutes

Number of words uttered between me and Roseline in the car:
4.25 ("I don't know, uh, breathe!")

The number of moments it takes for any hope that you had to be gone:
1

Driving experience I'd had on the petrifying roads of Haiti before taking the wheel to get to said hospital:
0

There was no time for tears as I walked my mom and Roseline to Roseline's car. She had been parked not too far away from where our ceremony took place, and as I took my mom by the hand and wrapped my other arm around Roseline's shoulders, I clamped down on the feeling of despair that was attempting to overwhelm me. I got behind the wheel and took a calming breath. There was no question that I would be the one to drive. By the time we arrived at the hospital, I was pretty sure that Roseline was ready to give birth right there in her seat. I left the car running and ran inside to get the nearest nurse.

I don't know how we got to the hospital without running anyone or anything over, but we made it. To be honest, it might have something to do with the fact that I was driving no faster than twenty miles per hour. I thought it would be best to limit our reasons for going to the hospital to a birth and not numerous broken bones. Early onset Alzheimer's not included.

"Baby...being...born," I said to the first nurse I could find, trying to catch my breath. A large woman in a light blue uniform sprang into action. She called for one of her fellow nurses and they ran to the car, one of them stopping to grab a wheelchair on the way. I hurried after them, and when Roseline was settled in the chair, they wheeled her away. She gave one last howl of pain and then she was gone into the hospital, whisked away to the maternity ward.

I'd be lying if I said that I didn't consider just driving away from the hospital right then and there. Yet I somehow found myself parking the car and heading back inside with my mom, if only to prevent Roseline reporting her car as stolen. One criminal in the family was enough.

We made our way to the waiting room and, after giving my dad a call to let him know where we were, settled in to wait for him to pick us up.

Just as I rested my head against the wall behind me to go to sleep and attempt to forget the morning, my phone buzzed in my bag.

Jason - Work, work, work, work bae

JASON 10:02am:

> Hey Alaine.
> What are you up to?

ALAINE 10:03am:

> Hey. I'm at the hospital.

JASON 10:03am:

> Hospital? Oh no!
> What happened?

ALAINE 10:04am:

> One of my mom's cousins
> went into labor while we were at the Citadelle.
> Everything happened so fast that I was the one
> to drive her to the hospital.

JASON 10:05am:

> That's insane.
> Are you ok?

ALAINE 10:07am:

> Yeah. I'm fine.

JASON 10:08am:

> Driving through
> the streets of Haiti must've been
> traumatizing...

ALAINE 10:10am:

> I was pretty scared.
> But that wasn't even the half of it...
> It's been a long day already.

JASON 10:12am:

> How much longer
> will you be at the hospital?

ALAINE 10:13am:

> I'm not sure. My dad

said that he would be here soon.

JASON 10:14am:

Ok. Well I'll leave you
to it then. I'm sure there's a new baby
that's ready to come into the world
right now that you're dying to meet.

ALAINE 10:15am:

Uh-huh. Ecstatic. I'll
talk to you later.

The Life and Times of Alaine Beauparlant

Me? Dying to meet Roseline's baby? No, someone else already had. Tony died because Roseline believed that his death would result in a curse-free life for her child. He died because I thought that breaking this family curse would help my mom get her memory back. He died because I was so lost in the idea of preventing anything from happening to Dad, or *Tati* Estelle, or stupid Andres, or Félicité, or any of the other relatives I had taken upon myself to save. He died because I blindly put all of my hope in something that I didn't even fully understand. And not once did I take a step back to realize that Roseline had been feeding me half-truths the entire time, just enough to keep me moving forward but never enough to see the full story.

I was a fool.

I slipped away silently as my mother slept in the seat beside me. It might not have been the best idea to leave her alone, but I figured that she couldn't get into too much trouble in a hospital. My aimless steps led me to the cramped maternity ward. The hospital had done the best it could with its limited resources and kept its cracked tiled floor spotless. I looked down the row of the thin iron beds, at the new mothers in various stages of euphoria and exhaustion, and swallowed the bile I tasted when I saw Roseline. The joy on her face was unambiguous. She rocked the wrapped bundle in her arms gently and laughed when tiny fingers clasped her own. I wondered if Tony Juste had been there for the births of his daughter and son, or if he had missed them like Roseline's husband, Pierrot, because it had happened too quickly. My head throbbed.

"Who are you looking for?" A nurse appeared out of no-where, smiling widely as she made to usher me to the row of beds.

"Oh, no, *merci*. I—I...already saw them," I said, pointing wildly at a bed near the entrance.

I spun on my heel and speed-walked to the waiting area... and collided into a hard chest.

"Oof— Hey!

"Jason!" I didn't think. I just hugged him, so happy to see him that I could feel my eyes well up with the tears that had been threatening to spill over since the Citadelle. I tightened my grip around him, burying my face deeper into his chest as I let out a trembly sigh. He didn't let go.

Finally, I stepped back a little to look up at him. "What are you doing here?"

"For starters, I figured that you might need a hug after braving those Haitian roads. It seems I was right."

I smiled as he squeezed my hand a bit tighter, letting him lead me to the nearest seats. When we were settled, he continued, "Don't laugh, but the reason I texted you was because I wanted to ask you out. Like, for real, for real, and not as a group with my cousin or standing up for a food truck at work. Before you leave. But then as I was reading your texts, I could tell something was wrong. I had to come make sure you were okay."

Playing it cool was not an option. Not after everything that had happened in the past few days. I didn't try to think of every possible scenario before acting, or worry about what I must look like after flinging dirt into a fire on a windy day at the Citadelle. I turned to Jason in my seat, placing my hand on his chest as I looked up into his eyes. I could feel his heart beating under my palm, feel his chest rising as he breathed in sharply and met my lips with his own. When we pulled back a few moments later, the silly grin on his face mirrored my own.

"Does that mean you'd like to go with me? On a date?" he asked.

I smiled again. "I'd love to."

"If there's one thing I've learned about what happened to Tony, it's that I've got to be more explicit about my feelings…"

I nodded, because I didn't trust myself to speak. I completely understood.

"I almost forgot," Jason said as he extended a small bag that I hadn't noticed he was carrying. "Here. For the new mom."

I peered inside, and a plump teddy bear gazed back at me with shiny onyx eyes. "I'm starting to think you have a treasure chest of kiddie toys that you still play with or something."

"My mom would be disappointed if I didn't demonstrate my home training and come with a gift," he protested.

I was about to tease him some more when I heard a familiar throat clear.

"And who do we have here?"

Jason and I looked up to see my mom and dad walking toward us.

"Jason, this is my dad. You met a few days ago when Tony…" My voice trailed off as I let the rest of my sentence remain unsaid.

"Come," Mom interrupted. "Let's get a snack. Jules only uses that faux intimidating voice when he's hungry."

Jason and I followed my parents to the nearest vending machine. I couldn't help but grin as I watched my mom be her normal self, asking Jason a million and one questions as we each ate a bag of chips. But my smile slipped slightly as worry tempered my glee. She was lucid now, but for how long? Would I always be torn by warring emotions when-ever she was feeling all right, waiting for the moment when she would slip back into the fog?

"Let's hurry and see Roseline before visiting time is over," Mom said, grabbing Dad's hand and walking to the mater-nity ward just a few steps away. We meandered through the tight row of beds, the nurse I'd seen earlier looking confused when she saw me walk past my "relative" near the door and toward Roseline. She was tucked all the way in the back of the room, in the final bed nestled into a corner, and was still looking down at her newborn baby in awe.

"So many visitors just for you," Roseline said softly, smil-ing down at her daughter.

Just then, we heard a loud clatter as someone made his way up the aisle. Pierrot was disheveled as he raced over to his wife and child. He gave Roseline a kiss and lifted the baby gently from her arms.

"Thank you! Thank you!" he said, clearly overcome with emotion. I wondered if he knew exactly what he was thank-ing me for.

Each person came in close to coo over the baby and kiss Roseline. I wanted to stand back but knew that would be too conspicuous, so I stiffly bent my face down to hers when it was my turn. She took my hand and stuffed a piece of paper in it. It took everything in me not to ball it up and throw it in her face.

"*Félicitations!*" Dad said as he handed Pierrot a vertical gift bag that he had hid behind his back. "Enjoy this bottle the first time your daughter gives you a headache."

"What's her name?" Jason asked.

"Nadège Alaine Giraud," Roseline said quietly. "After my mother. And…of course."

"She's named after Alaine? Oh, then I will have to send you three more bottles!"

Everybody laughed. I retreated from the bed.

"Where are we going?"

"Home."

"Are you sure? I don't recognize this way."

"We always have to drive through the gate to get to the house, Mom."

"Oh…yes, of course."

Dad looked in the rearview mirror as he braked and met my red eyes from where I sat in the back seat. As the gate creaked open, he shifted his gaze to inspect the side of Mom's face. She turned to him and smiled.

"That baby was adorable. What did they decide for the name again?"

Alaine,

I have had a difficult life. The trauma I've experienced at the hands of people claiming to have noble intentions stays with me wherever I go. You weren't there. You will never know hardship like I have. That is a blessing. But because of your knowledge gap in this regard, I didn't expect you to understand what I needed you to do.

You really do have an honest face. At Jacinthe's birthday dinner, you looked desperate for a solution to your mother's problem. Estelle had approached me a few weeks before and said that we could help each other. She's no friend of mine, but she had that same air that told me she was serious. I thought of my baby. I remembered Celeste once being the only beautiful thing in my life. I agreed.

As you get older, you will come to learn that the vast majority of people will always operate with their own interests at heart. It's best to conduct yourself with this in mind. Tony's family would've done anything to save him from his fate, even if that meant sacrificing someone else. It's the circle of life.

There's power in faith and there's no need to pretend you didn't believe in this curse. You saw it all around you. My mother used to say history tends to catch up with itself, even if it takes a few centuries longer than expected. Tony's time was marked. If it weren't him,

it would have been one of his children, or another de-
scendent. They have nothing to fear anymore. And now
it is our time to live life in the sun. Make the most of
the time you have with your mother and I will give my
own child the life I wish I had when I was younger.
One like yours.

I know you don't want to hear this now, but thank
you.

Roseline

UPDATED TO-DO LIST
FROM ROSELINE'S PLACES TO VISIT

~~Bois Caïman~~

~~Sans-Souci Palace~~

~~Labadie~~

~~Citadelle Laferrière~~

RUNNING LIST OF 5 STAGES OF WHAT GOES THROUGH YOUR MIND UPON REALIZING YOU'VE BEEN LIVING A LIE

DENIAL

- No, no, no, no, no, no, no, no, no, no, no, no, no, no, no, no, no, no, no, no, no, no, no, NO!

- This can't be right… Of course it worked. We just need a little more time for it to work.

- It's completely understandable that Mom called Roseline Estelle. Right? Right.

- My name is pretty uncommon. I can easily see it slipping anyone's mind.

ANGER

- WTF

- Why didn't it work?!

- I bet Roseline only did this for her child and knew that Mom wouldn't get better. How could she?!

- Shut up, Dad. Whatever sage advice you think you're

offering is pure garbage. I am not going to start meditating "to clear my mind" because that's not going to change anything.

BARGAINING

- But I thought I saw...

- Okay. What if Roseline did it wrong again? She was distracted. Her brain was addled with pregnancy hormones, I'm sure that's a thing. If I could just get her to redo her part... I could go back to the hospital and see if they have any more of that dirt from the jar Mom smashed, for some reason. She's kinda famous...maybe they kept some. Crazier things have happened.

- I bet Mom needed to be on board for this to be successful... If I just explain to her more clearly than I have in the past...then she'll get it and she'll be back and everything will be normal and I'll get my busy mom back and I won't ever complain about not seeing her again.

- Mom just needs to focus more. I could give her brain a pep talk. We could start meditating *together*.

DEPRESSION

- Mom was right. What was the point of doing all this?

- What the hell was I thinking?

- Tony.

ACCEPTANCE

- What is that?

PART IX

PADON SE PA SELMAN NAN PALE

(FORGIVENESS IS NOT ONLY IN SPEAKING)

LETTER *TATI* ESTELLE SLID UNDER THE DOOR OF MY ROOM THIS MORNING

Chérie,

Things are not always black-and-white. I understand that relations will be strained between us for some time... I will not try to change this fact. But I do want you to know that I love you and my sister. You are like a daughter to me and I truly believed that doing this would bring Celeste back to us. Give it time. I think it's important to keep our faith.

You're leaving tomorrow and still upset with me so I won't be shocked if you see this on your floor, recognize my handwriting, and throw it out. But on the off chance you don't, I wanted to leave you with this letter to clear the air before you return to Miami. We will miss you in the office. As for what you saw at the wedding, I do not owe you an explanation for that.

You'll learn what I mean very soon, but I am no thief. Creating PATRON PAL was the best thing I've ever done. I never thought I would touch so many lives and will work my hardest to make sure that more kids get the chance to reach their potentials and have decent futures.

Love always,
Estelle

The Life and Times of Alaine Beauparlant

I was done "giving it time." It took my mom seeing five doctors and forgetting a piece of a recipe to accept her fate. It took me a little longer, but I had finally arrived at the same conclusion. She had Alzheimer's, and I wasn't able to stop the damage it was doing. I refused to spend any more time thinking of curses and *madichon*, about whether they were real, or only partially real, or fake. For Roseline's baby's sake, I did hope it was fake, or at least broken. Perhaps Roseline will one day tell her daughter the story of how *Maman* saved *Papa*'s family from a centuries-old curse. Maybe she wouldn't, because it was no longer a concern of hers. But she would have a better life. It wasn't my problem.

All I knew was that my mom was here with the brain she had, and I needed to make the most of the little while we had left together. That moment when Roseline went into labor kicked the air from my lungs. And our ride home from the hospital provided the death blow that destroyed any hope I'd developed. Just. Like. That. I spent the next week watching Mom closely, explaining away any difficulty with normal activities or memory lapses as a coincidence. Getting angry that the same things kept happening. My denial was persistent at first. But I can't ignore it anymore.

Now we were working on the new project I'd suggested. I was still heartbroken, but it felt good to be spending quality time with my mother doing something she loved. Her mind wasn't gone yet. And when I got back to Miami, I wouldn't be afraid of awkward silences anymore. Compiling her nuggets of wisdom and all her recipes was something concrete we could do to give us all a little more joy. We would reveal our big idea at my farewell dinner that night with the assorted relatives who couldn't say no to a free meal (or potential drama), along with my new friends (or more-than): Jason, Marc, and Félicité, whom I—I couldn't believe it either—would miss.

Florida Senator Arrested in Shocking International Embezzlement Ring

By Colt Rivers, *The Capitol Post*

In the end, the allegations of Florida senator Andres Venegas misusing party funds had been grossly exaggerated—padding miles driven to political events for gas reimbursement here, dozens of custom-made Gucci suits written off as expenses there. Nothing unsalvageable.

But in an astonishing twist, federal officials have arrested Venegas for his role in a wide-ranging money-laundering scheme spearheaded by a Wilhelm V. Peeters to fuel Venegas's reelection efforts. Peeters is far from a household name, but he is known mostly in Caribbean circles as the middle son of a minor crime family in Aruba. Peeters was forced to flee the country eight years ago after divorcing the beloved daughter of the boss of a rival clan.

Often considered the "Fredo" of the family, Peeters escaped with $16 million worth of stolen diamonds, including his ex-wife's engagement ring, which he often wore around his neck. According to urban legend, the gaudy former amateur bodybuilder invested the money into building his own illicit empire of drug trafficking and online sports gambling in Haiti. He recently ventured into a new business: app development.

Venegas claimed in interviews that his investment in PATRON PAL, the wildly popular donation platform, was purely innocent. The app was made to connect people who wanted to help indigent Haitians kids but eventually devolved into a shell company as a sink for Peeters's illegal revenue. Peeters, who had by then adopted the alias Thierry Dieudonne, became so invested that he joined as chief financial officer and moved into an office space in Cap-Haïtien.

"He thought he could have his shady cake and eat it too," said Tricia Jenkins, creator of *Beautiful Brown*, a social justice, fashion, and hair care blog that somehow first broke the story. "Homeboy thought he'd prove all his haters wrong and demonstrate he could be a major player *and* do good on the side, like some deranged Robin Hood."

"Homeboy" was wrong.

"Peeters set up a super PAC to back Venegas's first senatorial run as part of his pivot to grow his American influence," said Nathan Sullivan, a spokesperson for the Justice Department. "Venegas clearly owed him a favor or two and had no choice but to accept the cash funneling into the company."

No one expected PATRON PAL to reach the heights it climbed. A third of the proceeds went to its "Pals" as promised, but the vast majority funded a jet-set lifestyle of gold-plated pools, private jets, and giant yachts for Peeters and the rest of his "board members." The $10 million net worth publicly declared by the company was comically underreported. Law enforcement officials are still attempting to come forth with a more accurate estimate but expect it to be several times that.

Jenkins received documents from an anonymous source tying Peeters to Venegas and exonerating Celeste Beauparlant and Estelle Dubois for their roles. CP independently confirmed that employees of the company are being actively investigated. Authorities moved at hyper speed to catch the primary individuals involved and had a major breakthrough when Dubois stepped forward months before to help catch Venegas and Peeters, in exchange for a plea deal to avoid prison. They even staged an arrest at one point when Venegas became paranoid of her loyalty.

"It may not have been the best thing to get involved with them, but Estelle was thinking of the children and how long she'd been trying to secure funding," Jenkins said in her blog post. "She feared for her safety and worried about the kids who would lose their ticket to school and a better life. This would lead anyone to react to Venegas the way Celeste did on that infamous Sunday morning. She was trying to protect her sister."

Perhaps the two sisters had insight into their childhood friend's psyche and what led him to make those poor decisions. We may never know. As the media world erupted in a firestorm over unconfirmed rumors of Beauparlant fighting Alzheimer's, focus on Venegas waned. But the politician, often listed as a top pick on the annual "DC's Cool" list for his penchant for recalling nineties rap lyrics, hid a dark demeanor behind his amiable persona.

"He was obsessed with winning," one congressional aide said. "On election night, instead of celebrating with his family and team, he spent three hours locked in his office brainstorming ways to stay in office."

Said another, "Even at his highest point before any of this

went down, he thought it was only a matter of time before all his power disappeared."

Perhaps Venegas was onto something, because his prediction came true.

Friday, March 25
From: Alaine Beauparlant
To: Tatiana Hippolyte
Subject: Eat, Slay, Love

Guess who has a summer mother-daughter trip in the works?!

MEET ME IN THE HAITIAN SUN

Itinerary
Celeste and Alaine:
Get ready for the experience of your lives on the island of
Tortuga. You will dine, dance, and explore all the beauty Haiti
has to offer. We are pleased to be your guide.

*Wednesday, June 8 - Night of Departure: 8:00 p.m.–11:00
p.m. Welcome Party*
Head over to the Boyer Ballroom after dropping off your belongings in your suite for an evening of fun. Dress code is
semi-formal masquerade. Bring an appetite and mask. Become someone else for the night!

Thursday, June 9 - At Sea
Enjoy the time you'll be on this ship, because it's the most
you'll have for the remainder of your journey with us. Take advantage of the open bar, karaoke, and all-you-can-eat buffet.

Friday, June 10 - Tortuga
Visit the rebuilt city of Cayona, slip your toes into the deep
white sand, and then go rock climbing on its highest mountain peak.

Saturday, June 11 - Gonaïves
Haiti's "Independence City" has a world of patriotic landmarks to explore. You might as well start at the beginning, which is near Lacrois. It is in this city Jean-Jacques Dessalines declared Haiti's sovereignty.

Sunday, June 12 - Jacmel
The south doesn't get enough love. Start at Place Toussaint Louverture, Jacmel's town square, and visit the galleries showcasing some of Haiti's most expansive artists. Stop at a nineteenth-century town house for a cup of coffee before leaving from the Port of Jacmel.

Ou retounen, tande?
You come back now, you hear?

POTLUCKTICS
A BLOG BY CELESTE BEAUPARLANT

Welcome to POTLUCKTICS

Dear Everyone,

Thank you. Thank you for sticking with me and sticking up *for* me. My life has been a haze for quite some time now.

When I would poke my head out of the ditch it was hidden in, I'd catch a glimpse of support from one of you and know that I was going to be okay. Then I'd bury my head back in the sand, not yet ready to acknowledge everything that has occurred in these few short months.

Love and trust can trick you into doing difficult things. I know that firsthand. And after you determine what you are willing to do for those you love, that decision doesn't lie there, dead. It eats at you, gnawing at your ear and whispering until you acknowledge it. You can imagine how that could drive anyone to extreme measures, even something as radical as assaulting a man on live television. *[Editor's note from Alaine, awesome-sauce daughter and verbal blog post transcriber extraordinaire: she's a little rusty with the metaphors, people, please bear with us.]*

And what you've heard is true: I have early onset Alzheimer's and am dealing with what that means each day.

Thank you to Tricia Jenkins over at *Beautiful Brown* for being kind enough to share with me the list of people who signed her petition to get me back on the air. *[Editor's note from Alaine, awesome-sauce daughter and verbal blog post transcriber extraordinaire: Seriously, Tricia, you're incredible, keep being you, boo.]*

I wanted you all to be the first to know, because you continued to believe in me, even in the moments I didn't believe in myself.

I'm not returning to GNN. Journalism is a calling that I answered more than twenty years ago. It was loud and incapable of being ignored. I didn't want to admit it, but I haven't heard that voice in a while. This extended vacation has cleared my doubt and made it easier to accept that TV news is no longer my passion at this juncture in my life.

Instead, I have filled my days with food. As other things slipped away from me, my favorite recipes stayed mostly put in my mind. At least, they are now. Who knows for how long?

When I woke up the first morning I returned to my childhood home in Cap-Haïtien, I nearly floated from my room to our stove. My sister is very organized and her pantries are stocked with every ingredient you could think of and tools one might need in any context. I made a cinnamon porridge that morning and I knew I still "had it" as her chef smiled warily at me when he took the first bite. I began a list of all the things I loved to make and another list of dishes I've never tried to prepare before. My daughter, Alaine, suggested I share my journey with you. *[Editor's note from Alaine, awesome-sauce daughter and verbal blog post transcriber extraordinaire: the phrase I used specifically was "you should totally blog about getting your* 'Julie & Julia' *on".]*

But really, I do this for her, so a piece of me that she hasn't known growing up outside the public face will be here with her even when I no longer am.

This is how POTLUCKTICS came to be and I hope you'll join me on this journey.

And while I may no longer be on GNN, I've told people's stories on camera for so long that I don't know if my vanity could keep me away from lenses, lights, and a screen forever. I'll have a YouTube channel, where you can catch me giving advice on everything from how to whip the stiffest possible meringue peaks to step-by-step directions for baking my regionally famous spiced rum butter loaf cake. I'm excited. I know that one of the many side effects of this disease is that I will eventually forget the things and people that have brought me much joy in my life. I will continue to share my stories and the stories of others for as long as I can.

Last thing—I'd like to thank Alaine for her support. *[Editor's note from Alaine, awesome-sauce daughter and verbal blog post transcriber extraordinaire: I did NOT make her do this, I promise.]*

I see so much of myself in her but on much better shoulders. Such public displays of affection to most teens (including me at this age) would've been met with chagrin, but she thrives on it. Alaine, don't ever change. I would be remiss to not thank my younger sister, Estelle, whom I literally see myself in. Thank you as well to my ex-husband, Jules, for bringing me back to our happy (and often frustrating) place.

All the best,
Celeste Beauparlant

COLUMBIA UNIVERSITY
Office of Admissions

Dear Alaine,

Congratulations! On behalf of Columbia University, I would like to formally invite you to join us as a member of our incoming freshman class.

We believe your passion, intelligence, and academic success make you a perfect candidate to thrive on our campus. The professors you will learn from in your courses and the connections you will make with your fellow students will stay with you for a lifetime.

We are especially proud to accept you as one of our first Innovative Interlude program fellows and look forward to hearing of the great work you will accomplish in your gap year. Rebuilding and refocusing PATRON PAL from the bottom up with your aunt after the very eventful year it's had is a daunting challenge, but one we are confident you can successfully undertake. We are excited to witness its rebirth—or the creation of an entirely new venture!

Enclosed you will find additional information on the Interlude program and financial aid options, with more resources forthcoming. In the meantime, we await your decision!

Sincerely,
Katie Sanders
Dean of Admissions

PART X

PA BLIYE'M

(FORGET ME NOT)

The Life and Times of Alaine Beauparlant

Dear Sister Wagner,

Sis.

We know each other pretty well by now. Can I call you Patty?

Patty, if you're reading this, you've made it to the end of my assignment—or skipped to the end, which in that case, shame on you.

I'm not sure if you'll ultimately be content that I Learned A Lesson or more disappointed because of the way things went down. In case you're wondering, yes, I did pass that stuff along to Tricia (you don't know me well AT ALL if you didn't think that once I heard Jason mention he was deleting things off Thierry's computer that I wouldn't get my fave intern to restore what he could and give me the goods).

Roseline's baby is healthy and Roseline seems happy as a mom, and though I bear her no ill will, I have no desire to see her ever again. My dad is more shattered than he's letting on about my mom. *Tati* Estelle is still my aunt, but it will be a good while until I feel the way I once did about her. I hope we get there though, especially since we've adopted the same goal of fixing PATRON PAL.

My mom…well, she has the best attitude, considering. I'm looking forward to continuing Getting to Know Her. I'll never stop.

My Best Wishes, and May You Have Many More Students as Awesome as Me to Keep Things Interesting,
Alaine Beauparlant

★ ★ ★ ★ ★

Authors' Note

We always said we'd write a book together.

Our parents were of the strict immigrant variety who took us and our two younger sisters to the library on weekends and forbade watching television on weekdays. All we had were our imaginations, our books, and each other.

We wouldn't actually get around to starting and finishing an entire story—this story—until years later. (It took being locked in the house, removed from work and school responsibilities, and awaiting the arrival of a category 4 hurricane.) That storm thankfully never made it to Miami, but the words to share Alaine's tale did.

Oh, Alaine.

She came to us so clearly. Before we knew exactly what her story would be, we knew her. Alaine was smart and sassy, quick-witted and sarcastic. A young woman with a lot to say who was just crying out to be heard. She used humor as a way to communicate with others as much as she used it as a shield to prevent them from getting too close. A first-generation Haitian American who didn't quite know her place as a member of either culture, Alaine had equal parts of us both but was also her own person. And as we wrote *Dear Haiti, Love*

Alaine, the world that would shape Alaine's character fell into place around her.

We relished the opportunity to incorporate so many of the idiosyncratic experiences and superstitions that we grew up with. While we didn't include them all, the more we wrote, the more we realized that so much of our lives were made up of moments that people who aren't Haitian American would be able to relate to as well.

We couldn't wait to share parts of our culture with others who might not have been exposed to it before. But we especially wanted this story to be for the kids who grew up like us, the countless individuals who don't always see themselves reflected in stories that are not solely focused on suffering and strife. We wanted an adventure that hearkened to the specificity of our culture but also left room for Alaine to find a place that was all her own.

Writing with a sister has been a (mostly) seamless process. The only official rule we had was passion always won out. Though we were typically on the same page on what would, well, go *on* the page, there were times we would reach a creative impasse. In those cases, whoever was most passionate about her plot point and made the best argument got her way. We think *Dear Haiti, Love Alaine* is much better for it.

Ayiti Chéri, or "Dear Haiti," is a popular name of affection that Haitians use to refer to our home country. People will often first recall the destitution and sadness that resides within its borders. The pain and violence. But that is not the full picture and never has been. Haiti is the embodiment of strength and light and laughter and love. We set out to write a book that demonstrates this.

Dear Haiti, Love Alaine was inspired by our interests in the obligations of family, and our responsibilities to ourselves. So much so, that we created an alternate history where Marie-Louise Coidavid was able to return to Haiti after being forced into exile in Europe. How would the decision to follow her heart and not go through with her promise to Marie-Madeleine Lachenais impact her family (and specifically Alaine) all those years later? We wanted to explore what leads someone to believe the unbelievable and the power of women across generations. Those ideas may have been our starting points, but our minds roamed free. And while we pulled from lore to help create the framework for the Christophe family curse, we developed a magic and mysticism that was completely our own. We're so proud that we were able to tell Alaine's story and shine a small light into Haiti's intricate culture. But the beauty is that there isn't one, single story that encapsulates the entirety of a nation. This was a love letter to our dear, dear Haiti. It won't be our last.

Acknowledgments

Is this the closest we'll get to an Oscar's speech? Here goes:

Oh boy, thank you to God. Thank you to our parents Elisabeth and Louis for taking us to the library every weekend growing up. Thank you to our grandmother Esther who is always our biggest supporter no matter what, and hands down the coolest family member we have. Jessica and Lydi'Ann, you already know you're our soulmates.

To JL Stermer, our amazing agent: we could not have asked for a more wonderful champion. We're on the same wavelength and frequency and you've made this sell-and-publish-a-book thing so much easier and fun. Working with you is a dream. This is where we would insert a joke about the speed of light being $c = \lambda v$. Also, thank you Joanna Volpe for connecting us with our beloved JL as well as Cassandra Baim, Veronica Grijalva, Hilary Pecheone, Mia Roman, and the rest of the fabulous team at New Leaf Literary.

And a special thank you to Devin Ross for seeing something in our story and sharing it with the rest of the New Leaf family.

To Natashya Wilson, fellow Niall Horan fan and our awesomesauce editor: thank you for falling in love with this book and smoothing and coaxing out of us the moments that have made DHLA even better. You believing in us and our words means the world.

Please give a raucous round of applause for Gabby Vicedomini for coming up with a title for this novel that encapsulates Alaine's story so well, and as an aside, for having such a vivacious Twitter account.

Oh no, the music's starting and we still have more to say…!

Everyone at Inkyard Press, Harlequin, and HarperCollins who has had a hand in making this ~~movie~~ book what it is: Gigi Lau and Ubiomo Ogheneroh for our gorgeous cover, Shara Alexander, *Frasier* aficionado Evan Brown, Randy Chan, Bryn Collier, Ken Cotnam, Heather Doss, Jessie Elliott, Kathy Faber, Heather Foy, publicist extraordinaire Laura Gianino, Olivia Gissing, library lover Linette Kim, Karen Ma, Margaret Marbury, Krista Mitchell, Azir Morinaj, Kerry Moynagh, Andrea Pappenheimer, Jennifer Sheridan, Jordanna Shtal, Eric Svenson, Jennifer Wygand. Thank you. Thank you. Thank you.

We are forever grateful for the beautiful comments of all those who took the time to read the book and talk about it, including Kelly deVos, Ben Philippe, and Dana L. Davis. Ibi Zoboi, thank you for shouting about DHLA as much as you did as soon as you heard about it. That will stay with us forever.

And Edwidge Danticat, you are a legend in every sense of the word. Having you read our book and then say kind things about it after you've been our North Star in this world of writing our whole lives is an honor.

To sound like *The Golden Girls* theme song for a moment: (at some point or another) thank you for being a friend, Adaobi Ibida, Alessandra Franco, Alexandra Hughes, Dr. Ama Annor,

Brian Foster, Candace "Caking" "Work Bae" King, Grace Morales, Heather Phillips, Jessica Simmonds, Kendra Plummer, Kristi Patterson, Kristina Francillon, Dr. Lola Odukomaiya, Ludmilla Paul, Nichole Armah, Nyema Robinson, Rachelle Felix, Rashanda Wimberly, Rebecca Hildner, Ruth Dalberiste, Saisia Wade, Stacy Burroughs, Stephanie Douthit, Stephanie Figueroa, Steve Aubourg, Dr. Sylvia Morris, Wendy Diaz-Huarcaya, Zuby Syed.

To Anita Anantharam, Laura Castañeda, and Tace Hedrick, for being phenomenal and understanding professors.

To Janel Blanco, for being an amazing boss and willing to work with Maika's hectic traveling schedule. To Florida Reading Corps, for giving Maritza the opportunity to introduce the most amazing children to the world of literacy.

Thanks to our co-workers, classmates, and students (new and old) for listening to us squeal about the latest developments in *Dear Haiti, Love Alaine*.

Ginger and Lily, just because. Get to bed, you little rascals!

And to the Academy and anyone we might have forgotten, we love you.